CW01215763

THE MISTS OF MIDDLEHAM

Also by Brian Wainwright

Novels:

Within the Fetterlock
The Adventures of Alianore Audley
Walking Among Lions
Hanley Castle

Extracts:

The Open Fetterlock (Kindle only).

Short Stories in Anthologies:

Yorkist Stories
The Road Not Travelled : Alternative Tales of the Wars of the Roses.
Right Trusty and Well Beloved (Grant Me the Carving of My Name Book 2.)

(Factual)
Frustrated Falcons

THE MISTS OF MIDDLEHAM
(ALIANORE AUDLEY II)

BRIAN WAINWRIGHT

The Mists of Middleham

© Brian Wainwright 2023
All rights reserved.

Introduction

Alianore Audley (circa 1446-?) was the youngest daughter of James, Lord Audley (killed in battle 1459) and his second wife, Alianore Holland (c1404-?). Alianore was also the great-granddaughter of Edmund of Langley, 1st Duke of York, through his daughter Constance, (incidentally the heroine of my novels *Within the Fetterlock, Walking Among Lions* and *Hanley Castle*) and was thus a cousin (albeit at some remove) of King Edward IV and King Richard III. She was also closely related to Anne Neville, Richard's queen, a relationship strengthened by her marriage to the little-known but evidently significant Gloucestershire knight, Sir Roger Beauchamp, who was also a distant cousin of Anne. Alianore is remarkable for what was evidently a somewhat reluctant career as a member of the Yorkist intelligence service, the details of which were revealed to the world through the publication of her Chronicle of the era, under the title of *The Adventures of Alianore Audley*.

It will come as a surprise to many that a new version of Alianore Audley's Chronicle has been discovered behind the wainscoting of a crumbling manor house in remote Shropshire. Written entirely in Alianore's crabbed hand, it is a great challenge even to those who have attended advanced courses in palaeography. This is because much of it is in a form of primitive code.

For the present, not all of the work has been deciphered, and it's possible that parts never will be. In any case, many of the incidents described are barely modified versions of those already published.

However, there was one particular bundle of parchment was quite different from the others. It proved to be almost a separate narrative, and certainly the events described had not been touched upon at all in the earlier manuscript. Whether it is in any sense an authentic record of events or merely a piece of fiction that Alianore wrote for the amusement of her family is hard to determine and is best left to the judgement of the reader.

As before, I have rendered Alianore's account into modern English, but the extraordinary style is, as ever, her own.

Brian Wainwright.

*

The Mists of Middleham

I had never been so cold in my life; or if I had I had forgotten it. Riding pillion behind my husband, I clung to him as much for warmth as for security, his massive back protecting me from the worst of the icy blast driving in from the north-east. Two of our servants were bearing blazing torches before us, so we might pick our way through the all-enclosing darkness and thickening mist, but it was impossible for me to see anything of our surroundings, still less anything that might pass as a landmark.

'I know it's cold and I *don't* know how far it is,' Roger barked.

I was puzzled. 'I didn't...' I began.

'I know you didn't. You didn't need to.' Sir Roger turned a little in the saddle, his breath a small cloud of warmth in the freezing air. 'I know exactly what you're thinking, Alianore — that we were mad to set out in such weather. As it turns out, you're probably right. Have you any idea where we are?'

'No, Husband. Somewhere in Yorkshire, I suppose, but beyond that...'

'You were the one brought up in Warwick's household,' he said, with an edge of accusation. 'I'd have thought you'd know every inch of land around here, every tree.'

I laughed in astonishment. 'I thought you knew the way. We've been along this road a hundred times. You've spent most of the last seven years at Middleham, and you knew it even before that. It's where we met each other.'

'I'm not likely to likely to forget *that* little fact!' He paused for a moment then laughed himself. 'It seems to me this mist is thicker by the minute. I'm not even sure we're on the road any more, or in the middle of some fellow's field.'

Just for a moment, I thought I could see a shape ahead of them. I was just about to open my mouth to draw attention to it when it vanished again. The impression left with me was of a hooded figure. Not an animal and certainly not a tree. Yet the glimpse had been so fleeting, the mist so thick, that it seemed pointless to announce it to Roger. Instead I forced my eyes wide, and kept a careful watch ahead of us, insofar as this was possible. The truth was we were lost, and were likely to remain so until daylight at the earliest unless we stumbled on some village or other habitation.

I feared this was not likely. I knew the country, just as Roger had said, and was well aware of how thinly it was populated. Ripon and the village of Masham lay behind us and somewhere nearby was Jervaulx Abbey of the Cistercian Order, surrounded by many acres of rough pasture for the Abbey's sheep. Beyond the abbey, less than an hour's easy ride in normal circumstances, lay Middleham itself, castle and village. These places apart there was little in the way of habitation but for shepherds' huts and isolated farmsteads, and precious few of either.

It looked like a long, cold night. If we *had* wandered off the road – easy to do in such conditions – we might not even be headed in the right general direction. Too far to the west and we would find ourselves on high and dangerous moorland. It was not a comfortable thought. Such places had their own beauty on a summer's day, when you were riding with a hawk on your hand under a clear sky. They were not a place to wander in the dark, full of gullies and peat bogs, an unsheltered, icy wilderness.

'It's a monk,' I said.

'What monk?' Roger was terse, impatient.

'What I saw, ahead of us.'

'Nonsense! What would a monk being doing out here, wandering about in the dark? On a night like this, any monk with half a brain will be snug in his monastery, swilling prime beef down his neck and warming himself by the fire.'

Yet in a moment, the monk stood before us. Not a shadow this time but a man, quite solid in appearance. It was too dark to make out any detail, but it seemed to me that he was young and sturdy.

'Good Brother, could you put us on the road to Middleham?' Roger asked. (He had gone in an instant from not believing a monk could be present in such a place to asking favours of him.)

The figure nodded, pointed ahead of us and began to walk. He did not speak, nor yet did he respond to Roger's repeated attempts to discover from him exactly where we were. He simply walked before us, occasionally vanishing into the mist only to reappear a few minutes later. If the gap grew too large he gestured us on, but he said not a word.

'Here's an odd fellow,' said Roger in frustration. 'Civil enough to lead us on our way, yet lacking the courtesy to answer one word with another.'

'Perhaps he's under a vow of silence,' I suggested. I did not care, was just grateful to be on a sure road. Even the fact that it seemed even colder than before could not detract from that. I leaned against Roger's back, closed my eyes, and somehow, despite the cold and the discomfort of the saddle, I fell asleep.

I was woken at last by Roger's sudden cry: 'Middleham!'

The mists had all but cleared. But as I looked, I saw, not the castle as I knew it, but mere ruins.

'The Scots!' I cried. 'They must have done this!'

'What are you blabbering about?' Sir Roger demanded. He was more than irritated. An uncomfortable journey is not good for anyone's temper.

'Look!' I said, pointing. But as I followed my own finger, I saw the castle quite restored, quite in order, with Gloucester's banner flying above it, spread out by the wind.

I could not explain. I still cannot. I can only tell you what I saw.

*

The Countess of Warwick and the Guild of St. Anne.

Lady Warwick was of course at Middleham — she was living with Richard and Anne and had been for some time. She was my first cousin, although a good twenty years my elder, and as you know, I had at one time served in her household as part of what my elders were pleased to call my 'training'. (What they thought they were training me *for* I never deduced.)

In all the time of our acquaintance I had never heard her say anything interesting. (This is quite remarkable, because most people, however dull, can bring *something* to the table. George Clarence, for example, was a fool, but he could also be witty, and he certainly loved his wife and his greyhounds, so he wasn't *all* bad.)

It was therefore all the more startling when she announced that she had seen King Harry in the night. For King Harry, you understand, was safely dead, and had been for seven years or so, along with Lord Warwick, whose principal ambition had been to have Roger and me executed.

We were quite alone for some reason, sitting on the window-seat in the solar. Where Anne and the others were I have no idea. It doesn't really matter anyway. Perhaps visiting Lord Edward in the nursery, or walking in the town to see the church and enjoy a pie from one of the market stalls. It's irrelevant.

'Do you mean a dream, my lady?' I asked.

'No!' That was impatient. It was as if we were back in the days when she used to slap my head for looking at her the wrong way. 'I was awake. He came to me. Showing his wound where the murderer stabbed him. He's a saint now, you know.'

'Did he say so?'

'He didn't need to. I *knew*. He had a great, blinding light about him. Brighter than the sun.'

Too much cheese before bed, I thought.

'I knew him, you know,' she went on. 'I mean I *really* knew him. Not just as a king sitting on a throne. He was brought up in my lord father's household. He was like a brother. There was him, and my *real* brother, who was also Henry. Henry Beauchamp, Duke of Warwick. They murdered him of course.'

'King Harry?'

'No. My brother'

'*Who* murdered him, my lady?'

'The Duke of Buckingham. Not the one that now is — he's just a silly boy. I mean his grand-sire, old Buckingham. So the inheritance went to Henry's daughter, my niece. Then it came to me, when she died. Until Richard and George Clarence stole it from me.'

'It was King Edward's decision, my lady,' I reminded her. 'He put a Bill through Parliament, it is quite legal. Not theft.'

She glared at me. 'Legal theft? How can that be? In any event, Edward of York's days are numbered. King Harry told me so.'

'All our days are numbered, madam,' I said gently. 'But you know, it really is not wise to predict the death of the King. They call that treason.'

'It was not I who predicted it, silly — it was King Harry. And they cannot accuse him of treason, nor touch him, for he is a blessed saint. They've already done their worst.'

The Countess had founded something she called the Guild of St. Anne. It met, bizarrely, in one of the stone barns that are dotted around Middleham. Or perhaps it was a shippon. Who cares about such peasant pedantry? Not I! She invited me to join, but I hesitated. I know not why.

One day I followed her to her guild meeting, but was careful not to be detected. Within the barn — or whatever it was — were a whole circle of women. Mostly local gentlewomen, but with a few goodwives from Middleham to make up the numbers. There was a crucifix fitted on the opposite walls, but the prayers they were reciting were a little odd. After a short time I realised that Lady Warwick was trying to talk to the dead, and these women were assisting her. Indeed, one or two claimed to be possessed by the spirits of the deceased, and were claiming to speak on their behalf.

I withdrew rapidly to a prepared position. This is what the Church calls 'necromancy' and it is strictly forbidden. If the judge is in a bad mood you can be burnt at the stake. If he's a little kinder, you might be whipped three times around the church and heavily fined. Neither option was on my bucket list for life.

I reported all this to Richard. Not because I wished any harm to Lady Warwick, but because I feared that if I maintained silence I might myself be judged guilty of misprision of treason. Richard was the King's Officer hereabouts, so by telling him I made myself safe.

His sigh seemed to rise from his boots. 'I will speak to her,' he said. 'Not that it will make any difference.'

I knew what he meant. The Countess was not a woman to be gripped or pinned down. She was slippery as an eel, elusive as a fish. She simply ignored anything she did not want to hear. (This is a very common failing among all people, not just countesses.)

*

Security briefing

As ever, the Scots bore watching, and provided me with no small amount of work in my reluctant role as intelligence officer. (I was much happier simply living as Anne's lady-in-waiting, but, as you know, that was as much a cover story as an office.)

In theory, all should have been well. We had a truce with King James III, and indeed an agreement that his eldest son, also James, should marry Cecily of York, King Edward's daughter. So, *in theory*, at this time, Scotland was an ally.

Of course, life is never so simple. The Scots, being Scots, were not much in favour of peace with England. On top of that, King James was an odd sort of fellow. He was roughly the same age as Richard, and said to be handsome. (In my experience, most princes are handsome and it's only very occasionally it's admitted that they're ugly.) He had, however, a number of low-born favourites, much misliked by his nobility. These fellows may have been perfectly capable as ministers — from what I could gather from reports they were — but their low birth was still a thing. In addition, it was said, the King had a habit of going to bed with some of them. (I am not referring to sleep.)

King James also had two extremely awkward brothers, called Albany and Mar. Both of them *hated* the English, or at least they hated the peace. This hatred was probably political — no one becomes unpopular in Scotland by hating the English — but it still caused trouble. Albany, in particular, was behind many of the troublesome raids across our border, which persisted despite the truce. Of course, we raided back, because one has to, so as not to lose face. That's what the England/Scotland border has looked like since our first King Edward's time. It makes it uncommon difficult to administer, and it was one reason why Richard's face was already looking more lined than it should have been at his age.

You see, the problem is keeping the raids in proportion. So much is expected. Go too far and war breaks out, and the King and his Council are displeased. Do too little and the King and Council are also displeased, and the whole North country besides. Keeping these accounts in balance is extremely difficult.

Much of the work, of course, was delegated to Henry Percy, Earl of Northumberland and his underlings. This produced additional difficulties. Percy was a prickly fellow, who did not much care to be gripped. Notionally, officially, on paper, he was Richard's subordinate, but that did not mean he jumped when Richard said 'jump'. He might or he might not. Or he might jump too high, or in the wrong place. An awkward sort, Henry Percy. Always had been, always would be. No, he needed handling — and watching. I had agents on his tail. Several of them, in fact. He gave me almost as much work as King James.

Then, across the Pennines, down at Lathom House in Lancashire (or occasionally at Knowsley when Lathom was being cleaned) were our dear old friends Thomas Stanley and his delightful wife, Margaret Beaufort, Lady Richmond. You could not ignore this precious pair, not least because they both had inexplicable favour at court. The best that could be said for Stanley was that he was a dull fellow; he was also extraordinarily greedy. He was the sort who if you had made him King of Jerusalem would have asked for Constantinople to go with it. As for Margaret, her burning ambition at this time was to bring her precious son, Henry Tydder, brought home from Brittany and restored to the earldom of Richmond. She thought us unaware that she was in constant communication with the King's great rebel and traitor, Henry's uncle, Jasper Tydder calling himself Earl of Pembroke. Known to us by his Yorkist Intelligence codename Uncle Jasper. (It was a lot shorter than 'Jasper Tydder calling himself Earl of Pembroke'.) There was a standing bounty of 5,000 marks on that fellow's head.

The Stanleys had their own private network, including at least one fellow at Middleham. I had detected him — he was one of the under-cooks — and I took great pleasure in finding new ways to feed him with false information. The trouble was, you could never be quite sure there weren't others playing the same game, people that I had *not* detected.

One way or another, I had plenty to occupy me, although much of the information was trifling and insignificant, except as part of a larger picture. One afternoon, however, I received something very interesting from Scotland. It had come by indirect means of course. Outwardly, it was a bill of account from a merchant in Newcastle.

It was in our number 7 code, which we hardly ever used as it took an age to decipher. This was saved only for matters of significant importance. When I had translated it into plain English I took it at once to Richard.

He was, fortunately, in his office. This was unusual, as he liked to have a clear desk by noon and the rest of the day for leisure. I found him muttering darkly over 'something fish garths'.

'Your Grace,' I said, making my curtsey, 'there is significant news from Scotland. The Earl of Mar has been accused of witchcraft.'

'Witchcraft?' He gave me a quizzical look. 'That's a new one. What do you make of it, Alianore?'

'Witchcraft is a load of bullshit,' I said. 'Mar has been on bad terms with his brother for an age. He wants the truce broken and full-scale war with us. My guess is he's really accused of treason, but witchcraft is easier to establish. It needs little proof. The accusation is usually enough.'

'Is this your work?'

'I'd like to claim it. I've been focused on trying to turn Albany. He's the more important, and the more unstable. He might jump any old way. Mar is, well, younger and lesser-known. I've barely tried to meddle with him. This is very good though. An enemy of England is taken out.'

'Witchcraft,' Richard mused. 'Do you know, some people claim the Queen is a witch? Even that she raised a fog to cover the battlefield at Barnet.'

'Well, it wouldn't have been much help, would it? Unless it was a *selective* fog? It would have made more sense to turn Warwick into a toad.'

He laughed. 'Maybe that was too much for her! As you said, Alianore. Bullshit. Some people will believe *anything*.'

'Yet I think there is a line in scripture,' I said. '*Rebellion is as the sin of witchcraft.* Therefore witchcraft must exist. To deny scripture is heretical, I think.'

Richard frowned. 'Samuel, if I am not mistaken. I do not deny it. I say that most accused of it would not have the learning to know where to begin.'

'Quite,' I said. 'I knew a witch, long ago. At least, one who claimed to be one.'

'Really? When was that?'

'In Wales, long ago. When I was but a girl. She was called Tegolin. She said I would be Queen of England — or could be. Look how that turned out!'

We both laughed. Then he began to pour out wine for us both.

15

'Any turbulence in Scotland calls for a small celebration, and especially when those hostile to England are suffering,' he said, placing a glass in my hand. 'Long live king Edward!'

I drank. 'Long live King Edward! England and York!'

'England and York!'

'Alianore,' he said, as I turned to leave, 'less worthy ladies than you have been crowned.'

It is pleasant enough to be flattered by a duke.

I made another curtsey. A full, court one. 'I could say something very similar to you, your Grace,' I said.

In my time I have known many men. Few better than Richard of Gloucester. It was odd to think that I had once turned down the chance to marry him. It was not my fate, and I knew it.

The Mission Begins. Christmas and its Aftermath, 18th Year King Edward IV (1478)

It had been a particularly dull Christmas at Middleham. The Earl of Northumberland and his lady had been among Cousin Richard's guests, and that hadn't helped, since Henry Percy's entire conversation was about himself and his own importance. The York Waits failed to turn up — wheel fallen off their cart while still in the snow south of Ripon — so there was no music apart from that provided by the ladies and gentlemen of the household. Who wants to listen to amateurs? The mummers were about as entertaining as a broken leg and the last cask of malmsey wine had turned sour. Even dear Anne, the Duchess, was out of sorts, while her mother, the Countess of Warwick[1], kept on talking about recipes for preserved fruit and her fascinating experiences as an amateur midwife. Richard was sulking because Lady Warwick had bought herself a fancy gold ornament without consulting him, and he'd just got the hefty bill for it from the merchant in York. I suppose it all went to prove one thing — it is actually impossible to die of boredom.

The last thing I expected to follow on from this excitement was a command from the King to go in search of the Holy Grail. It just goes to show that in this life one never knows quite what is coming next.

King Edward was not above consulting sundry wizards and necromancers — personally I am inclined to blame that so-called wife of his, Elizabeth Woodville, who had witchcraft in the family and claimed to be descended from Melusine the famous water demon. Anyway, one or the other of these lunatics had recently told him that the Holy Grail would be discovered somewhere within his dominions. No details of course, not even a rough map, of where exactly it was located, just *somewhere*. Needless to say, the story was that once he had his hands on it his throne would be secure, he'd conquer France and Scotland, and well, he'd be the greatest King of England *ever*.

---

[1] Alianore's repeated references to the Countess of Warwick, widow of the Kingmaker, demonstrate that she was living in Gloucester's household in the 1470s, and not under any kind of restraint.

But of course the Grail still had to be found, and it was not a job a busy man like the King, with six feasts, five hunts and three orgies written into his weekly diary, could undertake personally. So he worked through his list of assets until he found Roger and me — and he sent us a short letter and a long commission.

I suppose I should explain what the Grail is, for the benefit of anyone who has been asleep from birth. It's the cup from which Our Lord Jesus Christ drank at the Last Supper. Just about the most holy object you can imagine and it is said to have all kind of miraculous powers. For example, to drink from it is to have all your illnesses and ailments cured in a moment. The only snag is that it's lost. There are all sorts of legends about it, but no one has seen it in centuries.

'I don't think this is a mission we should accept,' said Roger.

'I disagree,' I told him. 'The traditional search period for the Holy Grail is a year and a day, and before that we'll need at least three months to research the texts. That's fifteen months holiday by my reckoning, and we can charge the whole cost to expenses. That strikes me as a nice little earner. All we need do is ride about a bit, have a few conversations with various weird punters, and write up a report. Money for old bow strings if you ask me.'

'But, Alianore — where on earth do we start?'

'Cornwall and Wales are the obvious places. Not that it really matters, because we aren't going to find it. It's ten to one on that the thing doesn't even exist.'

Roger was shocked. 'That's blasphemy! Or heresy at least.'

'No it isn't. I said it probably doesn't exist *now*, not that it *never* existed. Clearly, it did exist at one time. We are talking the ultimate relic — beyond price. People have been looking for it for over fourteen hundred years, and if they haven't found it then the chances are it isn't there to be found. Second favourite is that it's incredibly well hidden — it isn't going to be in some shop window, labelled 'Holy Grail'. It could be literally anywhere on earth, or below it. Built into some castle wall for all we know. Then there's another little matter. If we *did* find it, imagine how dangerous it would be. Neither of us is worthy to touch it for a start. We're sinners, not saints. Even *looking* at it might be a risk, if it's even half as powerful as it's supposed to be. Think it through. We don't want to find it — the thing is way too scary.'

Roger took his cap off and scratched his head; being a knight and all that goes with it he didn't like to admit that *anything* was too dangerous. Against the rules of his guild as you might say — sort of an insult to his *amour propre*, or whatever it's called in Latin.

'So what you suggest is that we just travel around, ask a few questions and make a point of *not* finding the Grail? It sounds like fraud — taking the King's money for nothing.'

'Roger, my dear, did we *ask* for this job? No, we didn't. It's pretty much a royal command and it wouldn't be polite to refuse — duty and all that.'

He gave me one of his looks. 'You're not usually so unquestioning in matters of duty,' he said, as if he suspected me of extracting the Michael.

'Well, it will make a refreshing change from being frozen to death at Middleham and we can spent at least part of the time searching at Horton Beauchamp — after all, the thing is as likely to be there as anywhere else.'

He insisted on discussing the question with Cousin Richard, but Richard, once he had seen his brother's paperwork, merely shrugged and said that we must certainly go, and that he looked forward to hearing of our adventures.

'I wish I could go with you,' he said gloomily. 'To find the Grail would be a bit special, almost as good as conquering the Turks or capturing Berwick. However, I can't very well rule the North *and* spend a full year riding about the kingdom. God be loved, there's a whole new dispute just come in this morning — those damned fish garths near York again. People get very heated about fish garths. Though at least I know where they've built the things. Where on earth do you propose to start?'

'Alianore suggested Wales,' said Roger.

'Well if I had the job I'd have a look at Glastonbury. That's where Arthur is buried and the monks probably have some writings in their archive about him and the Grail. You know Joseph of Arimathea is supposed to have brought it with him on one of his visits to England? He's also said to have brought the Lord Jesus over, when Our Lord was but a child. There are books about it in our library here — at least a couple. You try reading them and see if they give you any ideas.'

The Mists of Middleham

I did as he suggested. In fact, I stood at a lectern in the solar and read them out to the assembled company, while Roger, who writes a much more clerkly hand than I do, kept careful note of any relevant points. The books about Arthur were very long, and most of the stories were irrelevant to our quest, full of knights shattering lances with other knights, of the damsels they rescued from danger and of various unlikely witches who raised fogs and lived at the bottom of lakes and so on and so forth.

After three weeks of evenings like this everyone had had enough.

'God be loved,' said Richard, 'if I live to be a hundred before I hear another tale of King Arthur and his knights it will be too soon. Even the disputes over the fish garths are more entertaining. The men of York include more amusing invention in their tales than the author of this collection of badger excrement.'

'Language, Dickon!' objected Lady Warwick, who sometimes forgot he was no longer a twelve year-old page in her household but Duke of Gloucester, lord of the North, Constable of England and all the other stuff. 'I wish I could remember his name — he used to be in our service. Do you remember, Anne?'

The Duchess was as puzzled as the rest of us by her mother's sudden shift from her usual narrow range of topics. She shook her head and looked puzzled.

'Oh, he was obsessed with King Arthur and always boring us stiff with tales about him — that is when he wasn't drawing parallels with the modern world. I believe he was writing a book — he read us part of it once at Warwick and it was certainly better than any of this. Of course, he must be an old man by now — seventy or more if he's still alive. What was his name? Ah yes — Malory. Thomas Malory. A knight I think.'

Richard frowned. 'Thomas Malory? He was a die-hard Lancastrian. I think Ned had the fellow headed. He was certainly one of those he excluded from pardon.'

It was an awkward moment. None of us like to mention that Lady Warwick's husband, Anne's father, had himself died fighting for Lancaster. Of course, there really had been three sides in the fight — York, Lancaster and Neville — and it was true that many men had followed Warwick for love of the Nevilles rather than loyalty to Mad Henry VI and his unpleasant son. What Richard meant by 'die-hard Lancastrian' was that this Malory had not been one of these men — he had been one of the Henry VI fanatics, like my brother, Sir Humphrey Audley. (Every family has sheep with wool somewhat darker than it cares to admit.)

'Parallels with the modern world?' I had picked up on that. 'What parallels, madam?'

Lady Warwick looked at me as if I were stupid. 'Why, he compared good King Harry to King Arthur. What else? The man was *loyal*.'

There was a very awkward silence. Loyal to King Harry meant enemy of York.

'Then this is *political*,' I said, 'and that puts another slant on the matter. I think I prefer not to touch it after all.'

'It makes it more important,' Richard said. 'That manuscript, if it exists, needs to be seized and destroyed.'

'Or at least amended,' said Roger. 'We can change it to something more suitable. Make the parallels with King Edward, make them positive and very clear.'

'His manuscript *may* still be extant,' Lady Warwick said, 'and if it is, it will certainly be worth finding. I expect his family still have it in their possession.'

We all agreed it was worth a check. Lady Warwick thought she might even have the Malorys in an old address book, though she wasn't sure as she'd left so much behind when she was in sanctuary at Beaulieu. Conversation turned to something else, probably the wind and rain that were hammering at the windows. Though it was very warm and luxurious in the private apartments, we were still in the northern part of Yorkshire, which can be like a veritable ice floe in winter. Especially for those of us fortunate enough to be born in the South or Midlands — the natives scarcely seem to notice it.

*

Signs, Portents and Madmen. 19th Year of King Edward IV (1479)

I insisted on waiting until the weather turned warmer before we set off, but the trouble is that in the hills of Yorkshire good weather has a bad habit of unpunctuality. In the end, even though April's sweet showers had not had time to pierce the sharp drought of March to the leaf, let alone the root, we chose a day when it was not actually raining and made our farewells. I had several layers of clothes under my gown as I had no wish to feel chills running down my spine at every hint of an omen.

Anne made me promise to write and her mother handed us a jar of rose-hip syrup, which she said were a sovereign remedy against cold. Richard gave us one of his solemn looks and said that he wanted us back for Christmas.

The children, of course, we left in Anne's nursery, for they were all very young and much better in the Duchess's household, where there were always plenty of playmates, than roaming the roads and tracks of England and Wales. Nevertheless, we made up a substantial party, for a knight banneret and his lady must make some show of attendance, in case anyone thinks they are running out of money. I had my gentlewoman, Juliana, with me, and a maid to attend her. Roger had his squire, and then there was our indispensable Guy Archer and half a dozen stout fellows in our livery. Apart from our riding horses we had a whole string of pack animals to carry the stores we had calculated we would need — changes of clothes for everyone, armour and spare weapons (including Roger's favourite lance) for the men, reference books, a substantial amount of ready cash in various bags, some iron rations in case we found ourselves caught between inns, and my private cask of useful herbs and accessories.

You will appreciate that such a cavalcade could not travel swiftly, but there was no great need for haste and as far as I was concerned the whole purpose of the adventure was that we should enjoy ourselves as much as possible. We did not stop at *every* inn — only the respectable ones — and I'm not sure that we quite managed to venerate every available relic along the way, though we did our best. Even so, it took us several days just to reach York.

York was — and I dare say still is — a bustling place where you could buy almost anything from a fine-tooth comb to an anvil. Its greatest beauty in those days was that the citizens *loved* Richard of Gloucester, all but worshipped the ground he stood upon. Anyway, the point is that if you could produce your White Boar cognizance (as we both could) you would get an immediate ten percent discount on any marked price, without even haggling.

(You know, when I think about it, the adoration of the people of York was so excessive it was almost *embarrassing*. Of course, they were common people, merchants at best, and one must not expect those of low birth to have a proper sense of what is, well — proper. But even allowing for that, I've never heard of any ruler, of any place, who was even half way so popular; the wonder is that Richard had no more than two children born on the wrong side of the blanket. I think I can say without fear of contradiction that if he'd been so inclined he could have had *twenty-two* just in York alone, what with all those adoring people, of whom at least half were female.)

Once I had bought all the essential things I needed for the journey (and for a likely appearance at Cousin Edward's court) we had to invest in another pack-mule. Then we visited the great Minster, particularly to make offerings at the shrine of St. Richard Scrope, the holy archbishop murdered on the orders of the evil usurper Henry Bolingbroke[2] in the year of grace 1405.

I told Roger that if we were to have any chance at all with our mission (and I thought we had none) then we had to get as many saints as possible on board, even Yorkshire ones. You never know when a particular saint's intercession is going to tip the scales, but in any case it's better to have them on your side than batting against you. Scrope is a particularly powerful saint, by the way; no sooner was his head cut off than old Bolingbroke was struck with leprosy — just as he deserved for being a wicked Lancastrian. When a saint has that sort of kick, he's well worth propitiating.

---

[2] King Henry IV of the House of Lancaster; hence Alianore's partisan report of Scrope's execution.

Inside the Minster is a stone screen with a row of statues of kings, ranging from William the Bastard to Mad King Henry VI. Around Henry VI were a number of lighted candles and sundry small offerings, and as we approached one of the vicars choral was shooing away some of the local people who had been kneeling before it. Even as the last of them turned reluctantly away, he caught sight of Roger and me and assumed a horrified expression as he took in our combined collection of livery badges. I suspect he'd have looked more composed if the Archbishop himself had caught him with a whore on his arm while dipping into the poor box for her fee.

'We spend all our time driving these wretches away,' he protested. 'I doubt they intend any sedition, it's just ignorance and superstition. Some false friars have been preaching that Harry of Lancaster is a saint, and so they come to his statue to pray and make offerings. The Archbishop has pronounced it an insult to the King and an abuse of the Church, and yet still they come. I hope you don't think that anyone in authority here approves, because we do not. We are all loyal servants of King Edward, and pray for him constantly. And for the good Duke of Gloucester, of course.'

We were at pains to assure him that we would not report the outrage to Richard, or indeed to anyone else, and you would have thought from his countenance that we had just made an offering of fifty marks. He was even grateful for my suggestion that the best way to prevent any more of these displays was to have the statue removed and preferably smashed.

'Of course,' Roger said to me, as we made our way out, 'you realise, don't you, that up until Towton they said roughly the same thing about St. Richard Scrope. He only became a saint once we'd won.'

*

We were just outside York on our way south when I had what I can only describe as a vision. I do not normally have visions, you understand and nor do I encourage myself in that direction. It's a step too near madness for my taste, and, apart from that, there's always the possibility that the vision is diabolically inspired. I suppose saints and other very holy people are allowed to have visions, but I make no claims to sanctity.

Roger saw the change in me, saw me drop my horse's reins, and demanded to know what was wrong with me. He was, of course, very worried, the dear man, but it was at least a minute or two before I even knew that he was speaking, let alone what he was saying. When I returned to this world I shook my head like a dog that's been soaked in water, but I kept what I had had seen to myself. Partly this was prudence; partly it was that I did not really understand what I had seen. It made no sense.

I still find it almost impossible to describe. I can only compare it to a sort of shrine, though there were no candles or offerings and certainly no sign of an attendant priest or monk. There were many paintings of Richard — Richard of Gloucester that is — not very good likenesses but undoubtedly of him. There were books with strange covers, also with paintings on them, and there were more White Boars than you could shake at stick at. There were other things there that I have no words for. Curious painted boxes. The strangest thing of all is that this shrine — as I must call it for want of a better word — seemed to be built inside one of the city gates.

I have thought long and hard on this question but still do not understand the meaning of this vision, and merely record it as a matter of fact[3]. This was the first of many strange events during this quest which I cannot explain. It was possibly a thing of witchcraft — an attempt to deter us from our path. Yet if it was, who was it that performed the magic? Few knew of our purpose, or so I suppose. It was a secret mission, and we have not told all and sundry what we were about. Even our attendants knew no more than they needed to know.

In addition to this, why would the witch have chosen to create so strange and inexplicable a vision? Why not summon up some creature of hell? That would have been far more effective, I can tell you. Demons frighten me, puzzles do not. Sir Walter Gloy, my faithful chaplain, has suggested that sometimes the Devil is content merely to confuse us; to throw sand in our eyes, as he puts it. Given that he is a priest and so on I suppose his opinion on these matters bears some weight, the clergy knowing more about evil than most of us.

---

[3] It seems Alianore had a vision of the Richard III Museum, which was formerly situated in the Monk Bar. Though she often mocks her supposed supernatural powers, it appears she possessed them!

The Mists of Middleham

On balance, I think the most likely explanation is that it was one of those peculiar dreams that trouble us all from time to time, especially when we have eaten too much cheese the evening before. I must somehow have fallen asleep in the saddle, if only for a few moments, and had a weird dream; yet at the time it did not seem like a dream at all. I had the impression I was most vividly awake.

Anyway, after I had managed to persuade Roger that I had no wish to return to York and lie down on a bed for several hours (with or without his company) we rode on. I should like to pretend that we had planned every detail of our journey in advance, but this would be a gross exaggeration. We had certain key objectives in mind, places we knew we were going to visit, but apart from that we were inclined to follow our noses. By dinner-time[4] our noses had led us to the field of Towton.

Sir Roger became very quiet, even by his own standards. He rarely speaks of the battle even though, or perhaps because, he was in the thick of it. You can still see the mounds where the dead were buried [5], and very impressive mounds they are too. The Chroniclers relate all manner of silly numbers when describing this fight. Usually when they say 'a hundred thousand men' they simply mean 'the biggest number we can possibly imagine'. Nevertheless the total must have been impressive because almost the whole nobility of England was involved, even Lord Stanley.

For the benefit of those who do not know, I should explain that at the time of Towton, where Cousin Edward won his crown, we Yorkists were mostly Southerners, while the adverse party were mainly from the North. (There were of course exceptions on both sides, especially if you count Warwick and his brother as Northerners.) Most of Yorkshire lost fathers, brothers and sons there, and chiefly as a result of fighting for Lancaster. This made King Edward less popular in the North than the very Scots. Yet his brother Richard won the hearts of these hard-bitten people and made them his own. It's all the more astonishing when you reflect that your average native of the shire is deeply wary of anyone born outside his village. Taming a wolf is child's play compared to gaining the trust and friendship of such folk.

---

[4] In Alianore's terms about midday, or a little earlier. There was no such thing as 'lunch'.

[5] This may have been true in the 1470s, but the mass graves are no longer evident to a casual observer.

We knelt and prayed for a while, as it seemed the proper thing to do, given that we were engaged in a holy Quest. I suppose it might have edged someone a little closer to the exit gate of Purgatory, and a charitable deed always goes straight to the right side of God's ledger. The only trouble was that it was very muddy on that field. It seemed obvious to me that the place needed a proper chapel to cater for such devotions and I made a note on my wax tablet to mention the matter to Cousin Richard when we saw him again[6].

These duties done, we came across a charming wayside alehouse with the sign of the Greyhound[7], and sat down for a quart of ale and what they described as a *ploughman's* — this latter comprised several thick slices of bread that seemed to have more millstone than flour in them, a hunk of the local cheese, which in fairness was quite adequate, and a pickled onion.

There was only the one room, no little parlour for the gentry or other hint of sophisticated trade. Roger was granted seisin of the only chair and endowed with a pewter pot of strong ale in honour of his knighthood. The rest of us had to make do with the benches and leather jacks of small ale. (Although it must be said that a similar brew would be sold in London as 'XXXXX Best' and charged at nine times the price.)

We set into our victuals with a good will and some of us, particularly Roger, fell into conversation with the yokels of the place. It appeared they had all fought at Towton, even those who by their looks were so young that, if they were there at all, they must have had one hand on a battleaxe and the other on their mother's breast. Even more improbably, they all claimed to have been on the Yorkist side — this I very much doubted, but it wasn't worth arguing about.

---

[6] Richard III founded just such a chapel on the battlefield, but due to the Tudor usurpation it appears never to have been completed. It is *possible* that Alianore suggested this foundation, but Richard's own piety needed little prompting in such matters.

[7] A public house of this name still exists in the village of Saxton, near to Towton. Whether it stands on the site of the one Alianore describes is a matter of conjecture.

This went on for quite a while, until the greater part of our company was at least moderately drunk, and even Guy Archer — who has a better head for ale than most men have for water — was blinking like a rudely-awakened owl. The sun was lower in the sky than I cared to see, and so I coughed and hinted in my modest way that it was probably time we were on our way. After much muttering and sundry delays caused by hurried visits to the back yard, the procession formed up again, with a fair proportion of our meinie leaning in their saddles at improbable angles, and even Roger looking a little more flushed than a gentleman should during daylight.

The local yokels formed a sort of guard of honour around us, lifting their ale mugs in salute and calling out their good wishes for our journey. One or two even asked to be remembered to King Edward. But above all, they cried out warnings that we should be very careful if our path took us through Barnsdale. Robin Hood, they claimed, was back in the robbery business in those very parts.

Now, given that the proceedings were being conducted in a sort of drunken haze, I was inclined to dismiss this warning as mere banter and merry quipping. My reasons for this were as follows:

Robin Hood flourished in the days of King John or Edward II, depending on which source you care to credit.

He must therefore have been dead for at least a century, and probably much longer.

He is normally associated with Sherwood Forest, not Barnsdale[8], wherever that might be.

We were travelling in a large group, mainly composed of burly men armed with sharp swords, axes and sundry bows.

Your average Yorkshireman likes nothing more than to wind up his social betters if he thinks he can get away with it.

---

[8] It is south of Pontefract, as we shall see.

The Mists of Middleham

Robin Hood is a fictional character, like King Arthur and Guy of Warwick. He did not actually exist at any time, let alone in my time. Moreover, his legend includes the story of his death at the hands of the Prioress of Kirklees, wherever that is[9].

*

We rode on to Pontefract Castle without further incident, save for the occasional fellow falling asleep in the saddle and dropping off. Pontefract (or Pomfret as the locals call it) is a strong fortress and a very fine lodging. Here the White Boar badge procured free supper, bed and breakfast for the whole crew of us. The rooms were comfortable after a long ride, and cleanly enough, being swept at least once a month in case Richard should choose to drop by, as he sometimes did when journeying about the North in the course of his duty as the local boss.

Pontefract is famous for three things: liquorice, rhubarb and the murder of King Richard II. The first two are plants grown for medicinal purposes (for no sane person would eat such vile-tasting stuff for pleasure) by the local monks. As for the Second Richard, the Constable of the Castle insisted on taking us on the tour, showing us the dungeon where the martyr king had been starved to death on the orders of the usurper Bolingbroke. It was as vile a hole I've seen in my life, and I've seen a few — and even been lodged in a couple in my time. I suppose the fact that Bolingbroke was not smitten with leprosy immediately, but only after the murder of St. Richard Scrope, proves that King Richard II was not a saint. (Though I'm sure he was a much better man and a much better king than the wretched Bolingbroke.)

In the morning, we set off down what is sometimes called The Great North Road; though it could as rationally be called The Great South Road when one is travelling towards London. It was, as roads go in this country, in excellent condition, never less than ten feet wide and never more than six inches deep in mud. We made splendid progress, as mounted parties do on such a surface, perhaps as much as three leagues[10] an hour.

---

[9] The Priory of Kirklees was near Huddersfield, Yorkshire, and still extant in Alianore's time. One wonders at her ignorance, unless she was being ironic; which is quite probable.

[10] This distance is, very roughly, nine miles, or 14.48 kilometres.

The country became increasingly wooded, and although by statute a goodly distance on either side of the road is supposed to be kept clear, no one had bothered with such a detail and the trees and bushes pulled at one's clothing almost continuously, while it was sometimes necessary to duck in the saddle below a low branch. Why Parliament insists on passing laws that no one obeys and no one even tries to enforce I do not know. Those who talk most in the Commons are damned, thieving lawyers, and I suppose it makes them feel important and gives them something to make speeches about. As my mother used to say, Parliament may vote a turd to be a rose, but a turd it remains[11].

We intended to spend the night in Doncaster, a pleasant town that is strategically placed to be about a day's comfortable ride from Pontefract. We did not hurry, and had a couple of leisurely pauses to eat and drink, so it was well into the afternoon before we came to a roadside sign which read:

>Welcome to
>BARNSDALE
>A gonne-free zone
>Beware of the Outlaws

This was all quite freshly painted, and it was such an unusual sight that we all paused to stare at it. We were still staring at it, jaws more or less dropped, when an assortment of strange-looking punters clad in vivid green outfits emerged from the undergrowth. They all had arrows notched in their bows, and made no little show of pointing the said arrows at our various hearts. My first thought was that they must be a bunch of deluded Lancastrians still hiding in the depths of the woods after Barnet and Tewkesbury, quite unaware that the war was over.

'Stand and deliver!' cried the leader of this merry bunch, a stout enough fellow who spoiled his appearance by wearing a ridiculous feather in his hat.

Roger reached for his sword, as a knight does automatically in such circumstances, but with no armour on his back and three or four arrows aimed directly at him, he had a swift change of mind.

---

[11] This is evidently an ancient saying. Robert Graves included it in his novel *Wife to Mr. Milton*, and as he did not have access to Alianore's manuscript he must have found it in another source.

The Mists of Middleham

'I am Sir Roger Beauchamp, of Horton Beauchamp, in the county of Gloucester, Justice of the Peace and adviser to his Grace, the Duke of Gloucester,' he said in his sternest voice—which is very stern indeed. 'I warn you that I am on an important mission for the King himself.'

'God save King Richard!' they yelled in unison, lifting their bows high in salute.

'It's King Edward, actually,' Roger answered. Rather pedantically I thought given that it's usually wise to humour dangerous lunatics.

'I'm sorry, sir,' said Feather-hat, 'but we get confused with kings' names. They do change quite a bit and we don't always get the news out here. Forgive me for not introducing myself. I am Robin Hood, and these are my followers. Little John; Friar Tuck; William Scarlet; Much the Miller's son; Alan-a-Dale; Maid Marian – and sundry others whose names need not detain us, since they're not included in the legend and just play a supporting role.'

He gestured to each of the wretches as he named them, grinning like an ape that has just received a very significant and unexpected legacy.

'What mummery is this?' Roger growled; he was growing impatient. 'Robin Hood has been dead for centuries, as any fool knows.'

'Sir,' replied the lunatic, bowing low, 'we mean you no harm; we are but re-enactors, keeping a noble tradition alive. As you are obviously a goodly knight, custom requires only that we give you supper and a night in the greenwood in return for a reasonable fee. We shall drink the King's health, and damnation to Prince John. Now if you were the Abbot of St. Mary's, York, we should have to beat and bind you. Or the Lord High Sheriff of Nottingham, well, that would be really serious stuff. You'd be lucky to get away with your life. But you are neither, so don't be a spoilsport. You like venison, don't you?'

'Only if it's cooked in a decent sauce,' said Roger.

'The best in all Yorkshire,' Robin promised. 'We've been recommended for the quality of our table; it's all locally-sourced produce, of course. You could not find a better inn for food this side of Stamford, though I say it myself. As to the charges, they're very reasonable. Oh, you can count yourself lucky to be held up by us, Sir Roger. We're not so much outlaws as caterers.'

I sidled my horse closer to Roger and said in a low tone, 'Look, my dear, whoever these peasants are, they're all clearly madder than a March hare that the other March hares point at and call eccentric. They're probably harmless, but I think it good policy to play along. I don't suppose they'll delay us long, and given that Lent is over and it isn't a fast day, I see no objection to a venison supper. It might even be quite amusing to view their rustic follies.'

The absurd rogues insisted on blindfolding us all, and we were, I suspect, led in circles for a mile or two before the horses halted and the blindfolds were removed. We found ourselves in a large clearing, with crude structures – not quite houses – built around the edges of it and, right in the centre, a very large table. Not the sort of thing you would find in a decent castle of course, but roughly knocked together from planks of wood, some of which still had pieces of bark showing along the edges. There were a handful of chairs, constructed in the same rough-and-ready fashion as the table, and an ample supply of benches. Camp fires were already blazing away in the background, and some more of the guild of lunatics were turning whole deer carcases over the flames.

We were invited to sit down, and some quite reasonable wine — obviously stolen — was served to Roger and me. Everyone else had to make do with ale, though from what Guy Archer had to say about it I gathered it was a decent quart and by no means to be despised. The fellow who called himself Alan-a-Dale produced a lute from some crevice and started to sing the kind of songs that make you cringe and desire to bury your head in your hands. Cheese is not the word. The whole of Wensleydale, working day and night for an entire winter, could not possibly have produced such a quantity of it. Apart from the vile choice of material, he had the voice of a ruptured goat. Frankly, I'm still surprised he didn't attract the cats from all three Ridings of Yorkshire.

(I should perhaps explain for the benefit of those who have never been there that Yorkshire is divided into three Ridings, plus the Ainsty of York, which is a few hundred acres controlled by the citizens of York. 'Riding' is an old Viking word for 'third' and has nothing to do with how far you can ride in a day or anything like that. Yorkshire is a very large county, and some parts of it are exceptionally remote. It's easy to get lost, and I speak from experience. I once tried to ride from Middleham to Richmond market and found myself so far lost on the high moors that I had to spend a long night in a ghastly alehouse used by sheep drovers at a place called Tan Hill[12]. And, given that the rain was coming down in icy sheets, and you could see no further than your horse's nose, I was very glad of the shelter at the time, though it took me three months to be rid of the fleas of the place.)

At last the starter was served. It turned out to be venison soup, or possibly venison broth, but Robin called it velouté of venison drizzled with freshly ground acorns and locally-produced sheep cheese. I suppose I have eaten worse, but it really was nothing you would record on vellum and include in a monastery cook-book. The conversation continued, and was quite entertaining given that considerably more than half the company were the sort of fellows who would have been thrown out of Bedlam for lowering the tone of the place. About every two minutes someone would rise to propose a toast to the King — they gradually came around to the idea that his name was Edward — and we would have to get to our feet to drain our cups, or rather our hunting-horns. The hunting-horn is a most unsatisfactory form of drinking-vessel, not least because while it has liquid in it one cannot put it down, which is damnably inconvenient when one is trying to eat. However, I gathered its use was traditional, almost to the point of being a sacred obligation. It probably came down from the culture — if culture is the word — of the Vikings, who were once mighty gossips in that neck of the woods.

I should add that some of the hunting-horns were larger than others, and I was glad that mine was one of the smallest. After quite a short while some of the company could no longer get to their feet when summoned. The punishment for this crime was to be hit over the head with a large sausage. Most of those around the table squealed with delight at every fresh episode of this, but unfortunately I was neither drunk nor mad enough to share in the joy of it.

---

[12] A public house still exists at this location. It is said to be the highest in England.

The main course followed on. This comprised pieces of venison in some kind of thick sauce. Robin described it as 'escallops of venison served in Friar Tuck's special jus, with a trio of Saxon-touch root vegetables, garnished with hand-picked dandelion leaves.' It seemed promising, but unfortunately the loyal toasts continued unabated, and fewer and fewer of the company were able to rise to them. The first sausage had broken long ago, and a new and thicker one was brought into play.

Then it began to rain. More precisely, it began to deluge. I have rarely in my life seen anything like it, except perhaps during the time of the Duke of Buckingham's Great Flood. If someone had been tipping whole baths of water over us, I doubt whether we could have been any wetter.

'This is the trouble with being an outlaw in England,' Robin shouted over the roar of the storm. 'The greenwood is all very well until it rains.'

Up until this point, I had, in a way, been enjoying myself. It was true that I was surrounded by drunks and lunatics, but this was nothing new to someone who had attended as many court banquets as I had. The food had been tolerable, and the company above average. But now, soaked through to the skin, and with the water dripping from my nose like the effect of a very bad cold, I was no longer amused. Roger, being a chivalrous and thoughtful knight, rose to his feet, covered me as well as he could with his cloak, and hurried me towards one of the shelters. Inside, it resembled a cow byre, except that no cowshed on our lands would have been allowed to fall into such a disgusting condition. The roof did at least keep out most of the rain, and I sat myself in a corner on the straw and dripped. Our people gathered around us, all equally wet and some pole axed by the amount of ale they had taken on board. Sleep was impossible, and I spent a miserable night getting more and more furious.

Dawn broke, with some of my companions, including Sir Roger, sound asleep. I rose and squelched outside to find a suitably discreet place to relieve myself. That's another problem with the greenwood; there are no facilities at all. The outlaws had not even tried to dig proper latrines. If anyone thinks that living under a tree is romantic, I make haste to disillusion them. It stinks — quite literally. I washed my hands as best I could in a swollen stream, wiped myself down, and prepared for combat. The lunatics had made no attempt to search me, and my service-issue poniard was in its place in my secret pocket, a little damp but otherwise perfectly in order. I drew it from its scabbard and tested its edge. (For some strange reason one is always compelled to try the edge in such circumstances — the habit has cost me many a cut finger.) I could, I believe, have given a man a clean shave with it, had I felt so inclined.

Robin was sleeping in one of the smaller hovels, alone but for the so-called Maid Marian. Taking a slight run-up, I kicked him as hard as I could in the fork of his legs. Then, while he was still trying to make sense of the sudden and unexpected agony in his gonads, I moved swiftly to kneel on his chest and hold the point of the dagger extraordinarily close to his face. (I should explain here, for the advantage of any young damosels who may be reading this text, that a knife should not be brandished at the maximum distance from your body, as though it were a poisonous snake that might bite you at any moment, but kept close; hence my choice of position for this piece of action.)

'I know what you're thinking,' I said quietly. 'You're thinking, "Can I get a grip of her wrist before she can drive that poniard through my eye and into my brain?" Well, this is a Mancini XII Champion, the sharpest blade in the world, specially imported from Milan, and I've been trained in its use by the King's own Knifemaster-General. I can have the point sticking out of the back of your skull quicker than you can blink. So, go ahead, pilgrim. Make my day.'

'This is — unexpected,' he gasped. 'Not remotely like any part of the legend.'

'I don't get angry very often,' I told him, 'in fact, hardly ever, but you have made me very, *very* angry, you silly little man. I'm soaked, I've not had a single wink of sleep, and it's six to four on that in a couple of days I shall have the chill of all chills, and quite possibly die of it. This gown — though admittedly not one of my best — is ruined through lying on your filthy straw and you have seriously inconvenienced my lord and husband, who is a noble knight engaged on a holy quest at the King's own command. Now, you pathetic sheep turd, what *exactly* do you propose to do about it?'

The pretended Maid Marian made her move at this point. Fortunately she came at me from my left, and I gave her a forearm smash in the face which set her nose bleeding, and she sat back to yowl with the pain of it. (I learned that particular trick on a Yorkist Intelligence training course, and very effective it is, even with the left arm. She was lucky not to come away with a broken nose.)

He shrugged. 'I suppose that, in the circumstances, we might offer you complimentary drinks. I think that might be fair.'

'I think I might introduce you to my friend, the Archbishop of York. Ever heard of the statute *De heretico comburendo*[13]? I think it covers people interfering with holy quests, especially ones authorized by the King himself, and I think you'll find the penalty is a bit more than a two bob[14] fine.'

'Well, I suppose I might give you a reduction — a *generous* reduction — on the food bill. Though I have to say, it's really not my fault that it rained. You can't blame me for that.'

'On the other hand, I might take the matter up with my kinsman and particular friend the Duke of Gloucester, or with the Earl of Northumberland, who more or less calls himself my brother. Either of whom would be more than happy to see you and your little chums quartered in Doncaster marketplace. You do understand that when I say "quartered" I am not using the word in the sense of "lodged"?'

'No charge at all, then,' he said, a little hesitantly. 'The meal and lodgings will be entirely complimentary.'

---

[13] Statute against heresy passed in 1401. Alianore was bluffing here, as it's unlikely the statute would have been interpreted as covering mere interference with a holy intention, as opposed to heresy.

[14] English slang for two shillings. The penalty under the statute was actually death by burning.

'Then there's King Edward,' I said. 'Did I mention he's my cousin? He takes a very dim view of members of the lower orders who mess with the ladies of his family. On top of that, you've caused delay to a project that he, personally, instigated. You know, I have this feeling he might not be very pleased. You certainly won't like the King when he's angry. By comparison, I'm a particularly amiable pussy cat.'

'And of course, there would also be financial compensation. We don't like any of our clients to leave unless they're entirely satisfied. Will five pounds be enough?'

I thought about asking for more, but five pounds is a useful amount of money, and one should always be generous in negotiation.

'We have a deal, my friend,' I said, 'and what's more, you need not provide breakfast. And I shall recommend your dining experience to everyone I know.'

I removed my poniard from the vicinity of his eye, and hauled myself back to my feet. What I did not appreciate was the size of the audience we had collected. Everyone was awake, and formed in a rough semi-circle behind us. Some of the outlaws had actually taken up their bows, and for a moment I thought the situation was going to kick off, big time.

Robin held up his hand. 'No — let them go in peace. It's the first rule of our company that we do not offer violence to helpless women. Nor do we have a quarrel with this good knight, her husband. It's been an interesting adventure, and we part as friends.'

'Alianore — put that knife away!' Roger said sternly. 'The rest of you, get ready to leave. We've work to do, and can't waste the morning entertaining the local peasantry. Now, move!'

No one stood around to argue. Roger is quiet by nature, but when he speaks he speaks with authority, and you can tell that he's fought in a few battles in his time.

As we rode out of the woods he said to me: 'My dear, I should appreciate it if you would let me do the fighting in future, instead of making an ass of yourself in front of the servants. It's bad for discipline, you know.'

'Yes,' I said, 'I'm afraid I rather lost my temper, and I ought not to have done. Still, what a wonderful world! We've been captured by Robin Hood and yet came away five pounds richer. Most people would call that good business.'

When we reached Doncaster, we booked ourselves into the finest inn available, *The Broken Oath*, got out of our damp clothes, and went to bed for a very long time. After supper we went back to it again, but I was up betimes next morning and made my way to the White Friars, where I laid out a fair proportion of the five pounds for a particularly heavyweight wax candle for Our Lady of Doncaster. I like to think that Our Lady of Doncaster was suitably impressed, as it was by far the largest of the many set about her statue, not that one should boast of such things. It was partly an offering of gratitude for our safe escape from those rogues, and partly a request for intercession for the good conclusion of our mission. I prayed for quite a while at the shrine before returning to the inn for a hearty breakfast.

*

It was while we were in Doncaster that we learned that King Edward's youngest son, George, Duke of Bedford, had lately died, supposedly of the Pestilence[15]. It was interesting to hear the talk of it. Some said it was a judgement on the King for executing his own brother, George Clarence, the previous year. Others that God's punishment was due to the King taking the Bedford title from Warwick's nephew, George Neville, so it could be bestowed on his own son. No one seemed to think it might just be a natural event. No one had much sympathy for the King, either. My general impression was that the people of Doncaster and the local gentry felt he deserved everything he got. Doncaster was one of the King's own towns, so the prevailing attitude was all the more worrying.

*

---

[15]Pestilence – bubonic plague.

It seemed to me that we now needed to buy mourning, as there is nothing more embarrassing than to arrive at court in bright colours to find that everyone there is wearing black. It's worse than being unfashionable. However Roger said we should wait until we hit London, and ask around. The little boy had only been two years old, or thereabouts, and mourning for such young children tends to be quite short. The mention of pestilence worried me also, but there is nothing much one can do about that except pray. You can drink goat's piss, or wear a necklace of pork sausages, or do one of a thousand other things that people suggest, but none of them really work in such a case.

*

I do not propose to describe the whole of our journey south in detail – where we lodged, which shrines we venerated, who got drunk, and who started unnecessary fights. For one thing it would be tedious, and for another I have long since forgotten the details and my records are incomplete, with many lacunae. That in itself is mysterious, as I have distinct recollection of making notes that seem, somehow, to have vanished. I should however mention that there were a number of strange portents along the way — and I do not refer to such incidents as Sir Roger almost riding his horse into a marl pit, or the meeting with the champion archer of Nottinghamshire, when Guy won us a good eighty shillings in side bets, to say nothing of a flitch of bacon.   For one thing I continued to have visions from time to time, none of which made the least sense. These worried me, hence my unusual willingness to light candles to every available saint and to make generous offerings to every religious house we came across. I had begun to suspect that demons were at play, and in such circumstances it undoubtedly pays to have God and his various servants on your side. Some of the visions, like the first outside York, concerned Richard, and made me wonder if at some future time he would be canonised, since they seemed to predict his veneration by whole hosts of people yet unborn. I could not — and cannot — square this with reality. I should be the first, even writing as I do in these dark days under the rule of Henry Tydder, to declare that Richard was better man than most, and that he was also quite exceptionally pious, like his mother and his sister, the Duchess of Burgundy. But to make him a saint — St. Richard of Fotheringhay — would be too much. He could not work miracles, not even for himself.

For another thing, Roger kept saying the most extraordinary things in conversation. I will give you an example which will serve to demonstrate what I mean.

We were riding along, talking about this and that when for some reason he mentioned a family in the County of Chester, the Dones, that has the right to strike off the heads of malefactors without any form of trial or legal process. They abuse this right by holding innocent men to ransom, and by this means make much of their annual income.

I had, in truth, heard of this family before, though I couldn't recall their name or the manor where they lived. Given my connections in the area, they are quite likely some form of cousin, but it doesn't really matter. I said it was a wrong and wicked way to make a living, and that if Richard of Gloucester ever had the power to end such an abuse he most certainly would do so.

He snorted. 'Some people would call that treasonable, Alianore, or at least disrespectful to the King's Grace.'

'Not at all,' I said, 'I've always been loyal to the House of York, certainly since my brother Audley turned his coat — and before that I was too young for my opinion to count. It's just that I am on the reform wing of the party, like Richard, and I don't like to see injustice. It brings the King into disrepute, and he can't afford that. Look what they were saying about him in Doncaster — they still blame him for Towton and the fall of the Nevilles.'

'My dear, the nation will hardly be rocked by the opinions of the people of bloody Doncaster, will it? Hereditary power is the whole basis of society, and the ransoms are reasonable — a sort of toll. You can't just put an end to ancient customs and deprive gentlemen of their inherited rights. It would be revolutionary — Jacobinism at its worst.'

I stared at him, bewildered. 'Jacobinism? What's that when it's at home?'

He shook his head, like one startled out of sleep. 'I haven't the faintest idea,' he admitted, 'but since starting on this quest I often find strange words coming into my head. Sometimes, like just now, I feel compelled to utter them, even though they make no sense at all. Last night I asked the innkeeper for a Bacardi and Coke. No idea what *that* might be, and he looked at me as if I were mad, but I couldn't help it' I can't but think there's magic involved, Alianore; that something is taking us out of our normal world. I think it must be some kind of witchcraft, and pretty powerful witchcraft at that, if it makes you see visions and forces me to babble nonsense. I think we are either going to end up in Bedlam, or we'll slip through the space-time continuum. See, there I go again. I've no idea what it means, but it sounds like something that might get me burnt for heresy. You have to help me. Somehow, we have to stop it.'

I will admit to you that I was shocked. I married Roger precisely because he was a sensible, down-to-earth knight — the sort who regards fighting in a bloody battle as no more challenging than dead-heading the bergamot or writing a letter to John Paston. Yet here he was, jabbering mystic nonsense in the middle of the public highway like some half-crazed alchemist from the back streets of Oxford.

Yet in a moment he was talking sensibly again. 'You can't introduce logic or reason into questions of ownership. People, particularly gentlemen and those who rank above them, have their rights. Once you start running a fine-tooth comb through whether things make sense or not, you end up with questions like why should my lands be mine, just because they were my father's? Why should the King be the King, just because he happens to be the senior representative of Edward III? Why can't beggars and servants have a vote for the Commons? The world isn't meant to be tidy and logical. England in particular isn't meant to be. We aren't tidy or logical folk. People hold lands by the service of presenting the King with a pair of spurs on St. Swithun's Day, or by giving a red rose to the Abbot of St. Albans on Midsummer Day, and so on. It's traditional and it's charming and people like it that way. Start by taking away a man's right to cut off some random fellow's head and you end up with — well, I don't exactly know what you'd end up with, but it wouldn't be pretty or chivalrous or Christian.

'I think you're the sort of person who thinks that everything can be reduced to a formula, and that somehow, when you apply that formula, everything becomes fair. Well it doesn't, because fairness is an abstract concept, like decency.'

'Or Chivalry?' I suggested, feeling provocative.

'Chivalry has a code, Alianore, as you well know, but it's interpreted by individual knights in the light of their own honour. It's not worked out in advance by some clerk sitting in an office in Westminster, playing with numbers and trying to be "fair" to everyone. If it were, it wouldn't work properly. You have to leave room for discretion; indeed, in the end you have to trust people to play their part — especially if they are gentlemen.'

Anyway, you can see that I had plenty of cause for my extra prayers and offerings, and I hadn't a clue what else to do about my visions or the strange additions to Roger's vocabulary.

Eventually we turned off the London road and headed down the Fosse Way until, with the help of a local guide, we found Newbold Revel, once the home of Sir Thomas Mallory, and, as we had learned from Lady Warwick, now the main residence of his widow, Elizabeth. The place is in Warwickshire, a few miles outside Coventry, set in the sort of rich woodlands and fair fields that make one's heart ache for home. (I hasten to add that by 'home' I mean Horton Beauchamp, not the barren mountains and moors around Middleham.)

The manor itself seemed abandoned — it was an ancient, stone-built house covered by ivy, and although we banged on the door like bailiffs with a sheriff's writ, there was no immediate sign of life. At least ten minutes passed before the door creaked open to reveal a grizzled servitor who looked old enough to have attended Richard the Second's Coronation. He stared at us, his mouth slightly open, but said nothing.

Roger spoke sharply. 'Well, fellow? Is Lady Malory at home?'

The man seemed to hesitate for a moment. 'I shall make enquiries, sir,' he said, closing the door again.

This set Roger fuming. He does not care to be left waiting by menials, and although he claimed that his indignation was on my behalf, that was only a front. I shrugged and allowed Guy Archer to help me down from my mount. I could see little point in cursing and kicking the door. We were, after all, in no great hurry, and the servant was doubtless only doing as he had been bidden by higher authority.

After some considerable time, the door opened again. (I almost wrote that it creaked open again, but I think you can imagine that for yourself.) The same servant bowed low.

'You and your lady are most welcome, sir,' he said. 'If you will give me your name, I shall lead you at once to Lady Malory. Your people may wait in the hall, if it pleases you.'

Sir Roger announced us with some force, not in the least mollified. The fellow bowed again, not in the least troubled by my gentle knight's reference to him as a 'cursed whoreson', and we followed him into the darkness of the hall, a place that stank of damp and disuse. There was so much dust on the furniture that you could have planted a row of turnips along the table if you'd felt so inclined, and an eerie silence hung over the house, so intense that I swear you could hear the death-watch beetles tapping away in the beams of the roof.

After a complete diagonal traverse of the hall, we proceeded up a spiral staircase that was festooned with spiders' webs, along a passage decorated with hangings that looked as if they'd been left there by King Harold and never beaten since, and into a large and relatively handsome solar, well lit by an oriel window. As is usual in such locations, there was a semi-circular bench built into the window. On this bench were many well-worn cushions, and one lady, clad from head to foot in black. She was many years my senior, but not quite as elderly as I had expected, and her face, which was perfectly amiable, wore a somewhat bewildered expression as her servant announced us to her.

'Sir Roger Beauchamp?' she repeated. 'You will be of the Warwick family I suppose?'

Roger bowed. 'Madam, I spring from a branch of that family, and am a distant cousin of my lady of Warwick. Permit me to introduce my wife, Lady Beauchamp, who is another cousin of the Countess, but on her mother's side. We belong to the household of the Duke of Gloucester.'

This information seemed to impress Elizabeth Malory no end and she nodded her approval and invited us to sit on either side of her. She despatched her servant to fetch us food and wine, which is always a good sign that one has been accepted in a house.

'Of course,' she said, 'I remember Lady Warwick's *father*; now he was a splendid man, and a great knight, though of course he was never much in England. He was always away in France, fighting in King Harry's wars, so that his lady hardly saw hide or hair of him from one year's end to the next. And then his son, the Duke of Warwick, the fairest young man you have ever seen. My dear husband was never the same after the Duke was murdered by old Buckingham. It broke his spirit, and his mind. Then the wars came, and he was ruined, because he stood by King Harry. Nothing has ever been the same since then.'

There was a great deal more of this, and some of it was half way to being interesting if you had an obsession with the history of the Beauchamp family or the wickedness of old Buckingham — that is the grandfather to that Henry, Duke of Buckingham we all grew to know and love some years after the time I describe here.

From what I could make out, old Malory had hated Buckingham with a passion, and this had led him to favour York for a time, since Buckingham had been Lancastrian to his rotten core. However, once York had started to win, Malory had developed a fanatical attachment to Mad King Harry the Sixth — possibly assisted by the death of old Buckingham at the Battle of Northampton in the year '60. Anyway, he ended up so exceptionally Lancastrian that Cousin Edward excluded him from pardon, and he was lucky to die a natural death before he could have his head struck off.

(As an aside I should mention that if Henry, Duke of Warwick — my first cousin, by the way, though I never knew him — had been allowed to live, it is most unlikely that the Yorkist cause could have prospered. Because Anne's father would never have been Earl of Warwick, and would not have had half the power he in fact possessed. Henry Warwick was apparently the bosom buddy of Mad Harry when they were young men together, so it's highly unlikely he'd have turned Yorkist. So if old Buckingham *did* murder him — and that might be stuff and nonsense for all I know — he unknowingly struck a mighty blow for the House of York that day. There's a thought to conjure with.)

Anyway, after this digression reached its close, Roger and I managed to turn the conversation to the lady's husband, and, more to the point, his work on King Arthur.

'The King's men took all his papers away,' Lady Malory said, shaking her head. 'I don't know what happened to his book of Arthur, but it certainly isn't here. He wrote some of it in prison, you know, but none of it was ever given back to me.'

Roger and I looked at one another in disappointment. We had expected something of a treasure trove in this house, and not one we would have reported to any coroner. There was no saying who had the book — 'the King's men' could mean almost anyone, from the Under-Sheriff upwards. We could not hope to trace those who had arrested Malory and seized his movables — it might take weeks of checking the records, and there was a fair probability that at least some of those involved were now dead. There was also a very good chance that the manuscript had been destroyed — if written on parchment, perhaps scraped clean and reused as a merchant's account book or something.

We persisted for a time in some gentle questioning, but it was clear that Lady Malory knew almost nothing about the work. Like many authors, her husband had kept his writing to himself, and in addition, she was not in the least interested in the tale of King Arthur or the legend of the Grail, or in literature in general.

It was annoying, but there was nothing we could do apart from accept her kind offer of supper and a night's lodging between the moth-eaten sheets of one of her spare bedchambers. Before we left, she gave us a very decent breakfast and asked to be remembered to Lady Warwick when we next wrote to Middleham.

*

Our Modest Expenses Claim.

London always looks best when viewed from the high ground to the north of it. From there it looks positively impressive, with its high walls and multiple church steeples — the great spire of St Paul's soaring above the lot. After that, the closer you get, the more it stinks. Hardly surprising, when thirty or forty thousand people and their animals are crammed together in close proximity to one another – it is positively unhealthy, and a perfect breeding-ground for the pestilence and every other vile disease you care to name. I believe Paris is even larger — it boggles the mind to think of it.

London has more foreigners than you can shake a stick at — Flemings, Hollanders, Burgundians, Bretons, Lombards, Danes, Castilians, merchants of the Hanseatic League, French, even Scots. You can see men, believe it or not, with skin burnt black by the sun, not mere Moors but from distant lands far beyond. There are streets where one rarely hears an English voice, and people wander about in all manner of ludicrous and exotic costumes, waving their hands about and complaining because the inns don't serve olives and anchovies.

The locals don't like it much, and every so often riots break out and some fellow ends up swinging from the gallows as an example to the rest. However, it must be said that these aliens bring in trade, and they are also an excellent source of news for events outside the kingdom. Quite a few were kept on the payroll of Yorkist Intelligence for that very purpose. Treacherous schemes do not all end at Calais; for example, at this time King Lewis of France was nominally at peace with us, and indeed paying a regular pension to King Edward and even to some of our nobles, including Hastings. But he still required careful watching; he was a crafty rogue quite capable of playing both ends against the middle. This was quite obvious to anyone who was not in receipt of his cash — those in his pay tended to close their eyes and hope for the best.

For the time being, Roger and I sought only for news of where the King might be found. The court is never where you want it to be; it's usually a matter of tracing it by gossip, or travelling to its last known location and asking for the forwarding address. On this occasion it turned out to be at Windsor, which is about as far from London as it ever goes except when on an actual progress. It could have been worse, but it was still annoying that Edward was not somewhere more convenient, like Westminster or the Tower.

Our next step, after booking lodgings in one of the better inns of Southwark, and enjoying the benefits of a fine supper and a good night's rest, was to call at the Great Wardrobe. This, I should explain, is a large stone building near St. Paul's, where various items of the King's property are stored. Not just his spare clothes, as you might think, but whole stocks of cloth ready to be made into liveries; weapons, armour and banners that are not needed between wars; bed furnishings, hangings and other pieces of furniture that are not currently required — all manner of useful stuff. Repairs and maintenance of these items are also carried out — there is, for example, a whole room full of embroiderers.

At this time, it also housed the main archive of Yorkist Intelligence, which was located in the cellars, behind an armed guard and a locked door. Naturally, Roger and I had the necessary credentials to pass this barrier and reach the confidential clerks who worked beyond it.

These gentlemen were busy at work, or at least they gave a reasonable impression of being so, a locked door being a great advantage to a clerk. There were two of them, their desks placed below barred windows that admitted a surprising amount of natural light into the vault. Naturally they were burning wax candles as well, as a matter of principle, but it's questionable whether they really needed to do so.

We showed our credentials again, although one of the fellows clearly recognised me from my last visit, even though it had been some years since I had last set foot in London. He respectfully offered us some wine, and Roger and I assented, just as a way of being sociable. The wine wasn't fit for the King's table, but it wasn't vinegar either — one of the perks of the job was a share in any smuggled wine that the Service managed to detect. Not all of us were entirely focused on political and diplomatic matters.

Anyway, before long we got down to business and asked for any papers they had on Sir Thomas Malory. It turned out there was quite a bundle, and it took the pair of them to carry it all out from the dark recess where they had been stored. Roger and I each took over one of the spare carrels and began to plough through this stack of dusty treasure.

As anyone who has ever undertaken this sort of exercise will know, nine tenths of the documents were dull account rolls and records of wool clips and that sort of thing. However, there were some extremely amusing letters, including contributions from the likes of Margaret of Anjou, Warwick and even King Lewis of France himself that gave me a better understanding of some of the plotting that had gone on while I was still a very junior operative. One of the descriptions of Cousin Edward was so scatological that I could not hold back from roaring with laughter, unseemly though it might have been. I had never dreamed that old Warwick possessed such a vivid imagination, and made a mental note to tell the tale to Duchess Anne when next I saw her.

'Found it!' cried Roger suddenly, and he brandished a wad of parchment. A disappointingly thin wad, I noted.

I hurried over and helped him scrutinise the find. I had expected a long, complete manuscript, but this was nothing of the kind. It was more in the way of a collection of rough notes. If you were very generous you could, I suppose, have called it a plan. I remember a work of Christine de Pizan, *A Writer's Guide for Ladies and Damosels* [16], in which she stated that a good author should marshal her thoughts into something called a 'plan' before writing out a substantive manuscript. I have always thought that stuff and nonsense. Can you imagine if the Monastic Chroniclers had worked like that? — they'd still be working their way through the wars of Stephen and Matilda. However, it was clear that Malory had been influenced by this dangerous idea.

'Is that it?' I asked, moderately appalled.

'It looks very much like it.' Roger shuffled through more of his pile, more in hope than expectation. 'Most of this little lot is just enquiries from his bailiff about tenants and sheep-shearing. There's just the odd letter that hints at Lancastrian conspiracy, back in the day. For the most part though it's pretty dull stuff; I can't see posterity being interested in a list of Malory's books or a draft of a letter to the old Duchess of Suffolk, asking about her grandfather. Apparently he was some kind of poet. Good Lord, imagine what the Duchess must have thought of that! We've all got obscure nobodies in our family trees, but no one enjoys being reminded of it.'

---

[16] Christine de Pizan is well known, but the work Alianore quotes has been lost.

'Well,' I said, 'I suppose we'd better take it, for what it's worth. We might be able to make something of it.'

The clerks made no difficulty about our removing the manuscript. As far as they were concerned, it was part of a dead file, and as long as they had a signature for it they were covered. So we returned to the comfort of our inn, and took turns reading Malory's work in depth. Neither of us could find anything in it that pointed us in the right direction, and Roger was all for throwing it in the Thames. I thought this an extreme step, so I enclosed it with my next letter to Middleham, thinking that it might amuse the Duchess, or at least give her something to put on the floor the next time she was training a puppy.

*

It took a couple of days to reach Windsor, riding with some degree of haste and scarcely bothering to visit a single shrine. At last the great castle became visible on the horizon, its towers crowded with banners, just like the illustrations you see in a particularly well-illuminated romance. The King was very clearly at home, and we were glad to have caught him, as one never knows with kings. They can be dragged about all over the place by the exigencies of the kingship service, to say nothing of any desires they may have to go hunting on a different manor, or get secretly 'married' in some remote chapel.

We claimed our lodgings, which, since we had only just arrived and Roger was not a duke, were somewhat cramped and dirty. After we had washed away the dust of the road and donned our finest clothes, the ones we could wear about the court without people pointing and sneering, we made our way into the main building to present ourselves to Lord Hastings, passing beneath a sign that said: *Persons of Rank ONLY*. When you think about it, that was a very silly sign, since everyone has some sort of rank, but apparently it was installed to keep out beggars and other particularly obnoxious plebs. (I dare say the Tydders will have introduced an admission charge by now — anything to make money.)

The Mists of Middleham

Windsor, in case you haven't been there, is an enormous castle, and even if you're reasonably familiar with the place (which I was not) it requires quite complex navigation. When the court is in residence it's packed to the gills with all the folk you would expect plus quite a few you would not. Here you might have the Duke and Duchess of Suffolk and their entire tail of hangers-on; there you might find an ambassador from Burgundy, with his servants laden with rich gifts for the King and the advanced draft of some complex treaty; in this corner perhaps a pack of overdressed knights and squires set around a table dicing their livelihoods away; somewhere else there might be the prioress of some obscure nunnery, virtually alone and desperately anxious to speak to *someone* about her collapsed bell-tower, and next to her the Mayor of Bristol and his aldermen, petitioning for a new charter. Liveried boys run around with messages, and servants carry this and that from one place to another. All of these and many more, and the one thing they have in common is that they stand about in groups, blocking every passage, every stairway and indeed most of the great rooms. And you are supposed to remember who outranks you (curtsey, depth adjusted to their relative importance), and who doesn't (polite nod or a slight dip will do), as well as updating every passing acquaintance with your life story. Even with the best will in the world (which I have never claimed to possess) it takes time and patience to work your way through a crowd like this.

After half-an-hour I believe we were completely lost, but Roger refused to admit it, probably for fear that it might diminish him in my eyes. But eventually we found the right stair, a relatively uncrowded one with a young archer on guard at the foot of it. He nodded us through, and on the first landing we found a door marked: *Lord Chamberlain's Office*. It was a decent-sized room, with Hastings' bed filling one corner. The man himself sat behind a big desk in the oriel, where he had maximum light to do his work. There were two smaller desks for clerks, and all three work-stations were a foot deep in paper and parchment, just as you'd expect. It was a bit like Cousin Richard's office at Middleham, except Richard was tidier, started work before breakfast, and usually got down to the wood before Sext[17].

'Ah,' said Hastings, 'you are here at last!'

---

[17] A Canonical hour. Alianore is suggesting Richard usually cleared his desk by what we would call Lunch. Whereas Lord Hastings, apparently, was in a constant muddle.

50

He made it sound as if we'd made a detour by way of India just to wind him up. Roger explained some of the difficulties we had met on the road, and told him what little we had learned, while I rooted about in my purse for our account of expenses so far. It was a very reasonable submission, I thought:

Expenses of Sir Roger Beauchamp, Knight, and his meinie, coming from Middleham to the court of King Edward's Grace. Videlicet:

	£.	s.	d.
Lodgings on journey	3	10	0
Purchase of essential clothing	155	14	8
Purchase of books and MSS about King Arthur	45	6	8
Purchase of an ass, to transport essential equipment	2	0	0
Donations to shrines, etc.	0	6	3
Payments to guides.	0	0	9
Laundry (Payments to laundresses).	0	5	2
Stationery – parchment, paper, ink	0	3	2
Food	2	7	6
Ale, wine, etc.	3	2	3
New horseshoes, including farriers' fees	0	4	2
Gratuities	0	0	3
Total owed by Crown to Sir Roger Beauchamp, Knight.	213	0	10

I will not say Hastings' face was purple as he read this, more a delicate puce.

'I can't possibly pay this,' he cried, holding the paper away from him as if it stank of pig muck, 'Over two hundred quid in expenses for a journey from Yorkshire to Windsor! Do you think the King is made of swiving gold?'

(He didn't actually say 'swiving'.)

I shrugged. 'Then we had better go straight back to Middleham. Neither of us asked for this mission, and if you seriously think we can track down the flipping Holy Grail for nine pence and three farthings then you're three leagues out of your tree, my Lord Hastings. This is not a job that can be financed out of the petty-cash box; it's going to take a serious number of gold Angels.'

(I didn't actually say 'flipping' either, but I should not want anyone to think me irreverent. I really am not you know, I say my prayers regularly and attend Mass at least once a month. Sir Walter Gloy will vouch for me, if he's still alive when you read this. Which, come to think of it, he probably won't be, so you'll have to take my word for it.)

Hastings grunted. 'Well, I suppose I can let you have something on account. But as far as the Grail is concerned, you do understand, don't you, that this is principally a cover story?'

'Ah,' said Roger and I in unison. The 'ahs' were however somewhat different in tone. I believe Roger was quite disappointed that our task was to be more prosaic than we had been led to believe. Whereas I was concerned that we might be expected to do some real work, as opposed to bumming around pretending to look for something that almost certainly didn't exist anywhere we were likely to find it. I considered I was too old, or more correctly too senior, to get involved in dangerous field missions.

Hastings spread his hands. 'Of course, it's true that the King has been told that the Grail is to be found in his dominions, and would very much like to have it in his possession. If, by some remote chance, you do manage to find it, that will be a very considerable bonus. Such a relic would probably secure the Yorkist dynasty for centuries – even if you discount its supposed miraculous properties, the prestige of owning it would be beyond measure. There'd be crowds fifty deep in Westminster Abbey clamouring to look at the thing, and we'd cut a deal with the abbot for a big percentage of the takings.

'However, the chances are you won't find it. Never mind. It gives you a cracking excuse to visit Wales and the West Country. And that's precisely where we have reason to believe Uncle Jasper is planning to land this summer.'

'Uncle Jasper' was a thoroughgoing nuisance and one of our *bêtes noires*. Part of every Lancastrian conspiracy there had ever been, he had actually landed in North Wales back in the year '69, raised an army and caused all sorts of mayhem before being driven out by William Herbert, the real Earl of Pembroke. Unfortunately Herbert had been one of those taken out by friend Warwick a few months later, and our reliable allies in Wales were now few and far between.

'I thought he and his nephew were more or less prisoners of the Duke of Brittany,' said Roger, and I nodded because that was also my appreciation of the situation.

'Officially,' said Hastings, with something approaching a wink, 'but there is always the possibility of some kind of *sub rosa* venture. Brittany is no great friend of ours, and the Duke is capable of any madcap scheme.'

'Wales, then, is most likely.'

'Yes, but the West Country is a definite possibility, according to our informants. You must remember there's still a big Beaufort and Courtenay influence in those parts, even though since Tewkesbury[18] the males of those families are mostly six feet under the sod. Some people never know when to give up, and Uncle Jasper is a prime example.'

'As far as Wales is concerned,' I chipped in, 'I foresee one big problem. Roger and I don't have a word of Welsh between us. Nor a word of Cornish if it comes to that. That being the case, it's going to be a tad difficult to pick anything up in conversation.'

'The gentry practically all speak reasonable English,' Hastings answered. 'There's no need to make your arrival inconspicuous. You're on the Grail Quest, and in addition Sir Roger will have commissions as Surveyor of the Earldom of March, the Principality of Wales and the Duchy of Cornwall. I think that just about ticks all the boxes, and if it doesn't there's quite a few pilgrimages you can claim to be on. St Winifred's Well for starters. Look a few more up in the *Book of Shrines*.'

'And what is it *exactly* that you want us to do?' Roger asked. I could tell from his tone that he was moderately cheesed off, to put it mildly. He had overcome his initial misgivings and grown increasingly excited during our journey about the prospect of searching for the Grail. It was such an ultra-knightly sort of thing to do, and at heart it appealed to him. Rooting around the backside of Wales looking for Lancastrian conspirators was, from his point of view, a gigantic come-down. Like turning up for a prestigious international joust with the Bastard of Burgundy only to find that instead you're expected to partake in mud-wrestling with the local goatherd.

---

[18] Hastings is referring here to the Battle of Tewkesbury, 1471. See *The Adventures of Alianore Audley*. Or pretty well any text book about the Wars of the Roses.

'Find the Grail, of course.' To Hastings' credit, he didn't even grin, though you could see from his face that he wanted to laugh like the Duchess of York when she first read the Woodvilles' pedigree. 'Look, we lack sufficient reliable intelligence. Alehouse murmuring is all very well, but it isn't *fact*. I want plenty of situation reports about what's going on in those God-forsaken backwaters, and especially any worthwhile information about the doings of Uncle Jasper and his little pals. Obviously, if you discover there *is* Lancastrian plotting going on, you should put as many spokes in their wheels as you can.'

I hoped to do a lot more than that if I came into contact with Jasper Tudor. He had treacherously slain my brother-in-law, Roger Vaughan of Tretower[19], at Chepstow, back in the year '71. This was personal as well as political.

We talked for a while longer, but it was very much a case of a meeting expanding to fill the available time, and little more was said to the point. One of Hastings' clerks made an entry with what turned out to be Roger's commissions, all beautifully written out and weighted with King Edward's seal. By the way, the fellow did not scurry. Indeed, in all my long experience of clerks, I have never known one who did. This particular clerk was more for unobtrusive sidling.

At last, after drinking about a pint each of Hastings' excellent claret, we withdrew for consultations. Roger said very little at first, which is always a bad sign, but I could tell from the set of his lips that he was several lettuces away from being a contented bunny. We found a small walled garden where there was no one about to overhear us, not even an under-gardener or a spare Woodville, and settled ourselves on a turf seat. One that was, unfortunately, as damp as an old dog's bedding.

'So,' Roger grunted, 'this is no noble quest for a holy relic of great importance, but a dirty spying mission; one that sits ill with the honour of a knight. I am half inclined to seek audience with the King's Grace, and tell him to stick the whole thing where the Sun in Splendour doesn't shine.'

---

[19] In *The Adventures of Alianore Audley*, Alianore is rather vague about her exact relationship with the Vaughans of Tretower. Here she is crystal clear. The inconsistency is puzzling, although it is a fact that Roger Vaughan was married to her sister, Margaret, Lady Powis.

I hate the word 'honour'. It makes me reach instinctively for the poniard I always keep (even now in my peaceful retirement) in the secret inside pocket of my gown. However, in dealing with Roger, diplomacy has always been the thing, and in the old Yorkist days, when it was still relatively fashionable, he held his honour very dear, and it was not a good idea to tell him it was all a load of outdated twaddle.

'My dear, that really would not be a good career move,' I replied, assuming the gentlest voice at my disposal. 'I know King Edward has this image of being an affable, hail-fellow-well-met sort of chap, but given that he had his own brother topped not so very long ago he's more than capable of ordering your summary execution. That would be inconvenient for the children and me, to say nothing of Cousin Richard, who has come to depend on your advice. Besides, you're still the King's knight, and he pays you £100 a year by way of retainer, which is not to be sniffed at. You owe him some sort of service in return, and to my mind your role in the team is to offer protection, to translate any Latin or French documents that come along, and, if necessary, to fight. None of these tasks is in any way unknightly.

'I will do any dirty work that comes along; as a woman, the concept of honour relates only to my chastity. Spying on the enemy is perfectly respectable; indeed, it makes me a sort of heroine, especially as the official secrets rules mean I can never boast about it to my friends. In any event, *we can still search for the Grail*. That is our real mission from the King, and I have to say it's the best cover story ever invented.'

He gazed at me suspiciously, as he often does when he thinks I'm spinning him a yarn. But then he gave a curt nod of acceptance.

'You're right of course. We've little choice, and must make the best of it. To be honest, Alianore, I just want to get out of this place. But I suppose we'll have to hang around until the King finds us five minutes for an audience, won't we?'

'Well, that is the normal custom before leaving court. I don't suppose it'll take more than a few days, and in the interim we can feast and dance and take part in the disguisings, and all the other stuff they do here. It's not exactly *work* is it? I dare say there are a few gong-farmers who'd swap places. In any event, we need to collect our expenses.'

*

Roger's discontent made me feel that I needed another quiet word with Lord Hastings. Fortunately an opportunity arose that very evening, while I was posing in one of the passages, listening to the music and wondering quietly to myself how on earth how the Countess of Pembroke[20] thought she could get away with her ridiculous Burgundian headdress. It was almost large enough to be stuck on top of a church tower, where it would have looked marginally less ridiculous than on her head.

Anyway, I digress. As luck had it, Roger had left me to find a discreet corner in which to recycle some of the quart and a half of the King's wine he had enjoyed over supper, and I was temporarily alone, or as alone as one can be in a crowd of over-dressed and over-perfumed courtiers. Who should hove into sight but Lord Hastings, with the delicious Mistress Shore on his arm. I seized my opportunity, and with it his other arm.

I explained, as quickly and in as few words as I could. To do him credit, Hastings was rarely slow on the uptake, and as luck would have it he was in an amiable mood. This probably had something to do with the company of Mistress Shore, to say nothing of an excellent supper with endless quantities of finest malmsey and Rhenish to go with it.

He said, 'I'll see what I can do,' and gave me both a nod and a polite bow before moving on through the company. I knew that was a promise, and, I might say, as good as the speeches of twenty orators. There were people at court who would have killed their own brothers to hear Hastings say so much to their petition.

Before the end of the evening, I had a discreet message whispered in my ear by a gentleman. No, it was *not* that sort of message. Wash your mind out with soap of Castile! I was to wait upon the Queen first thing in the morning, and attend her to chapel. In addition, Sir Roger was to hang about the chapel door until Mass was over, as she wished a word with him.

---

[20] Mary, Countess of Pembroke, was one of Elizabeth Woodville's many sisters.

In normal circumstances this would have puzzled me no end. It's true that I had been one of Elizabeth Woodville's women for a brief while, but we didn't exactly write to each other every day and to be very frank, without prompting I doubt she would have been able to distinguish me from Bona of Savoy. However, I reasoned that this was something arranged by Hastings as part of the plan to settle Roger's mind. Roger, who lacked the benefit of my knowledge, was deeply puzzled when I told him of the Queen's orders and kept me awake half the night with his speculations. This was not helpful, but given the circumstances it was unavoidable and I just had to endure it and try hard not to tell him to shut up and go to sleep.

Of course in the circumstances one had to get up somewhat before the first sparrow in order to be scrubbed and dressed in good time for the appointment. For waiting on a Queen is very well named; one must be prepared to wait for as long as it takes, while never making the Queen herself wait for a second. After a disturbed night's sleep and not a particular long one, you may judge that I was not in the best mood for the occasion, but one must do what one has to do.

After checking myself carefully in the glass to be sure that everything was present and correct, and after giving Roger a mild shake to remind him that it was more than time for him to get up, I made my way to the Queen's apartments, with only Juliana in company. The whole place was deadly quiet, with just a few servants stirring. At one point, confessing myself lost, I had to ask one of these fellows for directions. They came out as a litany, spoken in the accent of London. Turn left at such a place, go down those stairs, fifth door along, through the Great Library, climb the spiral staircase... Well, it was something like that. Eventually I found the place, and needless to say the Queen was not ready for me, but still in the process of dressing.

There was nothing much to do but hang about in the anteroom, with a choice of staring out of the window or looking at an unduly flattering portrait of Anthony Woodville[21]. Fortunately there was no more than half an hour of this joyous pastime before one of the Queen's lesser women was sent out to inform me that I could now be received.

---

[21] Anthony Woodville, by this time 2nd Earl Rivers, Elizabeth Woodville's eldest and most important brother.

I was admitted to the Bedchamber. For those of you who do not know the ways of courts, I should explain that this is a Great Honour. Normally you do well to get as far in as the Presence Chamber, the Bedchamber is like — wow, you are supposed to be *seriously* impressed. Unless you are a duchess or something, in which case it's your due, like dining two to a mess.

Queen Elizabeth — for it was thus we all thought of her at the time, before it came to light that King Edward had committed bigamy when he wedded her — was her usual elegant self, and there was nothing to hint at the fact that she was barely out of bed. She sat in a richly-gilded and high-backed chair, her long fingers glittering with numerous jewelled rings, looking rather like an image of Our Lady at a particularly well-patronised shrine. She was with child at this time, but you would scarcely have known since the fashion then was for gowns to be high-waisted and cut rather full beneath the girdle, so the swelling scarcely showed. She was far too grand to allow any other outward symptoms to appear.

I made the requisite three reverences as I approached her, taking care not to approach too closely lest I be thought over-familiar. Royal personages almost always expect full formality in public — it is the norm, part of their image. But most of them are less punctilious in private, and the etiquette is relaxed a few notches, as long as everyone remembers his place — you mustn't slap them on the back, or call them Teddy, or anything like that. Elizabeth Woodville, however, liked formality at all times, and you just had to accept it as one of her odd little ways, just as I have to accept that Roger has hair growing out of his nose.

By the way, some Woodvilles were so fussy that they insisted on being spelt 'Wydeville'. Why on earth they thought their name should have a particular spelling when everyone else's name and title is changed just as often as the writer thinks fit I cannot imagine. I have seen Richard's ducal title rendered as 'Gloster', 'Glowster' and even 'Gloucestre', but never heard him complain about it once. I have in my own time been spelt as (for example) 'Alianora Audeley', 'Eleanor de Beauchamp', and 'Elinor de Bello Campo'. The truth is that well-bred people do not worry their heads about such trivial details — unlike the Woodvilles/Wydevilles/Widviles or whatever you choose to call them.

Despite what I wrote earlier on this subject, I have to say that I never saw any direct evidence that Elizabeth Woodville was a witch. This is strange, because I have lately heard the rumour that she was a very witchy witch indeed, who ensnared King Edward with incantations and love potions, and caused (besides the fog at Barnet) great storms at seas to hamper old Warwick. Frankly I don't believe Elizabeth was capable of putting together a mixture to ease a child's cough, let alone all the incredibly advanced stuff just mentioned, which even my mentor, the wise Welshwoman Tegolin, would have found a stretch. I shall write more of so-called witchcraft in a while, but for now I think it time to return to the matter in hand. The Queen gave me a gracious smile, though not a particularly expansive one.

'Lord Hastings has informed us of your little local difficulty,' she said, 'and we have agreed to assist, though Sir Roger Beauchamp's quibbles seem quite absurd to us. He ought to feel extraordinarily honoured that the King has been pleased to entrust him with so sacred a task, a quest close to his Grace's heart. That he should object to performing some more mundane duties at the same time is outrageous— the next thing to disloyalty. You will convey our private opinion to him at a suitable time. For the present, this is what we have devised to ease his prickly conscience...'

After those words, which I took on board as a moderately mild kicking, she outlined her plan for the morning's ceremony. It was a good one. I knew Roger would like it, and I said as much, which was a mistake, because her reaction told me that she considered my words impertinent. The atmosphere was suddenly colder than that you would experience by riding stark naked over the Yorkshire Moors during a particularly chilly February blizzard.

No further word was said, or was necessary — it was obvious from her whole bearing that she was *most seriously displeased*. Anyway, I hung around, and eventually attached myself to the back rank of her women as she set off for the chapel. The Mass was like every Mass you have ever attended, save that being at court the priests and their acolytes wore the most splendid of vestments, and there was a full choir of boys that sang very prettily. All I had to do was stay quiet, with one eye on the Queen to be sure that I knelt when she did, rose when she did, and so on and so forth.

When the service was over, she beckoned me over and placed a small, sealed document in my hands, as previously agreed between us. As we processed out of the chapel, there was Roger kneeling, his hat in his hands. The Queen gave him a nod, a suitably gracious one I am sure, and signalled to me with a brief gesture. I curtsied to her for the twenty-third time that morning, stepped forward, bent low to place the message in the top of his boot, and returned to my place. The ceremony, so far as we had rehearsed it, was over, and I followed the procession back to the Queen's apartments. She kept me hanging about for an hour or two, just to be irritating, and then sent me about my business with a few brisk words.[22]

The message, among other instructions, told Roger to take it to the King, which of course he did. I was not present at this meeting, which was strictly for boys only, but Roger came away from it grinning like a Stanley with the title deed to a new manor. Of course, Cousin Edward could lay on the charm a foot thick when it pleased him to do so, and I have no doubt that he did so on this occasion. Anyway, Roger's touchy sense of honour was satisfied, he was reassured that the Grail quest was centre-stage, with the dirty intelligence work just a minor sideline for his lady to deal with, and all was well with his world.

At a more practical level, he had also secured a goodly portion of our expenses, part in gold and part in letters of credit. The money came through the Chamber, as intelligence funding always did, so we were spared the hassle of hanging around the Exchequer for weeks, bribing clerks and ending up being paid out in tally-sticks. This pleased me greatly, as I reckoned that if one took into account the few exaggerations I had included in our claim, we were actually a pound or three in credit.

*

---

[22] Knowledgeable readers may detect some similarity between the ceremony described by Alianore and that recorded by Anthony Woodville, Lords Rivers, prior to his famous joust with the Bastard of Burgundy.

Dame Alianore de Beauchamp's Marvellous Discovery of Witchcraft

Witchcraft, my dears, is one part the use of herbs, and nine parts imagination. I speak as one who was trained in the craft by the famous Lady Tegolin of the Lordship of Newport in Wales. Albeit, I never qualified, and did not even take the Preliminary Certificate.

Herbs are extremely useful for medicinal and culinary purposes, and every gentlewoman should have a good knowledge of them. The alternative is to be completely at the mercy of physicians, who consult your horoscope, look at your piss, and charge you twenty pounds a visit. Most of these so-called doctors have as much notion of curing ailments as a cat has of the rules of chess.

However, herbs can also be abused. There really is no need of sorcery when a suitable dose of foxglove or monkshood can take out a horse. There is nothing magical or even secret in such methods, and I suspect that simple poison accounts for every death that has ever been attributed to sorcery.

Some people say a prayer over the medicines they create. I see nothing wrong or heretical in that, it is merely a way of seeking God's assistance in the process. Others prefer incantations, that are supposed to have power, but are truly no more than a jumble of words. Again, I see nothing inherently wrong in this, so be it that they are not a means of invoking some demon. To involve a demon is extremely foolish and dangerous, as well as heretical; if you imagine you can control demons, you are sorely mistaken. Unless, of course, you're a saint and if you're one of those you need no advice from me. Although if I were you, I'd keep it to yourself as the Church people can cut up very nasty with people who claim to be saints while they're still alive.

There are a few people (Tegolin was one I think) who can see into the future, or at least some part of it. This is a gift from God, but something that cannot be learned. I maybe have a small portion of it, but if so it's very weak. I never foresaw Bosworth, for example, though I did have a bad feeling about it beforehand. There are, as I mentioned, those who claim to commune with the dead. Necromancers, like Lady Warwick. Most of them are liars. The rest are better keeping their mouths shut on the subject as the Church forbids it. It would be heretical of me to say the Church is wrong, so I won't. I'm sure the Church is absolutely right, as it is about everything else.

Then there is alchemy, which is sometimes called science. Many learned men, including even doctors of the Church are involved in this, with the object of turning base metal into gold. I doubt this can be done, but it would be wrong to call it witchcraft.

Now, as for Elizabeth Woodville, I wrote earlier that she claimed to be descended from the demon Melusine, and that she had witches in the family. That much is true. Her mother, the Duchess of Bedford, otherwise Lady Rivers, was said to be one for a start. I think Elizabeth may even have enjoyed giving herself the *air* of witchcraft, as some foolish women do, for the sake of the power they feel it gives them over others. She certainly encouraged King Edward to consult all manner of soothsayers and necromancers and very possibly told them what to say to him. This is a very black mark against her, and has made many people understandably suspicious, but really a lot of it was Cousin Edward's fault for being so gullible.

But as for her *really* being a witch, casting spells and prancing naked in the moonlight, I cry you mercy! I can scarcely hold my quill for laughing at the thought of it. She is no more a witch than I am, indeed possibly less of one. She is now a 'guest' of the monks of Bermondsey, due to the kindness and generosity of her charming son-in-law, Mr. Tydder. Why would a witch of her supposed power tolerate such confinement for more than a day when she could so easily turn Tydder into a frog? Indeed, if you think about it, if she was *that* much of a witch, back in '83 she could have turned *Richard* into a frog; or a mushroom. She could have blanketed the whole of Yorkshire with a fog, and raised a storm to break down the bridges, and he wouldn't have been able to reach Doncaster, let alone London. Instead, she sent for her brother Anthony to bring a host of men from Ludlow, and thought she could stop Richard in his tracks with *them*. What manner of sorceress relies on mortal men, when magic can do the job at half the cost?

Ah, you may say, but Richard once accused her of witchcraft![23] And so he did, but only for political reasons, because she or her agents had tried to poison him, and it's far easier to persuade fools of witchcraft than poisoning. He never believed her a witch for a moment, for if he had you may be sure he'd have had her hanged, or at least paraded through the streets of London in her shift, with a penitential candle in her hands. Instead he cut a deal with her, and gave her a handsome pension, and promised to see her daughters decently married.

---

[23] See *The Adventures of Alianore Audley*.

You really should not believe everything you hear – or read.

*

Exorcise for Roger.

In all the circumstances I felt a need to consult the duty pastoral Bishop. Fortunately I discovered it was John Russell, Bishop of Rochester, a reasonable man and of sound Yorkist principles, who undertook the office of Keeper of the Privy Seal in his spare time. There were several on the Episcopal bench I'd not have trusted as far as I could throw them with one arm; although he that turned out to be the worst of the lot, Morton, had only just been elevated to it at this time. (Why Cousin Edward, who was no fool, whatever else he was, put trust in and promoted the stubbornly Lancastrian Morton is a mystery to me, but apparently the man was (and remains) a good administrator, as well as a teller of tall tales.)

I had spotted the appropriate door during my peregrinations around the court. It had a small notice on it: *Duty Bishop (Pastoral). Kick and Enter*. Fortunately he did not already have a client in the office but was amusing himself by studying a very thick book, probably one written in Latin about theology or something. I had just noticed it contained some very vividly coloured pictures of Adam and Eve when he slammed it shut.

He was a spare, scholarly-looking man, with the typical posture of a learned clerk, back bent from too much poring over books and manuscripts and a general air of competence.

'How may I be of service?' he asked, with something approaching a smile.

'My lord, that is a good question,' I answered, making my reverence. 'I scarcely know where to begin, but I think I need someone who knows about demons and their tricks, and the advice of a reverend bishop is likely to be a useful starting point.'

I told him of the quest Roger and I had been given, of my visions and of Roger's strange speeches. Indeed, I told him more or less every strange event that had happened since Middleham. Bishop Russell listened attentively, nodding occasionally as if to encourage the flow, his chin resting on his steepled fingers.

When I had told him everything he said, 'Does it occur to you, Lady Beauchamp, that this quest of yours might be greatly presumptuous, and an offence to God?'

'It occurred to me from day one, Bishop. My husband and I are sinners. I dare say there are worse, but we certainly don't rank as saints or even as exceptionally devout lay people. We are by no means worthy even to approach the Grail. It is, I think, more a task for some uncommonly holy father. However, we did not set out on this mission at our own behest, but at the command of the King's Grace. It seems to me that it was a lawful order, and not to be disobeyed. Am I mistaken in that?'

He gave that some thought, which surprised me. 'No – no, you are quite correct,' he said, with some reluctance I thought. 'The presumption lies with the King, and will doubtless be charged to his account. I doubt very much the Grail can be found by any mortal, even a virgin of blameless life and exceptional piety. In any event, it is better that it is *not* found. Such a powerful relic, in the wrong hands, could be most grievously abused.'

'Surely, you do not mean the King —'

He held up his hand. 'I say nothing against the King. I pray daily for his welfare, that he may have as long a life as God pleases. Yet he is not immortal, and his successors may well have the wicked numbered among them. Madam, I know you are something more than Sir Roger Beauchamp's lady and one of the Duchess of Gloucester's waiting-women. Lord Hastings has, from time to time, involved me in what we may call the more arcane aspects of his duties as Lord Chamberlain and Master of the Mint. I often read and analyse his intelligence reports when he is too busy with his wine and his women and his duties about the King. I tell you this so that we may speak freely, as colleagues in the same department. There are dark forces here at court. If King Edward has a fault, it is that he is superstitious. It's perhaps surprising in a man of his strong character and sharp intelligence, but if one puts before him some reasonably-convincing charlatan in the guise of a wizard or soothsayer, he's all too easily persuaded by their nonsense. There was one such that told him that his successor would be "G" and for that reason, it is said, he was persuaded to execute his brother, the Duke of Clarence, and give his own new-born the name George. Imagine what these people might do if they had the Grail itself in their hands! At the very least they might claim that it inspired the prophecies they invent. They might even dare to do worse. I mean, it might be used to work evil magic.'

'I should imagine that would not be a wise move' I ventured, 'given the power and holiness of the relic. I cannot imagine even putting my hand to it, still less daring to desecrate it.'

He nodded. 'You have some wisdom, my lady. But we are talking of people whose pride and lust for power know no bounds. We need not name names — suffice it to say it will be better all round if the Grail stays safely in its hiding place until such time as God Himself puts an end to human wickedness. It certainly should not be allowed to fall into the hands of any temporal power, not even the most benign.' He paused momentarily for effect. 'Now, as to these visions and dreams of yours — from whence do you imagine they proceed?'

'Well,' I said, 'given that I am by no means saintly, and not in the habit of fasting for weeks while meditating on Our Lord's Crucifixion, I have a horrible feeling that they are diabolically inspired. On our journey here from Middleham I believe I have venerated more relics and said more decades on my beads than I have in the whole of my previous life, but still they have not shifted. I suspect they are the work of a demon, and a powerful one at that.'

He sighed. 'Well, I am pleased by your very proper humility. If you had said that it was all from Our Lady and St. Michael, or something along those lines, I should have thought you ripe for burning, like that wretched French girl back in my father's time. I concur with your interpretation, and it seems to me that the demon's intention may be to harass your quest.' He frowned. 'That implies in turn that God favours it, though I find that *very* hard to believe. As for Sir Roger, I'm afraid it sounds very much like a case of demonic possession, though not a particularly severe one. Unfortunately, it's a specialist field and not one I have really studied. I could do with my diocesan exorcist to advise me, but there are colleagues here at court with the necessary expertise. I shall consult them, and then I think we must hold a private ceremony of blessing before you depart. Your husband cannot object to attending that, and we shall take the demons by surprise.'

*

Roger was not happy when I told him about the blessing. He called it a waste of time, which I suggested was pretty shocking coming from someone who had been accusing me of heresy all the way from Middleham.

'Given that we are supposedly on a holy quest, I don't see how we can decline a formal blessing from Holy Mother Church,' I said. 'I grant you it may be tedious. Ceremonies often are. In truth, I had rather read a good book, or even a good intelligence report, than take part in the finest ceremony ever devised. But on occasions, one simply has to conform with what is expected; as a matter of duty.'

'Duty' was always a good trigger word to throw at Roger. He gave the sort of mournful look that a lazy old dog might offer when told to leave its place by the warm fire and go out into the rain, but I could see that he was weakening.

'I suppose you are right, Alianore,' he sighed, 'but I wish we were back at Middleham. I never thought I would say it, but I miss his Grace of Gloucester's company. He may be a solemn fellow, but at least he isn't *complicated*. He might cut your head off, but if he did, it'd be for a tangible reason. Here at court I don't really understand half what is going on, and the other half seems *contrived* — that business with the Queen, for example; the more I think about it, the more it seems as if the whole thing was but a play, with a script that everyone had rehearsed except me.'

'It was intended as an honour, and a sign of the high favour in which you are held. There's no more to understand than that. This blessing is the religious equivalent; and very important at that — a sort of spiritual armour you should wear.'

'I hope there isn't going to be a crowd,' he said miserably.

'Oh, no, Bishop Russell said it would be quite private.'

'Good! I hate being stared at by bloody Woodvilles.'

After supper, we gathered in St George's Chapel. Of course, this was not the one which exists now, which is more in the way of a small cathedral. King Edward had only recently approved the architect's plans for that, and it had barely risen above its foundations at the time of which I write, though there was plenty of wooden scaffolding in place to accommodate the masons. No, this was the old chapel, which although much smaller than the one which has since replaced it was by no means the poky little oratory you find in many castles.

It was strange to be alone in this holy place with only Roger and Bishop Russell's chaplain, who had led us there. It was lit only by the candles that burnt around the various altars, and in particular around the high altar, to which the chaplain ushered us. We entered the chancel, where the banners of the Garter Knights hung high above, and where their stalls were located, each with a plate for the different knights that have sat there over the years, bar some that have been torn down for treason, or for resisting the Lancastrian usurpers, which was not really treason but was still treated as such. At last, at a gesture from the bishop's chaplain, we knelt on the cushions before the altar rails, and waited in the silence, looking at the big statues of Our Lady, St. George and St. Edward, the patrons of the place. In the dark, their faces looked grim and impassive and I lowered my head in prayer, wishing that I had chosen a more modest headdress. The one I was wearing felt like it was made from enough house bricks to construct Tattershall Castle.

It seemed to me that we were there for a very long time, and I was just beginning to get impatient when the tramp of footsteps on the painted tiles announced the arrival of Bishop Russell and his assorted acolytes, coming towards us in a suitably solemn procession. I could see nothing of them at first — for I felt obliged to keep my head reverently bowed — but when they reached the altar I saw that the Bishop was wearing his full canonicals, bright with embroidered scenes from scripture, his mitre a mass of jewels and gold thread. I don't know if the demons were awed, but I certainly was. I somewhat less impressed by the presence of the bishop standing behind him — it was none other than Dr. John Morton, lately elevated to the see of Ely.

I must admit, I had no idea what the staffing requirements were for an exorcism, but I instinctively judged that it didn't need a pair of bishops. Even if it did, the last one I'd have roped in was Morton. I'd seen his security file, and, given what he had told me earlier, I had an idea that Bishop Russell must have seen it too. He might just as well have invited Margaret Beaufort along to the show, and her worshipful brother-in-law, Uncle Jasper, into the bargain.

However, in the circumstances, there was little I could do or say about it. A woman — or even a layman — cannot very well start to tell a couple of bishops their business in the middle of a sacred ceremony, security considerations or not. So I kept my mouth shut, and watched as they began to celebrate the Mass.

The Mists of Middleham

Roger had broken out into an actual sweat, quite an achievement given that the chapel was notably chilly, especially when one had already been kneeling in it for a good half hour or more. I was wearing several layers, but was still shivering on a regular basis and wishing they would light a few dozen more candles.

'My lord Bishop,' he protested, 'I cannot take the sacrament. I am neither fasted nor shriven.'

Bishop Russell smiled, what I can only describe as the smile of a professional clergyman. It was almost as if he had expected this protest. 'Your reverence for the Blessed Sacrament does you credit, my son. However, it is after midnight, a new day, and you have not yet broken your fast. We have advanced the canonical hour for the purpose of this blessing. As to shriving, Bishop Morton here shall hear your confession at once, and I shall hear that of your lady. Nothing shall hinder our sacred purpose.'

It is extremely difficult, from the posture of a penitent, kneeling in a dark corner of a particularly chilly chapel, to find the right words to inform a bishop that he is an idiot.

'Bishop,' I said, after a pause to compose my thoughts, 'you may have been to a university and collected a degree or two, but there are sheep wandering lost around Coverdale with more common sense than you possess. You told me with your own mouth that you're an officer of Yorkist Intelligence. You must have seen Morton's file, and even if you haven't you must know that he is a Lancastrian at heart, and hand-in glove with Lady Richmond. God be loved,' I picked one of Richard of Gloucester's favourite oaths, 'up until Tewkesbury he was Margaret of Anjou's right hand man, and if he isn't on corresponding terms with the rebel, Henry Tydder, and with King Lewis of France, you can call me Alice and put me in charge of a dairy. If Sir Roger is possessed by devils, there is no telling what secrets he may let out. There's more to this mission than seeking out the Grail.'

Bishop Russell sighed deeply. 'I am well aware of that,' he said, in a put-Alianore-in-her-place tone of dry exasperation. 'All here are sworn on holy relics to secrecy on pain of treason. Bishop Morton's past loyalties I do not deny; but the King has pardoned him and made him a member of the Council. Do you have the effrontery to suppose that you, a mere knight's wife extracted from the depths of Yorkshire, know the King's business better than he does himself?'

'Ah, you're playing the 'you're-just-a-stupid-woman' card are you, my lord Bishop? Well, that sits well with me. I'm more than happy to yield up my commission and go home to Horton Beauchamp. I've never wanted anything more than to sit on my window-seat, watching the bees drift in and out of the open casements as I cast my household accounts. My betters, King Edward and Lord Hastings, forced me into playing this unnatural part, and not any ambition of mine.' I paused for breath, panting with the struggle involved in keeping my voice relatively low. I was blazing with anger, and but for the fact he was a bishop, and I was kneeling before him in a church, I'd have really told him what I thought.

'I do not say you are stupid, or that your services are not appreciated,' he answered calmly, before I could speak again, 'only that you should remember your place and not presume to choose the King's counsellors. Quite apart from that, Bishop Morton is the only priest immediately available with the necessary skills. Qualified and experienced exorcists do not grow on trees. It is an extremely specialised field. Besides, as I have told you, the man is sworn, and on pain of treason. Such an oath is not lightly broken.'

I tell you, my children, at that moment I just wanted to get to my feet, walk out of the door, to find my horse and ride away from Windsor, even though it was the middle of the night. I was talking to a supposedly intelligent man, who thought that a creature like Morton could be bound by the simple administration of an oath, as though he were William Marshal or El Cid or a paladin of that kidney. At times like this, one despairs, because there is quite literally nothing one can do. Authority Knows Best and you can speak to it with the most golden of tongues or write an entire book on the subject, and nothing will change.

Well, what more is there to say? The conversation turned into a traditional confession, and I ended up with penances for pride, wrath and vainglory just for starters. That's the trouble with having priests in position of power; they always have the last word — unless you happen to be the King, of course, when you can have them thrown in the Tower at the drop of a bonnet, and even cut their heads off if you choose. By the time Russell had finished with me I was developing a degree of sympathy for Henry Bolingbroke in the matter of Archbishop Scrope. Not that I said so, of course.

Eventually Roger and I knelt before the altar again, and everything seemed to be going swimmingly, bar for the fact that my knight was sweating profusely, like an armoured pig in the heat of a particularly sunny July afternoon. This struck me as odd, but nothing prepared me for what was coming.

The sacred Host was no sooner placed on Roger's tongue than he spat it out as if were a red-hot cinder. What's more, he reacted as though it had been, screaming, cursing, and rolling about on the floor like a man possessed; which, of course, was exactly what he was.

The bishops exchanged knowing looks, and then rushed towards him, followed by their acolytes. Two or three of the lesser clerics wrestled with Roger, struggling to hold him down. This would have been inadequate force at the best of times, but they were flung off as though they were little children, or mere puppets. Sir Roger climbed to his feet, his face an unrecognisable mask of fury, and he laughed, deeply, horribly, in a voice that was not his own.

'Sod you all, you miserable turds,' he roared. 'You and your pathetic God have no power over me. I am stronger than all of you put together.'

There was a great deal more of this, all loud enough to wake both castle and town. I shall spare you the worst of it, but he cursed their parentage, described their personal habits and private tastes in great and spectacular detail, and blasphemed sufficiently to curl the hair of a drunken sailor. Of course, you must understand, it was not Sir Roger who said these dreadful things, but one of the demons he had swallowed.

It took all of them, including both bishops, to subdue him, and they had not only to work together but to persist as he punched them, clawed their faces, spat in their eyes and called them every name you can imagine and quite a few that you cannot. They showered him with holy water, which made him scream and blaspheme, censed him with incense, and prayed over him, long and loud, with Morton leading the ceremony.

What was I doing while all this was going on? Very little, to tell you the truth for I was far too stunned by events to do anything useful or even to speak. I watched with horror, wondering whether Roger would ever be the same man again, or indeed whether the Church would throw him into prison, or put him on top of a bonfire. At length, I managed to pray, although it was pretty much by rote, because my mind was certainly in no state to come up with any conscious petitions. Of course the special prayers recited by the two bishops were much more important anyway, and I don't suppose my small contribution made any difference either way.

It may sound like an exaggeration, but I believe it was a full hour before the first demon was cast out, amid much celebration by the clergy. However, it was by no means the end of the matter, as it appeared that there were quite a family of them lodging inside Roger. He spoke now with a woman's voice, utterly different in tone to the deep bass that had preceded it, but equally foul in its language. Indeed, if anything, the taunts were crueller, more insulting than those of the first demon.

'Lilith,' roared Morton, above the noise, 'mother of devils, depart from this good knight and return to your dwelling-place in hell.'

'Indeed, it is I,' said the woman's voice, 'and I love my little knight. Why then should I leave him?' There followed a laugh so piercing that it was almost a scream. (Roger's own voice could not have pitched such a note had you paid him in gold.) It filled the whole chapel, so that the very windows trembled in their lead surrounds.

So it went on, hour after hour, demon after demon. For it appeared that there was not just one demon inside Sir Roger, but a whole parliament of them, and a particularly obnoxious parliament at that, say one that had had all its grievances rejected and been asked to grant five tenths and five fifteenths to a particularly unpopular king. The praying, the censing, and the application of holy water were repeated each time, as was the cursing, the screaming and the physical struggles. A strange mixture of religious ceremony and wrestling match that it would be tedious to describe in every detail, even if I could remember the names of the demons or the torrents of Latin prayer, which I could not do the next day, never mind after all these years.

Dawn was breaking before the struggle ended. Roger seemed to go limp, and for a moment I thought he had died, so still, so silent was he, so unexpectedly innocent and placid the expression on his face.

'What am I doing here?' he asked, shaking his head like a dog that has been doused in water. I hurried to him, and took him in my arms, overjoyed to hear his natural voice instead of that of one of the demons. We knelt there together for what seemed like an age, the clergy standing around, breathless from their exertions, Morton sweating like an overworked pig, Bishop Russell leaning against a pillar as if he could barely stand on his feet.

It was over. The demons were banished, or so it seemed. In the early morning light Mass was celebrated to completion, and Roger and I took communion without any further complications. I thought the worst was over.

*

Uncle Jasper

As we made our way out of Windsor, I noticed that Patch, the King's Fool, was standing at the side of the road holding up a sign which said: *'Reinstate the Windsor One'*.

Intrigued, I drew my horse to a stand. 'What joke is this, Patch?'

Patch was of course his stage name. His real name was Wodehouse, and he had a little daughter called Emma. He knuckled his belled cap. 'No joke, my lady. I've been sacked; for telling the Rivers gag.'

I shook my head. 'Well, it was bound to happen sooner or later. Do you not think mocking the Queen's family is just a little bit too — edgy?'

'It's no use being king of jesters and jester to the King unless you push the boundaries. It was the Duke of Clarence's favourite joke. I told it at Tiverton once, and he quite literally wet himself. And when I say 'literally', I'm being grammatically correct, not exaggerating.' Patch looked at his feet, quite crestfallen. 'I don't suppose, ma'am, that by any chance you've got a vacancy for a jester, fool or support artiste in your household?'

I felt pity for the poor man, I really did. 'I'm sorry,' I said, 'but I can think of quite enough funny things for myself without paying a professional. However, if you wish, we'll give you food and shelter, and you can keep whatever you make on the side. Where we're going there's a chance not everyone will have heard your material.'

I was rewarded by the toothy smile that transformed his face and by his happy skip as he thanked me. It seemed he still had a horse of his own, and I told him to fetch it and catch up with us on the road to Reading.

'What on earth did you do that for?' asked Roger, who was still looking rather grey.

'Oh, on an adventure like this,' I said, 'it is practically compulsory to take along a few eccentrics. The nearest we have is Guy Archer, and he's only marginally odd, with his deep drinking and his obsession with shepherdesses. That's practically normal. We should have at least a mysterious gypsy woman, who can see the future and fight with a knife, a Jewish physician who cures every ailment and a Moorish astrologer who says wise things. These types of people are difficult to find in fifteenth-century England, but at least Patch is an eccentric of a kind. He may even prove useful — a jester can be relied upon to lighten the mood, and he was the King's fool, which ranks him high in his profession. I think he's worth his keep.'

'And you'll put him on expenses anyway?'

'Of course; Patch is the fool, not me. I think it a positive duty to claim for everything we can. I'd put building our new duck house at Horton Beauchamp on the list or having the moat cleaned if I thought I could get away with it, but even I don't have that much cheek.'

*

My faithful chaplain and literary adviser Sir Walter Gloy has suggested that it would be better if I wrote in the present tense. He tells me it would make the story 'more immediate' whatever that means. Now Sir Walter is a good priest and a useful clerk, but I do find myself wondering on this point. Even if I do use the present tense it will not bring you, my dear future reader, back to the point where I was writing this. Still less to the time when the adventure took place. However, my mother used to tell me to listen to priests, so out of respect to her memory, and to Sir Walter's cloth, I shall give it a blast, as the common saying runs.

Right then, so here we are on the road outside Windsor. The road is quite dusty today. The horses kick up much of that dust, and we find ourselves coughing. You will be coughing too, dear reader, because the immediacy of my writing means you are actually here. I'm sure you are suitably excited to be in the year of Grace 1479, or as it is more commonly known the 19th year of King Edward, Fourth of that Name since the Conquest. Unfortunately we have not got a horse for you, so you shall have to imagine one. Or perhaps you are a quick walker.

I am already fed up with the whole bally shooting-match. I want to go home, preferably to Horton Beauchamp, or failing that, Middleham. I have a sore arse from all the riding we have done since leaving Yorkshire, and I stink of horse sweat. So does everyone else, and as a result no one notices. You probably stink of horse sweat too. At least you jolly well should do. You should be *drawn in.*

Sir Roger and I are in the middle of an argument; by our standards a relatively fierce one. He says we ought to go to venerate Mad King Henry's tomb at Chertsey. I point out to him that it is in the wrong direction, and King Henry is not a saint recognised by Rome. 'But there have been miracles worked at his tomb,' he says, 'and if it comes to that, St Richard Scrope is not recognised by Rome either, and you were keen to venerate him.' 'My dear, be reasonable,' I say. 'St. Richard Scrope is a *Yorkist* saint. He turned the Usurper Bolingbroke into a leper, which should be proof enough of his sanctity for any sensible Pontiff. Whereas King Harry the Extremely Loopy was a *Lancastrian*, and so cannot *possibly* be a saint. It stands to reason. Remember what the priest said at York about the Archbishop's ban on his cult. As to these supposed miracles of his, what are they? I'll lay six to four he hasn't done anything more impressive than cure a sprained wrist. If he was a *proper* saint, Cousin Edward's face would be a mass of unsightly pustules and bits of him would be dropping off all over the court. You'll be calling Margaret of Anjou "Venerable" next, or be talking about the "Blessed Butcher Clifford".'

'Alianore,' he says, 'whom do you address?'

My answer is a little sharp perhaps, because I am irritated. 'You, my redoubtable lord and husband, Sir Roger Beauchamp of Horton Beauchamp in the County of Gloucester, and also the back of my horse's head and that scarecrow over there. What a ridiculous question!'

'Well I did wonder,' he says, 'because you are talking more like a dim-witted waiting-gentlewoman than an intelligence agent, and I thought it might be deliberate. Of course King Harry was a Lancastrian. That's the whole point. Where are you more likely to hear word of conspiracies than at a Lancastrian shrine?'

He is right, of course. Annoyingly right, as only a husband can be. I want to slap myself for my own stupidity in not thinking of that possibility. It is all part of the absurdity of our mission, of course. For some reason my mind is focused on the impossible Grail quest, when it ought to be firmly fixed on Lancastrian plotting.

*

No, sorry Sir Walter, you may be a priest and all, and be blessed with the miraculous ability to turn common bread and wine into Christ's Blessed Sacrament, and I respect you as such. However, on literary matters you have no more idea than my shoe; possibly less. It just doesn't work. It reads like a parody, and I refuse to write a parody. This is a *serious* chronicle of events that *actually happened* to me, Alianore, Dame Beauchamp of Horton Beauchamp. The point is these things *happened in the past*. Moreover, by the time anyone reads this, they will be even *further in the past* and therefore the correct tense is the *past tense*, and that is what I shall use. Fashion be hanged — it's probably something invented by the Tydders anyway.

That reminds me, I want to tell you about the Tydders. Not the present ones, but their ancestors, to show you what lovely people they descend from.

I had this from my father, which may surprise you given that great men do not normally have much to say to their young daughters. The late Lord Audley was something of an exception to this rule. He would talk to practically *anyone* when he was in the mood and I, his youngest, he considered a good audience for his tales. Unlike at least one of my brothers, I never implied that he was a garrulous old fool. Partly because, when I was nine years old or so, I didn't know what 'garrulous' meant.

(As an aside, I should mention that Anne — that is to say Her Grace the Duchess of Gloucester, later Queen of England — told me that her father, Warwick, was similarly forthcoming. You could have knocked me over with the proverbial feather when she told me this, as I never thought old Warwick that sort at all. But apparently, from when she was only eight years old, he started telling her all his secret plans and ambitions. Stuff which might have got his head cut off if she'd not kept it to herself. She wrote it all down in some kind of secret book, but I believe it got lost when we left Middleham for the last time. Her working title, I recall, was *Under the Hog*.)

Anyway, this tale of the old Tydders, or Tudors, or as the Welsh say the Tudurs of Môn[24]. These fellows lived on the island of Anglesey, which is one of the most fertile areas of Wales. Good crops are grown there, and cattle and sheep live on rich pastures that are almost as good as those in Gloucestershire, but not quite. These Tydders were accounted gentlefolk, though their livelihood in terms of cash was something a Kentish yeoman would laugh at. Like all the Welsh (or at least the gently-born Welsh) they were proud of their pedigree which traced back very far. I dare say a fair bit was made up, as most pedigrees are beyond a certain point, but they were definitely respectable and descended from that Ednyfed who was steward to Llewelyn the Great.

When Owain Glyndŵr rose in rebellion against Bolingbroke, these Tydders joined his cause. I see no fault in that. Anyone who hated Bolingbroke cannot have been all bad. They captured Conwy Castle, and were besieged in it by Henry Percy, calling himself Hotspur[25]. After a time, they ran out of food, and were granted terms. They, the Tydders, were allowed to go scot-free under the articles of surrender. But in return they gave up several of their followers to be hanged, drawn and quartered by the English.

They bought their own lives with the lives of those who depended on them. Need I say more? Can you imagine Richard doing that? Or King Edward? Or even Warwick? No, and nor can I.

*

---

[24] Alianore mangles the Welsh language barbarously. I have tried to correct her errors to the best of my ability, but I apologise anyone with a good knowledge of modern Welsh for any shortcomings.

[25] Hotspur later changed sides and fought against Henry IV at the Battle of Shrewsbury 1403. See *Within the Fetterlock*.

We reached Chertsey at length, with Patch catching up with us along the road, a remarkable achievement given that I had sent him off in the wrong direction altogether. He immediately began to entertain the troops by singing *The Nut-Brown Maid* which was, as I soon established, his favourite ballad. He had a clear and melodious voice — if you like that sort of thing — and Roger admitted that there might indeed be benefits in allowing him to tag along. A lusty song, he said, was often good for morale on a long march, and a song always benefited from being led by a competent professional. All we needed now, he suggested, was someone to play the bagpipes[26] by way of an accompaniment. I rather thought not.

Chertsey Abbey is not the most impressive of monasteries — sacked by the Danes in the ninth century it has never really recovered. I should describe it as somewhat run-down and in need of significant investment, and that would be generous. It is hidden among trees and sundry fish ponds and located down a narrow and muddy back road, so is just the place to bury an unwanted king with an inconvenient reputation for sanctity. How the Danes ever found it I do not know — perhaps they had particularly good maps in those days.

I was surprised to find quite a long queue of pilgrims gathered around the Abbey gate. They watched us warily, as if half expecting to be arrested. (I don't suppose Roger's Yorkist livery collar helped in this regard, to say nothing of our tail of armed men.) It wasn't precisely illegal to visit old Harry's tomb, but it certainly wasn't encouraged, except by the monks of Chertsey, for whom it was a useful source of income.

We entered the church — or more precisely Roger and I did, leaving our attendants to hang about outside. We had no wish to give the impression that the place was being raided by the King's officers. It was very much a case of softly, softly, catch the monkey — although privately I thought we should be very lucky to find a monkey to catch.

'Thinking about this,' said Roger quietly, 'it might be better if you go on to the shrine alone. The sort of people we are trying to trap are not likely to open up in front of one of the King's knights; they might be more careless with you. I'll go and have a word with the abbot, ask him if he knows anything about the Grail. I don't suppose he does, but you never know. These places have libraries, and in a library you can find almost anything.'

---

[26] Bagpipes were common in medieval England and were by no means confined to Scotland.

This was his long-winded way of saying he didn't want to be involved in the spying, at least not any more than he had to be. It did, however, make a certain sense, so I nodded and let him go off on his own before asking a friendly monk to point me in the way of King Harry's tomb.

The good monk not only obliged, but regaled me with a succession of tales about the miracles that had been worked there. He couldn't for the life of him understand why the Holy Father was hanging back on canonisation. To be frank, I thought the reason pretty obvious, but then again not all monks do politics. Some are actually quite unworldly, and I suspect he was one of that kind. Anyway, I smiled gently, slipped a coin in his hand — remembering to double it for expenses — and said something about my poor father who had died for King Harry at Blore Heath, and my good brother who had had his head cut off after Tewkesbury. It was true enough, after all, and when one is giving a false impression of oneself in order to draw out confidences it is good practice to steer as close to reality as possible. I must have been convincing, as he looked at me with a degree of awe that might better have been reserved for a vision of a particularly saintly saint.

He was in the process of ushering me to the tomb when we were met by a fellow walking in the other direction. He wore the clothes of a gentleman – though not a markedly wealthy one — and was, I guessed, about fifty or so, with a face that had certainly travelled through a few storms and collected the odd battle souvenir. He was heavily built, and not much under six feet tall, with green eyes and hair the colour of an aged fox.

The monk blocked his path, seeking, I supposed, a further contribution. 'Do you leave us, sir, now that you have seen the shrine?' he asked. 'I'm sure that Father Abbot would welcome you at table for dinner.'

'I fear I must be on my way,' said the man. 'I've many miles to cover before dark, and cannot linger here. I must content myself with having seen the place where good King Harry lies.'

He was Welsh, though the accent was not particularly pronounced. I looked for any hint of a livery badge, that I might know which lord he served, but there was none.

'This lady,' said the monk, gesturing in my direction, 'lost her father at Blore Heath and a brother at Tewkesbury. She is another pilgrim seeking King Harry.'

'Indeed?' The green eyes flickered over me, with a degree of interest. 'I sorrow to hear of your losses. Perhaps I may have known your father, if he was of our party in the wars.'

'My father,' I said, 'was James, Lord Audley. It is possible you did know him, sir, for he had lands in Wales, and indeed some kindred among the Welsh. But I do not recall you being among his followers.'

He bowed. 'I am Edmund ab Owain,' he told me. 'I do of course remember Lord Audley, a most loyal and gallant nobleman, but you are correct — I was neither his tenant nor his servant.'

The problem with Welsh names is that they don't reveal very much. Had he been English, I could have said 'Ah, yes, you must be one of the Owains from near Chipping Campden,' and I could have placed him very well. As it was, I knew only that his father had been called Owain. There are as many Owains in Wales as there are Williams in England, and they by no means all related to one another, any more than Will Smith the blacksmith at Horton Beauchamp is related to Lord Hastings.

'The world may yet change again, madam,' he continued. 'I have never known a night so dark that there was not a dawn to follow it.'

'The House of Lancaster is quite extinct,' I said, pretending that I thought this a tragedy. I dabbed at my eyes with a corner of my veil, and tried to think of one of my dogs dying, for I did not have a raw onion to hand. 'Nothing more than pale ashes.'

'Not quite,' said the gentleman. 'There is my — my lord Henry Tudor, Earl of Richmond, in Brittany. From what I hear, he has not yet given up all hope.'

The monk muttered something in Latin, which I took from his tone and expression to be a blessing.

'My husband serves King Edward,' I said, 'but I have cousins who would be very interested to hear of any news of Henry Tudor.'

Again I was not lying, except possibly in my tone of voice. King Edward and Richard of Gloucester would indeed have been *very* interested. For a moment I thought my Welsh friend was going to say something useful. He cast around with his eyes, as if checking that we were not being overheard.

'You mistake me, my lady,' he said at last. 'I have no news to give you.'

He bowed and walked silently away. The monk went with him, probably to see him to his horse, although quite possibly in the hope of a tip. For my part, I was not sure whether to be annoyed or not. If there was a plot, it seemed the fellow knew nothing about it, so I had wasted my time talking to him. On the other hand, perhaps there *was* no plot. I knew I ought to have spent time checking Hastings' sources in more detail. It might all be rumour and wishful thinking. Some of our agents out in the sticks had vivid imaginations. They hated to report all was well in case their fees dried up. So instead they blew up every whisper of discontent into a conspiracy against King Edward.

I moved off in the direction the monk had indicated, seeking King Harry's tomb – or shrine as he had called it. I found it close to the high altar, almost hidden from sight as I approached it by a great pillar, one of many that supported the vaulted roof of the monks' church.

A little woman was kneeling before it, very well dressed, with two attendant ladies ranged behind her, their hands clasped reverently in prayer. I staggered against the pillar with surprise, and only just managed not to cry out. The principal of the three supplicants was Lady Margaret Beaufort, Countess of Richmond.

The last time I had met Lady Margaret, matters had been rather awkward between us, to put it mildly. She was the very last person I wanted to encounter, and I considered the advantages of making a tactical withdrawal, given that it is not really good etiquette for two ladies of breeding to start kicking seven kinds out of each other in the middle of a holy abbey. There was every possibility it might come to that, and I was outnumbered three to one.

Suddenly her voice raised in prayer, surprisingly loud coming from one of her small stature: 'Blessed Harry, hear my prayer. Bestow your blessings on my dear son. Let him come to the throne that was yours and should now be his.'

If a prayer can be treasonable, that must have been very close to it. It was no news to me, of course, that she had ambitions for her precious son, Henry Tydder, the so-called Earl of Richmond, but that she should actually express the wish in a public place, before witnesses — that was surprising. Of course, there was no proof — it was my word against hers. What's more, she was the Queen's very best friend. God knows why, but she was.

The Mists of Middleham

I don't like to admit it, but I was at a complete loss. Just seeing her there had thrown me back on my heels, almost literally. Yet at that moment, she turned and saw me, and I knew I had no choice but to be bold. I made her a deep curtsey — after all, she was a countess, and I wasn't.

'Lady Richmond,' I said, as though she were my very favourite cousin, 'what a delightful surprise to find you here!'

If looks could have killed, I'd have been stone dead, right there. However, she recovered well, rose swiftly to her feet, and gave me her finest imitation of a smile. (I doubt Lady Margaret has ever *really* smiled in her entire life. If ever she did it's a clipped penny to gold angel that her face would fall in half. She is not the smiling kind.)

'My Lady Beauchamp,' she got out. 'The surprise is surely mine finding you in such a place. This is a pleasant morning excursion for me, no more than three leagues from my house at Woking. You, on the other hand, are *very* far from home, and even further from your mistress, the Duchess of Gloucester.'

'Sir Roger has business with the abbot, or rather the abbot's library,' I said. 'We have come straight from the court at Windsor, on the King's business. We are in search of the Holy Grail.'

'So I have heard.' She nodded, rather briskly, like a dove picking at a crumb. 'I have many friends at court who keep me informed; as you may know.' She gave me a meaningful look. 'But this is a very strange place for you to choose to come, and I wonder at it. There are no books in the library here that will be of any use. However, as it happens, there are a couple back at Woking you might care to look at. I have an interest in the Grail myself and have made quite a study of it. If the King seeks it, then it's my duty to assist him if I can. Come home with me. Stay a day or two. You will be very welcome.'

I was so astonished I could barely keep my countenance. It is very annoying when enemies are polite and courteous, as one is quite disarmed by it. A part of me wanted to fling her invitation in her teeth, but the other part said that this was a chance not to be missed. If there *was* a Lancastrian conspiracy, then Woking was quite likely to be at the centre of it. There was even a chance that there would be something useful about the Grail in those books she had mentioned. So I forced a smile and an accepted the offer.

Thus, when Roger eventually made his appearance, it was to find me walking arm-in-arm with Margaret Beaufort, a sight scarcely less astonishing than a greyhound sharing its dinner with a hare. However, to do him credit, he took it in his stride, and greeted Lady Richmond like a long-lost sister. We rode together to Woking in perfect amity, and even more perfect hypocrisy.

*

Woking Manor — or Woking Palace as Lady Margaret called it — belonged at one time to the Holland family. It would have come down to the Audleys if Parliament had not been bribed rotten in the year '31, but there's no use crying over split milk, especially since in any event after the death of our mother it would have belonged to my brother, Sir Humphrey Audley, rather than me. And thus would almost certainly have been forfeited after Tewkesbury, when the silly fool got himself beheaded for fighting on the side of the House of Lancaster.

It was a splendid mansion, with a moat around its tall, stone walls, set in extensive grounds in which great herds of deer were roaming around — far too fine a place to belong to the likes of Lady Richmond. The sight of its gilded pinnacles and towering chimneys annoyed me no end.

The good news was that Lord Stanley was not on the premises. Lady Margaret told us he was far away, at Knowsley in Lancashire, busy with estate business and local affairs. From her off-hand way of speaking I doubted very much she was pining over his absence, though I made a point of saying that it had to be very hard for her to be parted from her dear lord by so many long miles.

Roger and I were shown to a very fair bedchamber where, after we had been left alone but for our attendants, I gave him a thorough situation-report while keeping my voice low in case we had eavesdroppers. (Nothing would have surprised me in Margaret's house, not even if she or one of her minions had been crouched behind a secret panel in the wainscoting, listening through a crack in the wood and taking notes.)

For his part, he had found nothing of value in the monks' library, which was apparently a very thin one, without so much as a decent copy of Geoffrey of Monmouth. It seemed he had spent most of his time listening to the abbot droning on about the abbey's poverty and the dire need to get King Harry canonised. To which he had apparently replied very little, not even something about the need to distinguish between sanctity and stupidity. (Sir Roger can be very tolerant, even when dealing with fools. Though he has never been particularly patient with me, I have to say.)

After that, we went down to supper, which, I must admit, was a splendid meal, almost as good as a feast. There were lampreys in vinegar, salmon in sweet syrup, a pike that must have weighed fifteen pounds, and tench and eels in a quite delicious white sauce, which had the taste of leeks and parsley about it. There was an almond pudding that must have had half a pound of sugar in it. There was a great deal more that I have forgotten. Even at the lower tables there were whole plates of oysters, mussels in cheap wine and plenty of quite decent bread. The service was equally impressive – plenty of fellows smartly turned out in Margaret's livery – courteous and well skilled at carving the fish. As for wine – well, we could have swum in it, and even King Edward would have thought the quality a bit on the special side.

Roger, completely disarmed, was thoroughly enjoying himself, saying more than once he had not eaten so well since leaving Middleham. For my part, I remained suspicious. The company was a little tedious. Most of those at the high table were either clergymen or ancient knights and squires who could remember Agincourt without difficulty. In addition, Margaret had some Dominican friar reading to us at length from a remarkably commonplace book of sermons, a practice which does tend to dull the conversation.

However, I had put Patch on notice to entertain us all, and when the good friar had droned to his wearisome conclusion, the new addition to our household stepped forward from the shadows, rigged out in his full kit, bells and all, skipping and prancing around to make sure he was noticed.

He had arranged for Guy to announce him. 'My lords, ladies, gentlemen, yeomen, lowly serfs and beggarly oafs, *direct* from the court at Windsor, England's funniest man, the one, the only, Patch the Jester.'

Patch bowed low, and began his routine with a clever little dance, while at the same time providing a musical accompaniment by drumming away at a pair of nakers he had suspended from his belt. It was an impressive performance in its way, requiring no small amount of energy and coordination, and when he concluded by leaping clean over a stool and making a low bow, there was a reasonable amount of applause to reward him, and even a few small coins from the company. These he picked up with effortless skill, making it seem no more than an extension of the dance.

As you know, I am not easily entertained. However, Patch was a real professional. I can't recall the half of his act, but at the time it was very funny indeed. All those old knights and clergymen were rolling about in their seats like ten year-old boys and Sir Roger was in tucks, literally weeping with laughter. I leaned against his shoulder, very content, and found myself quite helpless at times.

Patch did not just tell jokes — he was an accomplished mimic. It was not just the tone of voice — he somehow captured the way the person walked and stood and held themselves. You should have seen his Lord Stanley — it was almost as good as his Elizabeth Woodville. He conducted imaginary conversations between his characters, and it was if they were there.

He ended the session with a display of tumbling that I have rarely seen equalled. Even the York and District Tumbling Guild are not so athletic. When he finished, with the deepest of deep bows, coins were showered at him from all directions, and not a few of them were gold.

The only person who perhaps did not enjoy the act was Margaret Richmond. She came close to a grin at times, but I knew she was only trying to fit in with the general mood of the company. I knew because I had been in the same position myself many times at Middleham, although the quality of the acts we had to endure up there were generally so poor that I had some excuse.

There was an intermission during which Margaret's musicians entertained us with tunes from their gallery. We relaxed, and recovered from our exertions, because laughing hurts if you do too much of it. We drank our wine and picked at the various comfits that had placed before us, while some guests slipped away for necessary purposes. As I said, grandfathers and great-grandfathers were disproportionately represented in the crowd.

Then Patch appeared for his second session. This time he was wearing boots that came up to his groin, and a very short tabard that left us in no doubt he was a man — though I suspect he had added a certain amount of padding. In his hand was a tall staff that reached above his head, and he walked with high, sluggish steps as though he was picking his way through a marsh.

I knew what was coming — I'd seen it before at court — and to be brutally honest it wasn't that funny after the first time. I mean, old Warwick would have laughed his hose off, but for anyone with a tad of sophistication this was a bit passé.

Anyway, Patch kept on walking about, waiting for someone to feed him, and eventually one of the very old knights asked why he was dressed like that.

'Why sir,' said Patch, 'I'd not have got here at all without my great staff. The Rivers are risen so high in this country I could barely make my way through!'

Of course, as you will all know, 'Rivers' was the main title of the Woodville tribe, held at that time by the Queen's delightful brother, Anthony. That was the point of the joke you see, it was a dig at the Woodvilles. Amazingly, most of this company had not heard it before; they almost burst their sides laughing. For myself, I thought it a bit lame. Margaret found it even lamer. As I have mentioned she was (inexplicably) a close friend of the Queen. Her face was probably enough to stop the clock at Westminster, thirty miles away.

This fellow Patch, I thought, has potential. I was glad I had taken him on.

*

It was perhaps the darkest hour of the night when I woke up with a start, and sat up in bed.

'Alianore,' I cried, 'you are the most stupid creature that has lived since Eve bit into that apple!'

You might have thought this outburst would have woken Sir Roger, but it did not. He merely continued to snore in his gentle, knightly fashion. I dug into his side with my elbow and with many groans and gurgles he demanded to know what was wrong with me.

'Roger,' I said, very softly as I did not want those outside the bed curtains to overhear, 'have you at any time in your life set eyes on Uncle Jasper?'

He asked me if I knew what the time was, which I felt was rather unhelpful in the circumstances. But as I persisted in my questioning, he admitted that he had, indeed, had the pleasure of the acquaintance, at the fall of Bamburgh Castle, back in the winter of '62, when the Lancastrian garrison had been hungry, just barely alive.

Jasper had been among those captured, but inexplicably — at least to my way of thinking — had been released to go off into the world and cause more trouble. It is the more surprising in that Warwick had been the commanding officer on our side, and Warwick was not normally one to let his enemies off with a warning.

'What did he look like?' I demanded.

Roger was not pleased with me, and just wanted to go back to sleep. 'What did he look like? How do you expect me to remember after all these years? He'd be about my height; with reddish hair and scars on his face. I don't know if I'd recognise him if I was stood next to him – he'd be much older now. Now, can I go back to sleep?'

It fitted well enough, though there was not enough detail to be sure. This was why Lady Richmond had been so inexplicably warm in her welcome, to distract our attention from her fugitive brother-in-law. He could be miles away by now, in any direction.

Part of me wanted to get out of bed immediately and write an urgent dispatch to Hastings. But what could I say? It was not certain the man was Jasper, and my ineptitude had allowed him to escape. No, I persuaded myself, there was no point in making a report, as it might be false, and it would certainly show Roger and me in a poor light, however I dressed it up.

Yet in my heart of hearts, I was sure it was Jasper, and that Margaret was laughing at me, delighting in his escape. She would never admit it, of course, and there was nothing I could do to make her confess. Nor would there be any proof to be found here at Woking. She was too careful for that, her servants too loyal. I should just have to hope that we could pick up the trail again, before too much damage was done.

When morning broke, I admitted by suspicions to Roger, and was dismayed when he insisted that we must send word to Hastings after all. One ought not to argue with one's husband (except for very good reason) and I am sure that my habit of doing so will add to my time in Purgatory. When a man is as pig-headed as Roger can be on occasions one really has very little choice in the matter.

I gave him my reasons, those that I have rehearsed above but in greater detail. I stressed that the man in question might well not be Uncle Jasper at all, but some random Welsh gentleman with Lancastrian sympathies, of whom there were hundreds wandering about.

We spent a good hour before breakfast agreeing to a suitable draft, and what it came down to was a simple statement that we had reason to believe Jasper had been at Woking, and a recommendation that Margaret's household be watched. I thought that if Hastings knew his business he would already have a spy or two in place, but one never knew with the fellow. Sometimes it is a good idea to state the blindingly obvious.

*

Another vision — and Glastonbury

From Woking we made our way to Reading Abbey, which is a very splendid foundation with extensive lodgings for pilgrims and a fine selection of relics to venerate. They have a hair of the Virgin, an arm of St. James, a piece of the True Cross — not a very big piece, but still —one of Christ's sandals and a piece of crust left over from the feeding of the five thousand. All well worth seeing. Just down the road at Caversham there's a shrine to Our Lady — a really famous one — and a holy well belonging to St. Anne. We said a lot of prayers and heard a lot of Masses, but all this gave us was a tranquil mind. It's amazing how much better you feel for an absence of demons and a sense that God is not exceptionally angry with you.

While I was at Reading I took the opportunity to visit my grandmother's tomb, which is in the abbey in a right first-class location, just next door to our mutual ancestor King Henry I. The tomb has a very classy effigy as well as even more classy shields of quarterings, because my grandmother was the granddaughter of two kings and the source of much of my own top-quality blood.

It must have cost a fortune, that tomb, and I spent a long time just gazing at the effigy, which was beautifully crafted. Her Despenser husband lies next to her, although his bones are at Tewkesbury, and their hands are joined. I wondered if my grandmother knew that a king of her blood was now sitting on the throne of England. She had spent much of her life wrangling with that toad, Bolingbroke, so I was sure she would be pleased that the rightful line had been restored.

Something drew me to touch the joined hands of the couple. As I did so, I had a vision. I know not how else to describe it. She stood before me, tall and blonde and stately, making the effigy seem quite prosaic by comparison.

'Forget the Grail, Alianore,' she said. 'Leave it be. It will be the ruin of us all.'

Then the vision faded, as quickly as it had appeared, and I was left alone in that great church, shivering as if I had just been pulled out of an ice bath.

I tried touching the effigy again, in hope of a repeat performance. Nothing happened. It was as if I had imagined it all. Perhaps I had. Perhaps it was a waking dream. The vision dwelled with me for an hour or two and then, as happens with dreams, it gradually faded from my conscious mind, until I quite forgot it.

*

Glastonbury is a very fine abbey, and we were made very welcome by Abbot Selwood and given lodgings in his house and places at his table. When I say 'we' you will understand I mean Sir Roger and me, our people had to make do with the pilgrims' inn. But even that was no mean lodging, recently-built in the local stone, with rich carvings and statues around the main door and glass in every window, so it was not as if they had to sleep in the stables with the horses.

Nevertheless, rank has its privileges, and the Lord Abbot's table was a very fine one, as was the food and wine placed on it, and we really could not have expected better hospitality if Roger had been a duke. The fact we had been appointed by the King to search for the Grail did our status and credibility no harm of course, and it certainly gave the Abbot a great deal to talk about over our baked trout and eels in galantine. He told us the Grail was almost certainly within a mile or two of the Abbey, but very well-hidden.

According to him, when St. Joseph of Arimathea visited Glastonbury he had not only planted his staff (which miraculously turned into the Glastonbury Thorn, which flowers at Christmas) but also brought with him the Grail itself, which he had concealed beneath Glastonbury Tor. He said there was a spring named after it, that the locals drank from because it was said to be miraculous, but there was no knowing where the Grail itself might be hidden. Digging up the whole of Glastonbury Tor was simply not possible.

He consoled us after supper by leading us into the Abbey church, and showing us the supposed tomb of Arthur, which is built into the high altar. On top of the tomb was a large cross, crudely fashioned from lead, with strange uneven lettering upon it. Roger squinted at it for a while but could not make sense of it, although he said it seemed to be Latin. The Abbot, smiling complacently, said that the English translation was*: Here lies the famous King Arthur, buried in the isle of Avalon.* He went on to show us a pair of skulls, which he claimed were those of Arthur and Guinevere.

That was pretty much the end of the evening's entertainment. Roger and I had an early night, and I remarked that although the tomb was very pretty, everyone with any sense knew that King Arthur had never existed, and therefore both the tomb and the cross set on top of it must surely be bogus.

'I catch the whiff of heresy again,' he said with a patient sigh.

I frowned, 'Not at all. I don't question any of the doctrines or dogmas, or whatever you call them, of the Church. I believe every word, down to the last comma, and even if I didn't I'd still swear I did, as I've no mind to be burnt at the stake over some minor quibble of conscience. That doesn't mean I believe that every cleric since St. Peter has been free of sin; far from it. Anyway, the trade in relics is notorious. Consider the True Cross. If you assembled all the pieces held in various parts of Christendom, there'd be enough timber to build a carrack[27]. Given that the Cross must have been no larger than something one man could carry, it follows that some of the relics must be false. Not all of them, but a proportion, and the dodgy relics will mostly have been created by men of the cloth. Let's be generous and say that they do it out a mistaken desire to strengthen the Faith.

'Imagine you are the abbot of this God-forsaken backwater. One day, one of your monks says, "Father Abbot, what we need is a great relic to draw in the crowds and thus the offerings of the pious." And you dwell on this for a while, and ask yourself what is our unique selling point. Eventually it dawns on you – King Arthur. It's a famous legend, everyone has heard of him, and some of the tales are rooted in this part of the world. All you need is a grave with a man and a woman in it – not exactly something in short supply – and an old sword. Great, you think, one of the old corrodians [28] left behind his grandfather's sword. It's got a few jewels in the hilt—that will do.'

'You are forgetting the cross, Alianore. That strange cross found in the grave with the bodies, the one with King Arthur's name on it; to say nothing of the skulls.'

---

[27] A carrack was an ocean-going ship with three or four masts, the largest type of this era.

[28] Corrodian – a person in possession of a corrody, the right to live in and be maintained by the abbey for life; usually purchased, though sometimes created by the founder as a condition of patronage, a corrody was an early type of provision for retirement.

'Oh, any local craftsman could have produced that for sixpence. In fact you'd probably choose the most incompetent chap in town, as his style, if you call it that, gives the impression of primitive antiquity. And as the inscription is in Latin, the fellow won't have a clue what it's about. Come to think of it, he might not be literate in English, let alone anything else. It could say "This way to the bog" for all he knows. As for the skulls, they could be from any pair of random skeletons planted in the last thousand years; Romans or Vikings or whatever. And when you've put the package together, you announce it to the world by sending the sword off to the King. Except that the First Richard isn't that impressed, and promptly gives it away to some acquaintance, and what with one thing and another the expected throughput of pilgrims never actually materialises, and the offertory numbers stay as flat as a fluke.'

Roger shook his head sorrowfully and said, 'How ever did you learn to be so cynical?'

I said, 'We live in an absurd world, nothing is ever quite as solid as it seems, and life has taught me to be wary of appearances. Anyway, one thing is sure — the Grail isn't here, at least not in the monastery. The good abbot is probably kicking himself that his predecessor didn't have one made as part of his Arthur tomb hoax. Probably the fellow didn't dare go that far. The Grail is not something to be mocked.'

'I'm glad there's something you regard as holy, after what you've just said about the True Cross.'

'My dear, if part of the *bona fide* Cross were before me, my reverence would be second to none. Indeed, I should venerate a piece that I knew for a fact was bogus, as a matter of conformity and good manners. Just as I might declare the most hideous baby born to be an angel of perfection rather than upset its mother. However, the point is that the Grail — if it can be found – is a relic of relics, if even a tenth of what is written about it is true. It will speak for itself — perhaps quite literally. There is no way such a thing can be faked.'

'And it may be somewhere under the Tor,' he reminded me. 'The Abbot said as much, and if he's right there's little point in going any further. We could do with hiring some miners from the Forest of Dean, the sort of chaps used to undermine walls in sieges. They could make tunnels, and we might just find the thing.'

'Did you not notice the size of that hill as we rode in?' I asked. 'The miners could burrow away at that for a hundred years and still not find anything of any use. I feel sure that if we are anywhere near the Grail, and God wants us to find it, He will send some kind of sign. There's been nothing of that kind, and in any event, we have other business in our hands. I doubt very much that Uncle Jasper intends to land at Glastonbury, and so far we've heard not a whisper of Lancastrian conspiracy anywhere.'

*

Horton Beauchamp — A Peculiar Discovery

We lodged for perhaps a fortnight at Horton Beauchamp, which was an ideal forward base for our preparations, whether we decided to go next into the West Country or into Wales. I focused on reading and re-reading the paperwork we had assembled, which by this time was quite voluminous, as well as turning my mind to the matter of logistics. We had quite a substantial party to keep fed along the road — or rather, in many of the places we were going, the sheep track — and there was also the little matter of keeping in touch with Hastings. Miles consume messengers and one can only make a limited use of carrier pigeons. The damn things are a nuisance in the field, always requiring to be fed, and a standing invitation to any hungry thief. They also make a confounded row and fill their cages with shit, and at the end of the day you can only expect them to carry a very short message, nothing in the way of a two page report. They are also very apt to fall victim to birds of prey, and usually do so when the despatch tied to their leg is of capital importance. Their only advantage is that they are fast — far faster than even a messenger provided with fresh horses at regular relay points.

    Sir Roger, meanwhile, had had his thoughts marvellously concentrated by our little meeting with the absurd Robin Hood. He felt that our retinue was far too small to venture into such dangerous places as Wales and Cornwall, where the forces of law and order are very thin on the ground and invariably partial. Aided and advised by Guy Archer, he set about selecting half a dozen of the best archers from our younger house servants and the sons of tenants, to be paid day wages until we returned. I thought this would make our party a little unwieldy for comfort, but since it was essentially a military matter I did not press the point. Indeed, I began to practise myself with a crossbow and with the small longbow I sometimes used for hunting in those days. This latter was a feeble thing compared to those carried by professional archers, only about fifty pounds pull or thereabouts, but it could still put a nice hole in anyone not wearing armour of proof, particularly at short range. There was no point in my carrying a sword, of course, since I lacked the skill to wield one. There are few things more ridiculous than a gentlewoman attempting to use a sword, or even strapping one to her side. Of course, I did have the usual sharp poniard or two about my person, as you might expect.

Unfortunately, a day or two before we planned to set off, I fell ill. I know it would be better for the story if this had been some serious ailment — the pestilence for example, or child-bed fever — which was on the verge of claiming my very life when I received treatment from some mysterious infidel physician who just happened to be touring rural Gloucestershire. However, that would be to write fiction. The truth is that it was a minor inconvenience requiring a few days in bed and some moderate dosing with an herbal mixture that even Juliana was capable of preparing. I slept a great deal, and it would all have been over quickly — and not worth mentioning — had I not been struck by dark melancholy.

I had been missing my dogs, and even, to a point, my children, ever since London. Now I was overcome by a burning desire to see their little faces, and the impossibility of it made me weep and wish that I might never wake up. If it is possible not to be one's self, then I was scarcely Alianore at all. I turned my head to the wall.

Sir Roger suggested I was suffering from *accidie*, which for those of you who don't understand Latin means spiritual sloth. To which I responded with many rude and unsuitable words. When I had calmed down a little, I put it to him in my customary gentle and respectful way that as he was the one that had been taken over by a whole household of demons he was scarcely in any position to lecture me on matters of sin. Then I asked him very politely to go away and ride his best horse to Gloucester and back (I meant the place, not the person) as I intended to take an infusion of poppy juice and go back to sleep. I requested that I be not disturbed for a very long time, unless the house actually set on fire, or we were invaded by the French or something like that.

He flounced out of the room. No, that is not fair. Knights do not flounce any more than clerks scurry. Perhaps 'stormed' or 'stalked' is the correct word. Anyway, he was not best pleased, but at the time it did not bother me in the least. Frankly, my dears, I didn't *give* a damn. I reached for my cup of poppy juice and vervain and swallowed it in one gulp, after the manner of Guy Archer at the All-Gloucestershire Dry Cider Swilling Championship — which he won seven years running. Almost instantly I fell into a deep sleep.

It was during this sleep that I had a very strange dream. It was of the Welsh lady, Tegolin, who had taught me the basic arts of witchcraft and prophecy. (Although according to my brother, Bishop Edmund, not only did no such person exist, but our family was not in Wales at the relevant time. I do not pretend to know how to reconcile his version of events with mine, although even as a mere child he was an accomplished liar and since then has been trained as a senior clergyman.)

Anyway, it seemed to me that Tegolin was in the room, the room being otherwise exactly the same as when I was awake. She smiled at me in her usual, mystic way.

'Tegolin?' I said, not able to think of anything more interesting.

'Yes, my dear. I have travelled far to see you, knowing that you need my aid in your quest.'

'You know about Uncle Jasper?'

'I speak of the Holy Grail; your true quest.'

I shrugged, or at least I thought I did. I'm not at all sure that one really shrugs when one is in a state of drugged sleep. 'Oh, that. I suppose you're going to tell me that Owain Glyndŵr found it, and buried it with a unicorn on Bardsey Island. Or something of that sort, anyway.'

Tegolin paced around angrily, at one point actually merging with the wall hangings and stroking the head of one of the hounds as it stretched itself towards the fleeing stag. She had always been apt to do confusing things like that, even when she was real.

'Child, you have always been impossible,' she snapped, wagging a finger at me as though I were still ten years old. 'I put it down to your sluggish, Saxon blood — nothing limits vision and understanding more. If you'd used half your latent powers you'd be Queen of England by now, or a duchess at the barest minimum. It grieves my heart to see such waste. Look at you, wife of an obscure knight from the back end of Gloucestershire, running errands for William Hastings, a jumped-up squire! Glyndŵr knew where the Grail was to be found; he might have taken it into his hands, if he hadn't had to spend so much time fighting the tyrant Bolingbroke and his evil son. Now, do you wish me to help you, or not? You are draining my energy at a fearful rate — I am grown too old for this sort of visitation.'

I sat up. At least, I sat up in my dream. 'Of course I should like your help. I've no idea where to start looking for the Grail, and I doubt it even exists. But it would be much more useful if you would pinpoint the present location of Uncle Jasper given that he is a clear and present danger to the King I serve. And I should like to record my objection to your description of me as a Saxon. While I do have a certain amount of Anglo-Saxon blood, I am primarily of Anglo-Norman descent, with a strong infusion of Spanish and more than a few French ancestors. There may even be some Welsh in there, though I suspect it is rather diluted.'

'I am fully aware of your pedigree,' said Tegolin, her pedagogic tone quite undiminished by my protest. 'It is neither here nor there. To find your Grail, you must first of all seek out the Chapel of Moderate Risk. After that, you must find your way to the Tower of Mild Hazard. Climb to the top of the Tower, and you will find two doors. Behind the left hand door is the guidance you need to reach the Grail. Knock on it thrice. But whatever thou dost, do not knock upon the right hand door.'

With that, she simply faded away. Or rather, she merged into the wall hangings again, and walked off into the woods. And I awoke. Or I thought I did, because there was no obvious transition from sleeping to waking. It was growing light, and there was a big space in the bed where Sir Roger was supposed to be.

I climbed out of bed and looked at my glass. I was certainly not at my best. There were hairs growing at the top of my forehead, and my eyebrows looked as if they'd hadn't been shaved for a month. As for my hair – it was in a fearful tangle. I called for Juliana and told her to get to work with the razor and tweezers, and then help me dress. The way I looked at that moment I'd have been laughed out of every court in Europe. There is nothing worse for a woman's looks than spending day after day in the saddle, quite apart from the fact that it turns your arse to leather.

I thought about my dream. Had it in fact *been* a dream or had Tegolin actually made her way into the house. You know, the more I thought about it the less sure I became. Then I began to ponder on what I had been told, and whether I should mention it to Roger. On balance, I rather thought not. I had never heard of the Chapel of Moderate Risk, and I certainly hadn't read about it. I doubted it existed, and I had the idea that Roger would laugh at me if I mentioned it. Yet it had been a very vivid dream, and I had a lot of faith in Tegolin's power. She really was a witch, a professional one who could make things happen, not a pathetic amateur like Elizabeth Woodville who would have struggled to cover a battlefield in fog to save her life.

Then again, insofar as Tegolin had a political allegiance to anyone but the ghost of Owain Glyndŵr, she was a Lancastrian. God knows why, but there you are. (It was a highly illogical position to hold, given that old Bolingbroke was Glyndŵr's mortal enemy, but people are often illogical about politics.) She had refused to answer my question about Uncle Jasper, and yet I am quite sure that the real Tegolin could have found him with no more than a snap of her fingers and a handful of magic dust in the fire. Why would she want King Edward to have the Grail, the very thing that would make him unassailable? It didn't make sense. If the dream was real — in the sense of being some kind of magic communication, as opposed to my drugged fantasy — she was surely trying to mislead me. Like a lapwing that pretends not to be able to fly, so that it can lead the hunter away from its nest.

There was still no sign of Sir Roger, and so Juliana and I enjoyed a breakfast of manchet bread dipped in wine and washed down with a pint of small ale. After that, I toured the entire house, including the kitchen and brew house, and could still discover no sign of my knight — what was more, no one admitted to having set eyes on him. Even Guy Archer was unusually taciturn, and unusually sober.

It was puzzling, but it seemed somewhat early to order a search for a grown man who was more than capable of looking after his own welfare and so I merely gave orders for a horse to be saddled, and set off for a ride around the manor. It is always a good idea to keep an eye on what is going on about the place, especially when one is not normally resident. You can stake a purse of gold that some fellow will have neglected to maintain a hedge or a ditch, or that a tenant will have encroached on the lord's waste, or cut down trees without permission. The squire down the road (or even the local rogues) may be intruding into the park and poaching the deer. Indeed, the walls and ditches around the park may be broken down, and the deer half way to Bristol before you realise it. The warrener may be neglecting the conies, or taking some to market on his own behalf without accounting for the profit. It's even possible that the priest will have forgotten to celebrate Mass for a couple of months, or even that he will have ridden off somewhere about his own business and left his flock unattended for weeks at a time. Nothing should ever be taken for granted, and it is the plain duty of any lord (or lady) to ensure that everything is in its place and nothing is neglected. A manor left unsupervised for too long always goes to pieces. Servants — even the very best and most loyal of them — will only stir so far.

We had missed the traditional May Day celebrations — which in Horton Beauchamp principally involve the young men of the manor pressing the young women into the grass — but the month (one of my favourites in the season) was far from over. The blossom was already falling from the cherry trees, but the bluebells still flourished beneath the woodland canopy. I rode through pastures rich with our dark cattle, and with lambs just grown to a fit size for the table. I sat my horse for a while, enjoying the warm breeze and the sun in my face and the beauty of the green hills to the east. I forgot about the Holy Grail, and Uncle Jasper, and everything except my own contentment in the moment. This was home, and I never wanted to leave it again.

It was almost nine years since I had arrived here, dressed as an archer and in some danger of being burnt as a traitor if Warwick or the delightful Prince Edward of Lancaster remembered who I was and discovered where I was hiding. It didn't turn out that way, of course, or I'd not be writing this, and on the face of it I was very well placed. Lady Beauchamp, cousin of the King, favoured lady of the Duchess of Gloucester, an officer of Yorkist Intelligence, the mother of four reasonably well-made children and owner of many beautiful dogs and horses. Yet I was not content, because all I wanted to do was stay at home, manage my household and tend my gardens. Instead I was forever being dragged from one end of the country to another, or sitting behind some desk, scribbling intelligence reports by candle-light and getting ink all over my fingers (and sometimes my clothes) — all because to duty to the House of York.

'The House of York — what are they to me?' I said it aloud, although only my mare and possibly a couple of stooping swifts heard it. The answer came quickly — family for one thing; friends for another, at least in the case of Richard and Anne; your lawful King, in the case of Cousin Edward; and your husband's patrons and employers, not to say your own. The ties that bind, duty and loyalty, compel us to serve even when our hearts drag us in a quite different direction. You are lazy, Alianore, and always have been — you have ever sought ease, a corner by the fire with an interesting book, or a discussion with a man or woman of information. While others stitched, or spun, or said lengthy prayers, you dreamed, usually of rent-rolls and high titles. You are a neglectful wife and a disgraceful excuse for a mother, and even Duchess Anne — whom you call friend as much as mistress — you do not serve as you should. You skimp your prayers and attend Mass so infrequently it's a wonder you've not been taken up for a heretic. Even when you *do* attend, the truth is that half the time you're thinking of something else, even when the bell rings for the Elevation. All you want to do is sit on your arse in the back end of Gloucestershire, reading Chaucer and Langland or tending your wretched gillyflowers.

All this accusation ran through my head like a litany, and what do you think I said in reply?

'Yes, all that is true. And, yes, that is *exactly* what I want to do. So *stuff* you.'

I spoke aloud. A passing swallow looked at me with a shocked expression on its little face, and made an abrupt change of course. I watched its flittering passage until it vanished into the trees. There was an absolute silence, broken after some minutes by the gentle cry of distant sheep summoning their young.

I turned my horse and made my way at a walk, uncertain of where I was going. Indeed I believe I allowed my mount to decide, and she, delightfully placid creature that she was, chose a pleasant trail through the woods that ended near Guy Archer's cottage. His wife was working just outside the front door, milking one of their sheep. They had a decent piece of land as part of Guy's contract with us, and as he was rarely to be found there, Joanne Archer did most of the work about the place. Several small faces peered around the door at me, and by the look of her I judged that another was on its way. Fortunately, she was a strong, well-built woman, country-bred and more than capable of managing it all.

'Goodwife Archer,' I cried in greeting, 'I fear I have a thirst on me. Would you be so kind as to spare me a pot of your excellent cider?'

I'm not sure she was exactly pleased to see me, but she answered graciously and I dismounted and went with her into the house. It was dark inside, but everything was scrupulously clean and neatly arranged, allowing for the fact there were four or five little children — I forget the exact number — crawling about the place and looking for things to disturb, in the way of such babes. I patted the eldest, Geoffrey, on the head, and told him he was growing into a splendid fellow. It was no more than the truth, but it seemed to please his mother no end. She was smiling broadly as she passed the cider to me.

I took a careful swallow. It was as good as anything we had up at the Hall, and it was tempting to empty the pot in one, save that I feared to be thought unseemly. So again, I praised the product, and said it was as fine a dry cider as I had tasted in my life, which was the approximate truth. (My only real sorrow was that the pot held a pint rather than a quart, because I was feeling greedy.)

We sat and chatted for a while about what had been happening on the manor in my absence, who had married, who had died and which goodwives had had babies, and similar trivial matters. It provided me with a few mental notes as to which tenants I needed to visit during my time about the place, and what arrangements needed to be made to settle widows and see that the various farms and cottages were all properly tenanted and kept in good order. However, as the conversation drifted, she began to talk about Guy.

'I'm worried about him, my lady,' she said, looking straight at me. 'Since coming home, it's like I've been living with a different man. For one thing, he scarcely sleeps. He gets out of my bed in the middle of the night and wanders about. I don't mean he goes for a piss, either, I mean he wanders about, like someone out of his head. I've found him poking about the chicken shed, or sitting on a hurdle, or even roaming around in the woods. And when you ask him what the bloody hell he thinks he's doing, he looks at you as if it's *you* that's mad.' She paused, shaking her head. 'No, it's not what you're thinking. He's scarcely touched a drop, apart from small-ale, since he came home. All he does is sit there.' She pointed to the chair on which I was sitting, the only one in the house. 'He sits there and works on the new bow he reckons to be making. Well, I've seen him make bows before, but this one is taking a lot longer than usual, the reason being that half the time he does no more than sit and stare at it. And when he's not doing that, he's up at the Hall, teaching lads how to shoot.'

'I will send you a small cask of my special valerian mixture,' I promised. 'It will help him sleep, at the least. A couple of fingers' depth in a pot like this — no more, or it will either sour his mood or bring him out in hives. It's what I take myself at need. As it happens, your Guy is not the only fellow acting strangely. Sir Roger has quite vanished — no one has seen him since yesterday evening. That's one reason I'm out here. I don't suppose you have laid eyes on him?'

She shook her head. 'No, my lady, he hasn't been past here. Not unless it is that he rode by night, when I would be none the wiser.'

'Well, that is another strange thing,' I went on, 'because he didn't take his horse. He is on foot, and I'd not expect a knight on foot to get very far, as he isn't used to walking. Joanne, if it's any comfort to you, I'm as worried for him as you are for Guy.'

I just stopped myself from telling her about the exorcism at Windsor. It was better not to, as I feared the word would get about, and it would do nothing for Roger's credibility as lord of the manor if everyone knew that he had temporarily been host to a whole parliament of demons. It was not his fault of course, but people are still apt to be prejudiced in such cases.

'You are right in one thing at least,' Joanne said, 'a knight without a horse will not have gone so very far. That is certain sure. Nor, do I reckon, will he be sitting in a field, or wandering about the woods. If he's not in the church, the chances are Sir Roger will be in someone's house, or visiting one of the other manors nearby. You should find him in no time, if he isn't already back at home. In fact, that would be just like a man, to be storming about asking where *you* are, when he's the one that went a-wandering.'

There was sense in what she said, so after taking my leave and thanking her for her splendid cider, I rode on to the parish church. I found it quite empty, save for the parson, Sir Julian Lessing. He was busy saying a mass for one of Roger's ancestors, so I took a pew in the chancel and waited for him to finish. This was no great hardship, as it is always profitable to the soul to hear a mass, even if you are thinking about something entirely different at the same time. Like the nasty crack developing in the plaster above the high altar, just in the middle of the great painting of the Trinity that was put up there to celebrate the family's share of the spoils of Poitiers. I made a mental note that something would have to be done about it before it got any worse, even if it meant bringing in craftsmen from Bristol, who would need a huge and expensive scaffold and an endless supply of beef, bread and cider, quite apart from their fee. One cannot afford to allow God's house to fall down, as it's very bad for the family image. I wondered how much more I could add to our expenses as a contribution towards the cost. It would be money spent in God's service, after all.

Beneath it, painted Beauchamp bear cognizances held up little painted banners showing the arms of Beauchamp of Horton Beauchamp, just to show who had gone to all that expense.

Eventually Sir Julian finished the mass and noticed my presence. He hurried across, his manner somewhat unctuous, and spoke of his delight in seeing me in his church — Roger and I rarely set foot in it except on the highest of holy days as we had a perfectly adequate private chapel up at the house. I'm afraid to say that I was somewhat abrupt in cutting across his flow of compliments. I said I had urgent need of my husband, and wanted to know if Sir Julian had seen him.

He had admitted that he had, although it had been well before Prime. Sir Roger had spoken of going to the chapel in the woods where his first wife was buried. The chapel of St. Anne or, as the ignorant hinds called it, the Chapel of Moderate Risk.

The Mists of Middleham

It was a good job I was sat down at that moment, as I believe my legs would have crumpled beneath me. Swallowing my astonishment, I heard myself ask how the chapel had acquired such an unusual title.

He smiled, delighting in the tale. 'Long ago,' he said, 'very long ago, in the days of William the Bastard, or perhaps his sons, there were wolves and wild boars ranging this part of England; so many that the people went in fear of them. But in those days, my lady, it was in a very remote spot. This church did not exist, nor yet the village and people feared to visit the chapel, took a great risk in doing so. It was a place of pilgrimage, for the sacred spring next to it was far more famous than it is now. But in time the wolves and wild boars diminished — no doubt because Sir Roger's noble ancestors hunted them to extinction. So gradually the danger of visiting the chapel diminished, and it gained its vulgar name. I believe only the oldest of our people call it thus, and it is a long time since any pilgrims have made their way to it. To most, it is simply the chapel of St. Anne, and very properly so.'

This was all very interesting but it did not explain Roger's decision to visit the chapel, or the hours that had slipped by since he made it. I was worried, as it seemed to me that hunger should have brought him home long ago, if nothing else. I thanked the parson, and made my way back to my mare.

I was not exactly sure where to find St. Anne's chapel, although I knew it was somewhere in the woods. I had visited it once or twice, but we were so rarely at Horton Beauchamp, and when we were there were usually better things to do. I set off at a gentle pace, my eyes searching through the trees for some sign of a stone building, but I could only hope I was travelling in the right general direction. There was a reasonable path, but the tree branches hung low over it, and I frequently had to duck in the saddle to avoid collisions. I fear I did not escape without a few scratches.

After some time, at least part of which was occupied in riding around in circles, I managed to find the place. It was not at all impressive, you must understand. There were no soaring pinnacles, no lofty steeple reaching up to the sky. The chapel was (and is) ancient, small and squat and largely hidden beneath a mantle of ivy. A small hut stood a little way off, home of the resident mass priest. There was no smoke from its chimney and no sign of life. The fellow was probably away in Stroud, drinking his fees; that was his usual practice, anyway.

I dismounted, secured my mare, and made my way to the chapel door, which, rather to my surprise, swung back on its hinges without a sound, as though it had just been oiled. I stepped inside, and peered into the darkness. There was no sign of a single candle, the only illumination being provided by the rather narrow windows, and not very much at that, for the trees were close and the glazing was covered in painted heraldry and scenes from the life of St. Anne.

I almost stubbed my toe against the tomb of Roger's first wife. It was a rather fine monument, with her effigy dressed in the style of King Harry's time and very richly painted. I could not imagine why she had wanted to be buried in such an obscure place, but then she had been born into a cadet branch of the Courtenays, and they were always a strange bunch, and Lancastrians to boot. There's no accounting for taste.

The thought had barely crossed my mind when I heard the distinctive clunk of a chisel on stone somewhere not so very far away. To say I jumped is putting it mildly — I went about three feet backwards. Then I had a moment to think, and reasoned that ghosts and demons are not big users of chisels. So I drew out my poniard from its pocket, and made a stealthy advance.

Just around the corner, in a little cubbyhole that passed for a side chapel, some fellow was squatting with a small lantern beside him. As I watched, he thoughtfully raised a mallet, and hit the chisel once again, provoking a small fall of mortar.

'What the devil do you think you are doing?' I demanded, in a voice that filled the whole chapel.

It was the fellow's turn to jump, for my approach had taken him completely by surprise. As his face turned towards me, I saw to my amazement that it was Sir Roger himself.

We stared at one another for several seconds.

'I had an idea,' he said at last. 'My father used to say there was a great treasure here, guarded by a dragon. So I thought I'd look for it.'

'*You thought you'd look for it?*' That came out a bit loud, I'm afraid. 'I've been looking all over Gloucestershire for you. Did you not think to leave word?'

He stood up, and brushed himself down. 'It was the middle of the night when it came to me. Everyone was asleep, and you had given me the idea that you didn't want to be disturbed. So I thought of the tools that old Tom Lister left behind him when he died, and I found them in my storeroom and made my way here. I didn't think it would take long, and I didn't want half the manor knowing what I was about. There's no saying what I might find.'

'Someone's bones I shouldn't wonder. Roger, I don't know what you were thinking about, but is this not desecration?'

He shrugged. 'I don't think so. It's my chapel, belonging to my family from God knows how many years ago, and I've every intention of putting it all back in order when I'm done. Look, here's the dragon.'

He held up the lantern, and there was indeed a crudely carved dragon on a large stone. He had been chipping away at the mortar around it for some time, and it was almost ready to be dislodged.

I was having nothing to do with it. I returned my poniard to its place, took a convenient pew, and said very little.

Roger returned to his work. It seemed to take an age of nibbling away at the mortar, but at last he gave a contented grunt. 'It's only a thin stone,' he said, 'I can get the chisel behind it, and there's a void beyond. All I need do now is lever it out. Take my knife, and give me a hand.'

I was reluctant, to say the least. I've done many strange things in my life, some of them fairly sordid, but poking around in crevices in ancient, sacred places is not something I care to undertake; too much risk of disturbing the dead, or offending God, or both. However, Roger was insistent. With both of us prodding away, the stone came off with surprising ease. Behind was a void, and just for a moment I had the impression of movement within, as if we had disturbed some creature. But it was just my imagination toying with me.

All that was in sight was some old parchment; indeed, quite a bundle of it.

'Some treasure!' I exclaimed.

He grabbed it, and untied the ribbon that bound it. There was lots of writing, in a small, clerkly hand, and to my disgust I saw that every word of it was in Latin. I doubted it had any relevance to humanity, but that was only my instinct, as I have no more of that tongue than my *Ave* and *Paternoster*— though in truth the same can be said for many a country priest.

'This will take some time to translate,' Roger said, stating the obvious. He knew more of the language than I did, but when all was said and done he was an English knight, not a scholar. 'However, unless I am much mistaken, this manuscript was written by my father. He was something of a clerk, you know. Wanted to be a priest, but then his elder brother died and so he had to marry and become a knight. He bought most of the books we have — *all* the ones that aren't romances or chronicles. This could be important; remember what I told you — he spoke of a great treasure.'

'Hmm,' I said, considering that to be the most proper response. 'Well, I suppose you'd better set to work, and in privacy. If it's so important, it might be wise to keep it in the family.'

The next few days passed slowly to the point of tediousness. Roger shut himself in his counting-house, and scribbled and hummed away to himself as he tried to make sense of the papers. He drank ale sparingly, and hardly appeared for meals at all. At last I was reduced to taking him a slice of beef between two rounds of manchet bread.

It took him more than a Paternoster-while to even notice my presence.

'What's this?' he asked, sounding almost too weary to stay awake.

'A little meal I've just invented for someone too busy to come to the table. I'm thinking of calling it an "Audley".' 'Don't be absurd, Alianore! Do you seriously suppose that in all the long years since mankind was thrown out of Eden, no one until now has ever thought of taking meat between two slices of bread? On campaign, in the old days, we rarely ate anything else.' He paused and took a bite. 'I think I'm getting the sense of it now, if sense it can be called. It's not a treasure at all. Not gold, or jewels, and still less the Grail. But it is, well — sensational. I don't know what else to say. If I didn't remember my father and his ways, I'd say it was invention; crazed invention, and not to be believed. But he never imagined anything in his life. For all his learning, he was a very plain man; positively prosaic.'

The Mists of Middleham

I waited for the story to come out, while Roger wasted time shaking his head and sighing. 'My father,' he said at last, 'was in the Duke of York's service. You knew that, I think, that my family and theirs have been linked through four generations. Anyway, in the year '55, the Duchess had her last child; a daughter, Ursula. The times were dangerous, and my lady took it into her head that the child was not safe. A crazed imagining, no doubt, but women are that way sometimes, aren't they, especially after childbirth. So she chose to pretend that the child was dead, substituting the stillborn baby of some washerwoman while sending the real Ursula into deep cover. It seems my father facilitated it, made all the arrangements to convey the baby away from Fotheringhay. Later, when all was well, the Duchess realised it was impossible to resurrect a supposedly dead child, that it would be far too embarrassing. So she arranged for Ursula to stay where she was, in safe obscurity. Where, we must presume, she still lives until this day.'

'But that is ridiculous!' I cried.

'Did I not say so? I don't think it was only the Duchess who was temporarily crazed. It seems that even York himself was kept out of the loop. Apart from the Duchess, only my father, the washerwoman (who acted as Ursula's wet nurse) and the Countess of Warwick knew the full tale.'

'Lady Warwick?'

'Apparently she was in attendance on the Duchess at the time. And, as you know, she has some craft as a midwife. It seems she also has some skill at keeping a secret, although I'd not have guessed that of her. Perhaps our cousin is not quite the fool she appears. She apparently arranged for the child to be cared for by one of her husband's affinity. A clerk called John Rous, of Warwick.'

The name rang a faint bell. 'Is that not the man who creates books of family history for the Countess?'

'The same one,' Roger confirmed, 'or else a man of like name that just happens to live in the same place. The question is now, Alianore, what on earth do we do about it? This is a family secret and a big one. The King and my lord of Gloucester are presumably quite unaware that they have another living sister. Is it for us to break the news? Would we even be believed?'

'I should like to think about that,' I said. I was still taking it in, and considering all the implications, not least my dream of Tegolin that had referred to the very chapel in which we now stood. I sensed that this business of Ursula had some sort of link to the Grail quest, but I could not for the life of me imagine what it was. That is to say, I could not have put forward any kind of argument that would have made sense to Roger, or any other sane person, but somehow I knew the link was there, and that Ursula was part of it. Maybe it was inspiration; maybe it was merely an excuse for my simple curiosity to see what she looked like. I do not pretend to be perfect.

Next morning, over breakfast, I suggested that we should ride to Warwick. Rather to my surprise, Roger agreed with me. It was as simple as that.

*

Warwick and Guy's Cliffe

The journey from Horton Beauchamp to Warwick is as pleasant a ride as you could wish, through some of the most beautiful and fertile country in England, and the weather was almost entirely on our side. We travelled by way of Tewkesbury, and visited the great abbey, where I said prayers for my brother, Sir Humphrey, who lies buried there. As an obstinate Lancastrian, and an executed one at that, he needed prayers more than most and on a mission such as ours it was highly appropriate to be charitable.

I tried a few subtle questions on Abbot Strensham, in an attempt to establish whether he had had any Welsh gentlemen among his recent guests, but found him rather skilled at avoiding the subject. His talk over supper was mostly of the battle nearby, especially when he discovered that Roger had fought in it, but from his general tone I judged him a Lancastrian supporter, albeit a feeble one. He said much about the pitiable fate of Somerset and the so-called Prince of Wales, and even something about my miserable brother, but the fact that Sir Roger had almost died of wounds gained in fighting these deplorable wretches did not seem to register with him at all.

It would not have surprised me, therefore, had I found Jasper Tydder hiding in the bell tower. I did not, of course, but I set Guy Archer and Patch the Jester on the trail, had them questioning everyone from the cook to the cellarer, but they gleaned very little. The abbey had Welsh guests all the time — it was, after all, on the way to Wales — and not a few of them were middle-aged gentlemen. But there was no one who could be clearly identified as Uncle Jasper, and no one, even under the influence of strong cider, came out with anything remotely suggestive of Lancastrian plotting.

Next day we rode on by way of Evesham, calling in at the abbey there to venerate the available relics and pray for guidance. It is here that the famous Simon de Montfort is buried. Although one must deplore the fact that he invented parliaments, it must also be said that he rebelled in his time against a king called Henry, and therefore should be regarded as a sort of Yorkist. Anyone who hates a King Henry cannot be entirely bad — indeed, the monks of Evesham are half way to making Earl Simon a saint, which demonstrates my point.

We did not linger long, for it was still a fair ride to Warwick, and Roger said that he wanted us there before the end of the day.

Warwick is one of the most impressive castles in England. At this time it was in the hands of the Crown, because young Edward, Earl of Warwick, (Clarence's son) was still very much a minor. Nevertheless, Sir Roger and I both being family members in our different ways we were allocated a particularly fine suite of rooms and we settled in very nicely. I wrote letters to Hastings and Duchess Anne so that they knew where we were and because I didn't want to give the impression that they'd been forgotten. However, I chose not to mention the matter of Ursula of York. I thought that best kept quiet for the time being.

I would have been quite happy to stay a month and forget all about the wretched quest, but Sir Roger, being Sir Roger and full of such concepts as honour and duty, kept banging on about Guy's Cliffe and this dratted John Rous. So after only three or four days we rode out there. It wasn't much of a journey, the place is only a couple of miles north of the castle, so we didn't even bother to pack bread and cheese, while our escort was minimal.

Guy's Cliffe is essentially a chantry, although there are a number of ancillary buildings. The late Warwick planned to convert the place into a home for distressed gentlefolk — believe it or not — but due to his death at Barnet and subsequent redistribution of his assets this never happened. Poor old Warwick. I pray for him sometimes. Because although one of his key ambitions was to drown me, or burn me at the stake, he also had his good points. He was Anne's father for one thing, and he hated the Woodvilles for another. Had he lived long enough I'm sure he'd have hated the Tydders as well. There is some goodness in all of us.

Sir Roger's supposed ancestor, Guy of Warwick — who may or may not have existed — is allegedly buried in a cave near Guy's Cliffe. The job of the chantry priests is to pray for his soul and for the souls of all subsequent Warwicks and their families. (That is quite a lot of souls, as you can imagine, although I suppose some of the really old ones — if they were well behaved — will be out of Purgatory by now, or very nearly so.) In their spare time they compose illustrated histories. At that time their chief client was the Countess of Warwick, who loved books about her ancestors and would happily charge their exorbitant cost to Richard of Gloucester's account. Richard had no choice but to pay up. As he was enjoying the benefit of holding a very significant slice of her lands — due to the fact that Parliament had declared her legally dead — he could not really complain too much.

Master John Rous — for he was no ordinary priest, he had been to Oxford and collected a master's degree, which is more than most do — was about sixty years old, his hair sparse and white and his body equally lean. He was one of those priests who looks at you down his nose, as though you have just been dragged in by the cat. At first he was not inclined to be at all helpful, but then Sir Roger pulled out his multitude of commissions, all of them carrying King Edward's very impressive seals, and Master Rous suddenly became a lot more flexible.

'The lady you seek is here,' he admitted. 'She was placed in my care long ago by my noble patron, the gracious Countess of Warwick. She is quite safe and quite contented. She lives with her old nurse, and devotes her life to study and prayer, supported by funds sent to me by my Lady Warwick and the Duchess of York. I have no idea how you learned of her existence.'

'My father,' said Sir Roger, 'was Sir James Beauchamp.'

'Ah,' said the priest, 'that would explain it, I suppose. What exactly do you intend to do about it? I doubt very much that King Edward will thank you for raking up old family secrets. For it is a deep secret, you know, and potentially quite an embarrassing one.'

'It seems to me,' said Sir Roger, 'that the King has the right to know about his sister. What he does about it is entirely up to him. It's not as if I propose to put an advertisement in the *Court Circular*.'

'What of this lady?' asked Rous, pointing at me in what I considered a very rude manner. 'Women are not good at keeping secrets. It's their very nature to gossip, to give each other news about matters which were better kept to themselves.'

'My lady,' said Sir Roger, 'is more than capable of keeping a lock on her tongue. Do not be so hardy, priest, as to speak ill of her in my presence. You will bear in mind that she is the King's cousin as well as my wife.'

'So be it.' Rous said briskly, rubbing his hands together. 'I will not stand in your way. Go out and across the yard. You will see before you a tower of sorts — only three storeys high. It's part of an ancient fortification, created by the famous Sir Guy of Warwick, long, long ago, when armour was but chain mail and leather. We call it the Tower of Mild Hazard. No one knows why, although the stairs *are* rather worn. Go inside. Climb the stairs to the very top. Go carefully, as I said, they are rather worn. Knock thrice upon the left hand door. The *left*. There you will find her, and her woman. At this hour they will be busy with their embroidery frames. Do be polite. She is, after all, the King's sister. She is *very* aware of it.'

'Do you take me for an oaf?' snarled Sir Roger. 'I am a *knight*! I am courteous to all ladies and damosels, as required by the Knightly Code. Am I the sort of rogue who would omit to take off his hat, or sit down without being asked? Come, Alianore, let us get out of here before I forget what is due to this fellow's cloth.'

He took me by the arm and all but dragged me from the room, which was a great pity because I would have liked to have had a good look at the manuscripts Rous was working on. They did look very pretty, but as it was I barely got a glance at the drawings he had on his sloping desk.

We crossed the yard and soon found the tower, which was not a particularly impressive structure. The access door opened to reveal a couple of inner doors and a narrow, spiral staircase which led up to a similar arrangement on the next level. So it was up more stairs, Roger leading the way. At the top he strode across to the right hand door and knocked loudly upon it.

Why he chose the right hand door when Rous had stressed the left I do not know. For my part, I knew at once that something was wrong. The silence was intense.

'Wrong door!' I cried, but the words were scarcely out of my mouth before Roger was hammering it on again. This was a very bad move.

From somewhere within came a roar. When I say a roar, I mean a roar. Those of you who have visited the King's lions in the Tower will know what a lion's roar sounds like. This was like twenty lions roaring at once, and with it came the clomping sound of heavy feet crossing a wooden floor.

'Run for it!' I cried.

Roger was drawing his sword, for it was not his way to run off from danger.

'A Beauchamp does not turn his back on an enemy,' he said. 'A Beauchamp! A Beauchamp!'

'It will take more than a sword to stop this,' I said, as the roaring redoubled and the footsteps drew closer. 'Run!'

I was already on my way down those stairs, skirts kilted up to my knee so I could move faster.

'Oh, SHIT!' was the cry from Sir Roger.

Having considered his options, he was close behind me. Close behind *him* was what I can only describe as a Thing. A very horrible, scary Thing. Possibly a demon. I did not look back to check — the smell of its breath, exceedingly pungent, was enough for me. It was as if we were being chased by every jakes in London. We were out into the air in record time, and I collapsed in the courtyard, shaking and on my knees with Sir Roger standing over me, brandishing his sword. Fortunately for us, the Thing, whatever it was, was an indoor Thing. It did not follow us beyond the threshold, but was good enough to give up the chase.

'What in hell was that?' Roger demanded, as he helped me out of the mud.

'I think we can safely say it was not Ursula of York,' I gasped. 'It must have been her neighbour from the next apartment.'

The only thing to do in a situation like this is to get angry with the local official. We stormed back into Rous's room and banged on his table, setting his ink pots dancing and demanding answers.

He sighed, and put his head in his hands.

'You knocked on the *right* hand door, didn't you? You've only gone and disturbed the Boggart! It'll take at least a hundred Masses to calm him down again. Perhaps a full exorcism. He'll be out every night now, scaring people to death, causing cattle to miscarry and hens to stop laying, and it's all your fault! I'm going to complain to the Bishop about this, you see if I don't.'

Priests have a way of making you feel guilty about matters that are really not your fault, and Master Rous was highly skilled in this department. For a moment even Sir Roger looked bashful and Roger, for all his many shortcomings, is not given to bashfulness. Then he recovered himself.

'One brief moment, Master Priest. How we were supposed to know you had a boggart lodged in the tower? Why would anyone expect to find a boggart lodged next to the King's sister?' He frowned. 'It seems to me that *you* are the one with explaining to do. Is that thing even licensed?'

'The Boggart has been here for over five hundred years,' Rous replied. 'One of our jobs is to keep it under control. Usually it's well-behaved. The odd ritual, the occasional Mass, is all it needs or expects. But all it takes is one idiot, and it goes on a rampage. It will take weeks to calm it down. Perhaps months. In that time the local populace will be terrorised by the thing. That's your fault, with your blundering, not mine. Look, do me a favour and just go away. My colleague and I need to start the ceremonies, and we will be on our knees for hours because of you two. To say nothing of having to bless about twenty gallons of holy water to sprinkle around the entire district. You have no idea!'

With that he stalked off in the general direction of the chapel, clenching and unclenching his fists and looking a very unhappy little chappie.

Roger sighed. 'I don't even know what a boggart is,' he admitted.

'An evil spirit,' I explained. 'Most often found in country districts. Mischievous at best, evil at worst. They tend to plague the lower orders, not persons of quality such as ourselves. You must have heard the legends? They usually form themselves into whatever their victims fear most, because their own purpose in life is to frighten people. That's what they do.'

'Well, that Thing certainly frightened me,' Roger admitted. 'Let's get out of here. We can try again tomorrow. When you will be careful to knock on the *left hand* door.'

I could tell by his tone that he had already persuaded himself that it had been my mistake. The fact that I had been three feet behind him when he knocked on the door did not trouble him in the least.

We rode back to Warwick Castle in something close to silence, for we were both very badly shaken. If you are a woman, even a great lady, even a cousin to the King, there is no shame in running away from danger, and no one will think the less of you even if you scream your hennin off. It doesn't touch your honour in the least. Poor Sir Roger though felt *diminished*. Ashamed. The fact that he had nothing to be ashamed about, that any sentient being with a grain of sense would have run from that boggart was neither here nor there.

The Mists of Middleham

He relieved his feelings by writing a very long and moderately rude letter to the Bishop of Worcester, asking if he was aware that there was a boggart kept at Guy's Cliff, and whether he knew that it was so inadequately governed by Master John Rous and his fellows that it felt free to chase ladies of the King's blood down the stairs of its tower. What, he asked, did the Right Reverend Father in God John Alcock intend to do about it? Because, whatever it was, it had better be good.

Whether anything came of this letter I know not. Given the nature of the Church and its bureaucracy the chances are it was merely filed away and forgotten. The Church is like that. Though if there had been a fee payable for disturbing a boggart, you can be sure that there would have been a summoner on our case within a week.

For my part, I took a while to calm down. There was a jug of claret wine on the dresser, and I poured a fair portion of it down my neck. The great bed, with its magnificent hangings, began to look more and more attractive as the afternoon drew on. At length, I could resist it no more. I remember unpinning my headdress, stripping down to my shift. Perhaps Sir Roger helped me, perhaps I somehow managed on my own, I'm not quite sure. I had increasing difficulty in thinking. All I wanted to do was go to sleep. I climbed into bed — and I mean that literally, because it was so high of the floor that it had its own set of steps on either side. After that, things grew a little hazy. In truth, I descended into a well of darkness, many fathoms deep. I left the real world quite behind.

*

Ursula of York

We went back next day, of course. Master Rous was not pleased to see us. He said he had been up all night, saying Masses, sprinkling holy water and performing sundry rituals to lay the Boggart.

'For the love of God,' he said, 'be sure to knock on the *left-hand* door this time. Remember what I said about being polite.'

'Remember what I said about being a knight!' Roger growled at him.

It seemed a long way up those stairs.
This time Roger was very careful to knock on the *left-hand* door. (The other door now had a notice on it, with red letters, reading KEEP OUT — DANGEROUS BOGGART. I presume Rous had added this for the sake of everyone's health and safety.)

After a short wait the door was opened by a neatly-dressed serving woman, nearly old enough to be my mother, who smiled at us and welcomed us into the apartment beyond.

There she was. Her face was strangely familiar. Indeed, absurd though it is to make such a comparison, she resembled Richard of Gloucester, if, that is, he was exceptionally well shaven and clad in a woman's gown. There could be no doubt this was Ursula of York. Sitting behind a very large embroidery frame.

We made our reverences, remembering what Rous had said, and she beamed at us.

'No need for that!' she cried. 'I keep no state. Whoever you are.'

'I am Sir Roger Beauchamp, and this is my wife, Alianore. We are members of the household of your ladyship's brother, the Duke of Gloucester. By pure chance, due to papers left behind by my father, we discovered where you were, and thought it our duty to seek you out.'

'Really?' Ursula did something quite unexpected. She giggled as if she was fourteen years old, and was receiving a boy she did not quite know how to handle. I studied her with care. She certainly did not keep great state. Her gown was such as a waiting gentlewoman might wear on a working day, and she had nothing on her head but a simple cover-chief of ordinary linen. She wore no rings, no jewels; there was no sign at all that this was the King's own sister.

'Please sit down,' she said, indicating the cushioned stools opposite to her. 'As I told you, I keep no great state. I have very few visitors, and live simply. I do not even use my title. I prefer to be known as Crystal Plantagenet and I give out that I am not true-born. I'm sure you understand.'

'Madam,' said Roger, taking his seat, 'I'm afraid there's a great deal I don't understand. Are you aware that your royal brothers and sisters have no idea that you are alive? That they believe you died as a baby?'

'Oh, I'm quite aware of all that!' Once again, the giggles rose to her mouth. It was most disconcerting. What manner of creature was this? 'If King Edward knew I lived, he'd probably marry me to some horrid foreigner to advance his diplomacy. I don't want that! Nor all the fuss that goes with it. I like to wear loose gowns, not ones too tight for me to raise my arms. I like to be able to walk abroad in Warwick without being stared at. I have all that I need. My kind patrons, Lady Warwick and the Duchess of York, provide me with ample funds. Master Rous protects me, and has given me an education. I assure you I am perfectly happy. I have a wonderful life. I am *free*.'

'But madam —'

'Call me "Crystal."' To my astonishment, she reached out and patted his knee. That was certainly no way for a princess to behave. Or indeed, anyone above the rank of tavern slut.

Roger almost choked. 'Crystal. You must see we have a duty to inform the King his sister lives. He will wish to make provision for you, your ladyship.'

'Duty?' Again she giggled. 'Oh, that is a silly word. You don't need to tell anyone. Let it be our little secret. I've told you, I'm happy as I am. I don't want to live at court with all those ghastly people. Master Rous has told me all about them and their horrid intrigues. Besides, don't you think it would be very *embarrassing*? For the King, and even more so for the Duchess of York? How would you explain it? Can you *imagine* the talk? It wouldn't make you popular, Sir Roger. Or your dear lady. Not with the people who *count*. And I should be most *dreadfully upset*. I can tell just by looking at you that you're a very chivalrous knight, Sir Roger — I'm sure you don't want to make me *cry*?'

Roger just choked, and looked at me as if to say, for God's sake, Alianore, have a word!

'My lady —' I began.

'Crystal!'

'If you insist. Crystal, you must see we are in an impossible position. This is too important a matter to be kept secret. We might even be accused of treason.'

She snorted with laughter. 'Fiddle-de-dee! Treason! I don't see the problem. Hardly anyone knows I exist, or who I am. How does my little life touch the state? It doesn't. Please. Just leave me in peace.'

'We shall have to think on it,' I said. 'We cannot make promises.'

'Please do think on it. Sleep on it.'

'You know, Crystal, there might even be a compromise. What if you lived with your brother up at Middleham? That's quiet enough. It's a long way from the court. And at least you wouldn't be living next door to a boggart.'

She laughed again, a gurgling laugh like a child. 'Oh, the dear Boggart? He's no trouble at all, normally, if he's left in peace. He doesn't have parties until three in the morning, or get roaring drunk, or play loud music. You wouldn't know he was there. Besides, he scares strangers away, and that's no bad thing. He's as good as a guard of archers and far less troublesome.'

This one, I thought, is several courses short of a banquet. What on earth were we to do?

Ride away and forget all about it, I thought. *Not our business. Not our mission. There* was something about this girl I did not like. I could not put my finger on it, but she made my blood run cold. Apart from which, just by instinct, I hated her guts.

Suddenly, I felt very tired. All I wanted to do was go to bed. I made our excuses and left. By this time I was feeling decidedly unwell. Somehow, I rode back to Warwick. It felt like a journey of twenty miles. It was barely time for dinner. I had no appetite, however. All I could think about was that lovely bed. The sun was bright outside, the birds were singing in full voice, and I was asleep.

*

Lost

At some point during the next few hours, I developed a fever. To be quite plain, I was lost to the world. Not quite dead, but lost in dreams, in horrors.

From time to time, my mind reached the surface, as it were, and I could hear people talking. Sir Roger, of course, and various others.

'Her ladyship is gravely ill,' said a voice. I think I saw him, but perhaps I merely imagined him, standing there in a white cap or coif and a long grey robe. 'She may not live. I have bled her, but it is far too early to say whether there has been any effect. Her humours are quite out of balance.'

'Take me to Middleham,' I said. Whether the words were heard, whether they were actually spoken, I cannot say. 'Take me to Middleham. Do not let me die here. Not in Warwick! Not in Warwick! Middleham! Middleham! Middleham!'

'Is there *nothing* more to be done?' That was Roger. Roger at his most urgent.

'Prayers. Have a priest say Mass. Allow time for matters to develop. God's will be done.'

'Can she be moved? Can I take her home?'

'I would not advise it.'

'Middleham! Middleham! Middleham!' I cried.

Then there was darkness.

*

Crystal Plantagenet

I am shocked back into present tense.

I ride through a kind of mist. I know that isn't a good description, but this is no ordinary mist, though I find it hard to say why. Sir Roger appears at my side, dressed from head to toe in full armour, and carrying his lance. I can see his face through his open visor; it is calm, unsmiling. He peers ahead, looking for our way. He is riding his high horse, the destrier he normally keeps for when he is fighting. It is not a comfortable mount to ride on a casual journey.

I am wearing a white gown, which is very strange because (at this particular time) I do not possess a white gown and have no idea where it came from. The headdress matches it, a very simple cone adorned with pearls and free from veiling. I don't remember that either. Indeed I don't remember waking up, or dressing, or travelling to this place. We seem to be alone — not a menial servant in sight. It isn't quite silent. I can hear the horses' hooves on the soft turf; smell the grass they have cut through.

'Roger,' I say, 'will you be so good as to pinch me.'

'Why?'

'Just do as I ask for once!' I hear my voice rise in anger. He leans over and pinches me, and it hurts. Given that his hands are encased in steel gauntlets this is no surprise. We are not dreaming.

'This is not a dream,' I say.

'Did you suppose it was?'

I try to keep calm. 'Do you remember waking up this morning? Or anything after that, such as how we came to be here?'

He hesitates. He thinks. He turns his head towards me. 'Now you mention it, no, I don't. I sort of remember going to bed last night, but after that it all seems to be a blank. But we are here together, aren't we?'

I review the possibilities, and frankly, they all stink.

'We could have been drugged,' I suggest, 'though off-hand I can't think of anything that removes short-term memory and yet allows the patient to wake feeling clear-headed, and fit enough to manage a horse. The second possibility is enchantment.'

'Alianore, you scoff at such things!'

'No, you are mistaken. I scoff at the charlatans who *pretend* to work magic. I don't deny that magic exists, but in my experience it is seriously uncommon. This might be one of the rare exceptions, and a great, stonking enchantment at that. The other possibility is this: I read a tale once of a monk who doubted his faith. So he walked into the woods near the monastery and prayed to God to put an end to his doubts. Then he slept under the trees. When he was woken by the abbey bell, he made his way back and found he didn't recognise a single one of the other monks. It took them a while to figure it out, but it turned out it was hundreds of years later. He had been recorded in the abbey chronicle as one who had broken his vows and run away, and all the monks he had known, even the youngest of the novices, were long since dead and buried.'

'You mean there was a sort of — time-slip?'

I nod. 'If you want to put it that way; it was God's way of resolving the monk's doubts. It's *possible*, I suppose, that God is seeking to resolve our doubts by the same method. The bad news is, whether this is the work of God or the Devil, I have absolutely no idea of how we are to find our way back to our proper place. We appear to be extremely deep in the solid stuff, and without even a single servant to help us.'

Roger adjusts his hold on the lance. You could even say he *flourishes* it. 'Well,' he says, 'we must just face the adventure, and what it brings. At least I am armed, and I must have had a good sleep, as I feel fresher than I have done in weeks; quite ready for action.'

He is actually enjoying himself. I try not to be annoyed, but Roger has a way of living in the moment. He rarely troubles his head with what *might* happen. I suppose this is one of the reasons he is so brave, and I expect I ought not to fault him for it.

The mist still clings to us. It is an unusual colour, closer to green than grey. It stinks in my nostrils, and I long to be free of it, but we ride on. Slowly, almost imperceptibly at first, it begins to lift. Features of landscape appear. Trees first, a whole forest of them, then a river running darkly in a valley to our right, with gentle hills beyond, but there is no sign of settlement, not even so much as a shepherd's hut. If it comes to that, there are no sheep. I look in all directions, but do not recognise where we are. It could be anywhere; or nowhere. Given all the circumstances, we might not even be in England. There is simply no way of knowing. I notice one thing — no birds are singing; in my experience this is always a bad omen.

Sir Roger is not at all disconcerted. Indeed he gives his destrier a touch of spur, and the fierce horse rears in protest, then increases its pace, leaving me to follow in his wake as swiftly as I can. My gentle jennet is not made for high speed, but for an easy, comfortable pace, but she does her best, while no doubt wondering to herself about the unnecessary haste. Roger is a length clear, then two, and the destrier's hooves bite deep into the turf, flinging up great clods of earth and grass. It is almost as if we are pursuing an invisible stag.

This goes on for some time, and has a dream-like quality that is quite off-putting. I keep wondering where we are, and how we got there, but my mind fails to produce satisfactory answers. I increasingly wish myself back at Middleham. Middleham has its consolations, when all is said and done. One of them is that one at least knows where one is.

I see a figure on the horizon. Or to be more precise, two figures, and man and his horse, the former mounted on the latter. As we draw nearer I see he is wearing black armour. (I always think painted armour frightfully common — it implies that the owner is too mean to employ people to keep it polished.)

There is something sinister about this knight. Though if you ask me exactly what it is, I would struggle to define it. His visor is open, and as we draw closer, I see enough of his features to be reminded of the man I met at Chertsey, the one I later decided was Uncle Jasper. Is it Jasper? I am not sure. I will be honest, and admit that I am not sure of anything.

A bellow emerges from the Black Knight. 'Who is it dares trespass on my land?'

'Do you want to make something of it, you nameless Lancastrian dog?' Roger roars back. It is scarcely the language of conciliation.

'I spit on your mother's grave, Yorkist pig.'

'Is that all? I piss on your mother's; aye, and dump a huge, stinking sloppy turd on your father's tomb, then go off and drink fifteen pints of strong perry just so that I can have the pleasure of puking on it as well. You dare to block my path? I'll knock you and your spavined mount from here to Penzance.'

It is obvious where this is heading, and also obvious that nothing I can say or do will make the slightest difference. So I hold my tongue, and sit there, trying to look inspirational, while they bombard one another with insults for a good quarter of an hour. I decide not to bore you with a complete record of them, as there is nothing you have not heard before. Indeed, you probably heard most of it while still in the nursery.

Eventually they run out of insults and charge at one another. This is when I realise that something is *seriously* wrong. Roger is, perhaps, already a little past his prime as a jouster, but he is a skilled knight who knows his business. He certainly knows better than to drop his lance like a red-hot brand at the most crucial of moments. The impact of the Black Knight's lance bowls him clean out of his saddle. There is a terrible crashing sound as his armour hits the turf. Roger lies still; very still. For a terrible moment I think him dead.

Somehow, I dismount and attempt to run to his assistance. But I find my legs are like lead weights. I stumble, fall to my knees, get up again, and somehow make my way to Roger. He breathes, but he has been knocked out of his senses. What other injuries he has, I cannot tell.

The Black Knight looks down at me from his horse, his expression cold, not even triumphant. I no longer think he looks like Uncle Jasper. He rather resembles Anthony Woodville; handsome and yet, somehow, repellent with it. I try to persuade myself that none of this is real, that it is some sort of elaborate dream. Yet the grass beneath my hands seems very real indeed.

The Black Knight speaks. 'I shall send servants, and a litter, to bring you to my castle.'

With that he rides off. What castle? I ask myself. There are no castles anywhere near, apart from Warwick and Kenilworth, and it's certain that neither belongs to this insolent fellow. Near that is to the last place I remember in the real world. Before I can ponder the mystery, the servants arrive with the litter, so quickly that it's as if they were waiting in the trees all the time. I can make no sense of it at all.

Eventually – by what means I am not sure – we find ourselves in a turret room, by no means small, with a large bed on which Roger is placed by the serving men. He is still out cold, and I snap at them to bring feathers and a candle, and various other medical requisites. I burn the feathers beneath his nose, and at first there is no effect at all. I contemplate myself wearing black and a widow's barbe, and don't much care for the idea. The servants fetch food; manchet bread, slices of beef, a dish of salt to season it. They bring in a jug of wine and two glasses. I ignore it, burn more feathers, pinch Roger in places it's unseemly to describe in the hope of shocking him back to life. He merely grunts. I start to panic. I demand water and a cloth, and when these arrive, I set about applying a damp cloth to his forehead. I fear that he will never wake, that I shall be left alone in this evil place.

For evil it is. It raises the hair on the back of my neck, and brings prayers for protection unbidden to my lips. My flesh not only creeps, but trembles violently. I try the wine, and my hand shakes as I lift it to my lips, so that it spills down my chin. It fails to calm me, or to give me warmth in the belly. The room is cold, unnaturally cold, and when I shudder it isn't solely with fear. I order the wretched servants to fetch a priest, but they smile awkwardly and shuffle out, closing the door behind them. No priest comes to us.

Hours pass, or so it seems, and I am alone with my unconscious Sir Roger and a locked door. I burn more feathers, and convince myself that before long I shall run mad. If, indeed, I'm not mad already, given that nothing that has happened makes any kind of sense. It's as if we've accidentally found our way into one of those foolish tales of Arthur and his knights that I read to the company at Middleham.

At last, Roger stirs. It is a slow business, not a swift awakening. At first I think I am imagining the change, that it is no more than wishful thinking. He grunts palpably. His eyelids flicker open, then close again. He groans, and moves his arm. I watch intently for signs of progress. I pray long and hard. Eventually, his eyes still half closed, he speaks my name. His voice is questioning, bewildered, like that of a lost child, and I tell him to rest; to sleep if possible. He doesn't argue. I sense that the worst is over, that he will recover, and pray that I am not mistaken. He has no broken bones — I have checked — but there is always the chance of bleeding within, of damage to the brain. I am well aware that only time will tell.

It is then that she makes her appearance. The door is unlocked, and she walks in. Very tall, she wears a gown of rich crimson, trimmed in ermine, and a towering headdress which makes the one I saw the Countess of Pembroke wearing at court look positively restrained. Ursula of York.

'My Lady Ursula!' I cry. 'What do you do here?'

'You should rise to your feet and curtsey before you address me, minion!' she snaps.

I think this a bit strong in the circumstances, since I am her cousin and in a private room. I frown, stand up, and wait for her to go on.

'Ursula was the name my mother gave me,' she continues, still glaring at me as if I am a dog that has just laid a turd under her nose, 'but as I told you, I am known to the world as the Lady Crystal Plantagenet. The Duchess rejected me, my family does not own me, and so I choose to pretend — for now — to be my father's bastard child.'

'It is a very clever concealment,' I say.

I see suspicion in her eyes. 'Do you mock me?'

'No more than usual,' I say.

Her hand stretches out. It is as if a horse has kicked me; a particularly vicious and heavy horse at that. I literally fly backwards through the air, until my head hits the wall and I crumple in a heap on the floor. A not particularly clean floor, I note. It takes a Paternoster-while, or more, to get my breath back.

'A neat trick,' I gasp.

'There can be more, a great deal more, if you remain insolent.'

I decide this is a good time to say nothing, at least until I can figure out what on earth is going on. I watch her, sense that the energy she has used to floor me has left her slightly weaker; yet not nearly weak enough. I dredge my memory For Tegolin's lessons on the subject of enchantment, clutch at possible ways and means to escape.

'You,' she says, pointing at me in a most ill-bred manner, 'are going to fetch me the Holy Grail. I need its power if I am to take my rightful place as Queen of England. Sir Roger will remain here, as my hostage, until you comply with my command. After that, provided you both accept my authority, I shall see you suitably rewarded.'

I slowly make my way up from the floor. 'How generous,' I say. 'Yet I do not see what possible need you have of us. With your own great powers, it should be child's play to find the Grail yourself.'

She flicks her hand again. Once again the pain surges through my body, and I collapse to my knees.

'You would do better not to question me,' she growls. 'However, I will tell you that I have seen your destiny, and it is your fate to recover the Grail, though why such a gift should be granted to such as you is a great mystery. You will do as you are told.'

'But apart from anything else, I have no idea where the Grail is!' I protest. 'Anyway, I refuse to be of assistance. You have no right to the crown, and I am a loyal subject of your brother, King Edward IV. God bless him!'

Another jolt, but not as painful this time, and as I look up I see she is leaning against the wall.

'Do not mention that name in this house!' she cries. I am uncertain whether she means Edward, or God, or both. 'You will do as I say, or alternatively you will stay here, to entertain my men, while Sir Roger seeks the Grail. He will not abandon you to my care, I think!'

With this, she leaves us, slamming the heavy door behind her.

Roger groans with pain. 'Alianore, my love, why did you provoke her so? She has hurt you.'

I get to my feet again. 'Not so very much. Compared to childbirth, such pains are a pat on the head, I promise you. This is all an enchantment, Roger. A very good one, highly impressive, I admit, but just an enchantment. This castle does not exist; nor does the knight who fought you.'

He snorts. 'It certainly felt like he did!'

'It's an illusion; just an illusion. She is using all her power to create it, and that is why I provoked her, to weaken her. Our only way out of here is to break the enchantment.'

'Oh, yes,' he says, 'and how are we going to do that?'

'With a sort of prayer that Tegolin taught me, long ago. I just hope I remember it correctly, because if I don't it could turn out rather badly. Look, it's hard to explain, but we have to try, and I think we have to try pretty quickly too.'

'This is witchcraft, isn't it?'

'Well, it's under the same sort of guild I suppose. But in my view we don't have a great deal of choice. Can you stand up?'

He looks at me as if I have just insulted his manhood and his knighthood at the same time. 'Of course I can!' he snaps.

I take the salt and make a protective pentacle, all the while praying that I am doing the right thing. I know it is very dangerous, and would welcome the advice of a brace of bishops or the odd cardinal. Unfortunately no one of such authority is currently available. I tell Roger to join me inside the pentacle, and to hold me tight.

'Whatever you see, or think you see, do not let go,' I warn him as we embrace one another. 'We must begin with the Seven Penitential Psalms.'

'It's as well we both know them by heart,' he remarks, 'and that I even know what the words mean.'

'This is no time for boasting,' I say. 'Begin. *Domine ne in furore tuo arguas me, neque in ira tua corripas me...*'

We continue through the psalms, as I try not to hasten, to avoid any slurring of the words. I remember there is a demon — I forget his name — who collects such errors, and takes a great bag of them each day to his master, the Devil. We even remember to say the *Glorias* between each psalm. Already I feel safer, such is the power of prayer.

At last it is time for the magic words. I only hope that I remember them correctly. I take a deep breath, and then at the top of my voice cry out: 'Glory! Happier pig! On, wise liar! Unending clog!'

Immediately, the room is filled with a rushing wind, and darkness closes around us as the walls seem to dissolve. There is a sound like a thousand screaming souls in my ears, and I close my eyes, holding onto Roger as tightly as I can.

The cold is indescribable – one could dance naked on the highest towers of Middleham in February and be warmer. When I dare to look, I find that Roger has apparently turned into a hideous demon, replete with bright green scales and burning red eyes. I cling on, nevertheless, in the hope that this is an illusion, and am at once gripped with agonising stomach cramps. Something buffets me as we spin through the air, and my hold on Roger, for all my efforts, is broken. The darkness closes, and yet below me there is light. I fall into a burning circle of fire. The flames grow higher, reaching towards me. Then all is black, as I lose consciousness.

*

The Litter

I expect to wake up in the front row of Hell, between Wycliffe and Bolingbroke. Instead, when I come to my senses, I am on a swaying bed, with curtains all around. Juliana is sitting next to me. For some reason she touches, my forehead. Then pulls back the curtain.

'Sir Roger, Sir Roger,' she cries. 'My lady is awake.'

I realise I am in a litter. It jolts to a sudden halt, and almost at once, Roger is there, staring at me.

'Alianore, are you awake?' he asks.

'I think so,' I say. My voice sounds faint, even to my own ears. 'Roger, was it real? Do you remember the Black Knight?'

'What Black Knight?' He says. 'Are you still raving? You kept saying "Middleham". It was the only thing you said that made any sense. That physician said I was mad. But I thought —'

'You thought you would do as I asked. For once.'

'Why Middleham?'

'Safe there. Safe from evil. Roger, there is great evil about. Pray for us.'

Blackness again. I know nothing more.

*

A Bewildered Yorkist at King Arthur's Court

When I come to my senses, I am lying on sweet-smelling grass, staring in wonder at a patch of daisies. There is no sign of Roger, and the strange white gown I was wearing at one point has somehow been replaced with one of my own, something much more suitable for travel. I grope in my hidden pouch and find that all the essentials were there – poniard, picklocks, code book, horn of ink, tinder-box, small flask of gonne-powder. I sit up, and look around me. All that is missing is Sir Roger, and our people. I am quite alone. This begs a question. Where am I? England or Fairyland?

I am still sitting there like the village idiot when a fellow comes walking towards me, an old fellow with a long, grey beard. His clothes are made of fine cloth, but of ancient cut, like something you might see on a *very* old tomb. His expression is amiable enough—indeed he is smiling at me as if we are old friends.

'Are you the Devil?' I ask. Why I ask this I have no idea, except I half believe I must be in Hell, given that the spell has clearly not worked properly, and that magic is, at best, a very dangerous business.

He laughs. 'Of course not; I am King Arthur.'

For some reason it doesn't surprise me that he is talking some kind of Welsh. What *ought* to surprise me was that I can understand it. I told Hastings that I do not have a word of the language, but that is not strictly true. I have had Welsh nurses in my time, and been Tegolin's pupil for a while, and can say '*Bore da*' and '*Cariad*' with the best of them. What I *cannot* do, in normal circumstances, is conduct a conversation in the tongue.

'Good day to you, your Grace,' I reply. 'Permit me to introduce myself. I am the Empress of Cathay.'

'No you are not,' he says, lifting a reproving finger. 'You are Dame Beauchamp, lady of Sir Roger Beauchamp, Knight, of Horton Beauchamp in Gloucestershire, and you are seeking the Holy Grail. Do you really think I don't know these things?'

'King Arthur is a fictional character,' I say. '*Ergo*, you cannot be King Arthur. It stands to reason.'

'Alianore, Alianore,' he cries, shaking his head, 'does it not occur to you that there may be more than one reality?'

I pick myself up, ever so carefully, and check that my poniard is to hand. I have the idea that if this fellow is not the Devil, the most likely alternative is that he is a dangerous lunatic, and you never know what one of *those* will decide to do.

'It has never occurred to me,' I say, 'because I neither want to be burnt as a heretic nor shut up in Bedlam. There is the Earth, which God made, and there are Heaven and Hell, and Purgatory, so we are taught. But there is no such thing as an alternative reality.'

'Oh, yes there is!' he says.

'Oh, no there's not! Even if you were King Arthur, you're dead long ago, and therefore some sort of ghost.'

He takes my hand, and squeezes it. 'Does that feel like a ghost?' he asks. 'Alianore, the Church does not know the half of it. They are like a man who tries to confine a great ocean between the banks of a field ditch. There are alternative realities, and this is just one of them. This is the England where I am the Once and Future King.'

'With all due respect,' I say, 'I prefer the England of the nineteenth year of King Edward IV where I belong. By the way, where is Sir Roger?'

'Back in that very place,' says King Arthur, 'entirely safe. You need have no fear. You will find your way back to him in due course. First though, there are discussions to be had.'

'In Camelot, I suppose?'

'Where else?'

I decide I have little choice but to humour him, and so walk with him across the field. The ground dips before us, and suddenly I see two fine grey horses waiting to carry us, and a small host of knights and lesser attendants. The armour these chaps wear is primitive – just chain mail with the odd small piece of plate – but the knights carry lances and wear large swords at the hip, and there is a virtual forest of banners, including one that displays a huge, golden dragon. Well, I think, at least I am not in the hands of a solitary lunatic.

We ride for a little time, along the shore of a great lake and through a dense woodland, and then, down in the valley, I see a most improbable castle, with a ridiculous number of towers and turrets, each of which seems to be flying a banner of some sort or other. I note that the towers tend to be smaller in circumference than makes military sense, while some are far too tall in proportion, and I suspect that most would not stand up to artillery for very long. The whole thing is whitewashed, except for the roofs, which seem to be made of pink tiles. Where one obtains pink tiles I cannot imagine.

The small town built around the castle walls is unfeasibly tidy. There are no piles of excrement blocking up alley ways, no pigs rooting through rubbish, no rotting heads or quartered trunks stuck up on poles over the gates. Even the people seem clean, as if scrubbed under the pump that very morning, their eyes shine and they cheer King Arthur and wave little flags at him without any apparent organisation or compulsion. I conclude that the mayor of this town must be an exceptionally efficient fellow, and I wonder how he finds time to conduct his trade or craft.

Once inside the castle I am handed over to Queen Guinevere and her numerous ladies. The Queen reminds me very much of Anne Neville, indeed at first sight I am convinced she *is* the Duchess. Yet somehow she is not. These ladies are very courteous, but they treat me much as one might use an exhausted child. They feed me, give me a cup of wine, undress me and put me in a huge bed. I try to talk to them, but they actually have very little to say. I attempt to tell them I am not tired, but before the words are out I am asleep. The truth is that I am exhausted.

How long I sleep, I do not know. It is the deep, dreamless sleep of one who has not rested for a month. I awake, puzzled, to find myself in the same great bed, looking up at an azure canopy above me. The ladies — or at least a detachment of them — are watching me, and before I know it, they have me in a bath, and are scrubbing at me as though I am covered in soot. Then, reeking of rosewater, I am dressed in one of their antique costumes, and find that I am expected to wear a wimple, as though I were a nun or a widow. I protest at this, demand my own clothes, but find it is rather like arguing with the weather. I get used to the clothes after a while – the gown is actually quite splendid, made of a silken cloth that even Elizabeth Woodville would envy. The only problem is the temporary loss of my poniard and the other useful bits and pieces I usually carry around with me.

They take me to the Queen, who greets me warmly, and settles me at her right hand. The other ladies form a circle, and start spinning or sewing, and it soon becomes clear that they expect me to join in. I find myself trying to make a shirt for a beggar, listening to inconsequential talk in the strange local version of Welsh that they all speak. I wonder how long this state of affairs will continue, as no one seems to be in any haste to deal with the questions I want answered. They have an odd, polite way of avoiding a satisfactory response. Indeed, it is rather like dealing with a convention of Exchequer clerks, but for the fact that the clerks would at least be open to bribery. I am unsure whether I am an honoured guest or a prisoner in soft captivity.

If it is captivity, it is one from which I cannot hope to escape. The first essential in escaping is to know approximately where one is situated, so pursuit can be evaded by choosing the best direction of flight. But I have no idea at all where I am. I suspect it might be Purgatory, but if not it is possibly an enchantment within an enchantment. Breaking out of either is well beyond my powers.

Every so often we pause for a decade of the rosary. This persuades me that at least we are not in Hell. Pages in livery circulate with wine and wafers and sugared almonds, and for a time there is quiet conversation, led by the Queen, whose quite astonishing resemblance to Anne Neville makes it hard for me to avoid staring at her, etiquette or none. Then work begins again, and there is no noise at all but the occasional 'ouch' as someone is careless enough to stab her finger with the needle.

I reflect that in some ways it is like being at Middleham, without the intelligence work, the cold draughts and Lady Warwick lecturing on the best method of preserving quinces. All that keeps me from reasonable contentment is the lack of any news about Sir Roger.

The day drags on like this until it is time for supper, which seems to be the principal meal, taken in the great hall of the castle with the whole of the household from the King downwards assembled in the same place. A very old-fashioned arrangement I think as I sit at table with the rest of the Queen's ladies. Some of the knights are unmannerly enough to wear their armour to the meal, while others wear dirty tunics soiled with the rust from their mail. Sundry entertainers wander about, swallowing fire, juggling balls, plucking at harps, piping shawms and banging away at tabors, while dogs root in the floor rushes for discarded food. It is a kind of ordered chaos, although I suppose the lively atmosphere appeals to some.

Later the King hammers on the table for silence, and some fellow in a long robe drones on for an hour about some tedious episode involving a knight and a dragon. To make it worse, it is all in verse. When it concludes the company applauds wildly, as though it were Chaucer in person, and I pretend to clap so as not to appear awkward. I do not hear a sensible word throughout the entire meal, and the principal drink offered is some sickly mead. I shorten the odds on this being Purgatory from five to one to six to four.

The Mists of Middleham

The odd thing is, the King's beard is shorter than yesterday, and far darker, and the more I look at him the more I realise that if properly shaven he would look remarkably like Richard of Gloucester. This is growing ridiculous! All I need now is for Sir Lancelot to appear and remind me of the Earl of Northumberland.

The meal lasts at least three hours, by which time most of the men are blind drunk and even one or two of the ladies are giggling and pointing at the best-looking of the younger fellows. I don't know what to expect next, but the Queen rises to her feet quite suddenly, and that is the signal for her women, and me, to follow her from the hall. Those men who are still less than three sheets to the wind stagger to their feet and bow in an attempt at courtesy, but they soon sit down again and carry on with their drinking.

Before I know it I am back in bed again, and ponder on the fact that here at least I am honoured, as I have both it and the room to myself. I try to make sense of things, but fall asleep almost at once.

The next day begins much like the last. Just before noon a splendid dinner is served to the Queen and her ladies in her chamber. I realise that yesterday I must have slept through this meal, and imagined that what was in fact an afternoon was a whole day. There is so much that confuses me, and still no answer to my questions. After the meal, I am told the King wishes to speak to me. The fellow who brings this message to the Queen leads me through the castle, through various rooms until we stand before a doorway large enough for a mounted man to pass through. My guide opens one of the double doors, gestures for me to precede him, and then, once I am through, closes it behind me, so that I am quite alone.

Before me is a very large, circular table, which I realise must be the famous Round Table itself. (Henry Tydder has a replica hanging on the wall at Winchester, which I am told he has spoilt by repainting in his own ghastly colours. However, it *is* only a replica, and compared to this one a terrier pup to a full-grown mastiff.) I walk carefully around it. Each knight has his name painted on the surface to mark his place, and each has a large chair, painted and gilded. The cost of such provision does not bear thinking about. Then again, I say to myself, it's probably only an enchantment anyway, and not in any sense *real*.

I read the names, and they are for the most part what you'd expect: Sir Sagramore; Sir Kay; Sir Gareth. But then I find *Sir Roger de Beauchamp*. I haven't the words to describe how this hits me, but my legs buckle, and I stagger, my hand leaning on the chair that stands in Roger's place. Is this, somehow, a dream? Have I lost my reason completely?

'You seek the Grail?' It is King Arthur's voice. He has entered the room without my realising it, and has brought with him a short-statured fellow who looks like a clerk. I contrive a reverence of sorts, and he continues. 'What makes you think yourself worthy of such a quest?'

I sigh. 'Look, I have been through all this with Bishop Russell. Must I keep on saying the same thing over and over again? I don't even *pretend* to be worthy. Quite frankly, I'd much sooner be at home with my dogs. But I'm acting under King Edward's orders; it's a matter of *duty*. By the way, I'm not *just* looking for the Grail. I need to find Uncle Jasper, and keep him from raising a rebellion in Wales. Which he is probably doing at this minute, while we stand here, spouting nonsense at one another. Much though I appreciate your hospitality, and that of Queen Guinevere, I really do need to get back to the 19th year of King Edward IV.'

'You need not worry,' says the clerkly fellow. 'Here you are quite outside time as you understand it. Therefore there is no haste at all.'

'This is Merlin,' says Arthur. Except he really calls him Myrddin Emrys; I am translating for you. 'If anyone can assist you in your task, he can. Not only is he the wisest man at my court, he is a master of magic.'

'First of all,' says Merlin, 'I shall show you the man you call Uncle Jasper. He is certainly no uncle of yours, lady, and you seek his destruction.' There is a crystal bowl on the table, in the place marked for Roger. This he fills from a jug of water that stands on a trestle to the side. He points a finger at the water, which first grows translucent, but then slowly clears to reveal an image of the man I met at Chertsey Abbey. He is sitting in a dark room, a parlour perhaps, and with him is a woman, whom he holds close, lovingly. I had not thought Uncle Jasper (or any of his clan) capable of love, and yet I know, or rather sense, that he loves this woman dearly. He has travelled far to see her, and taken great risks.

The image fades away, so that all I see is a bowl of water, such as you might use to wash your hands.

'Jasper is in Wales chiefly for reasons of love,' Merlin says. 'He is no immediate threat to you, so I suggest you focus on the Grail quest. We are more than willing to help you. Indeed, for my part, I am willing to teach you the rudiments of magic, a necessity if your task is to be completed. This is not an offer I make to anyone, but it's clear, from the evidence I have seen, that although unschooled you have the necessary qualities.'

I shake my head. 'Sir, you are very generous. However, I read of something rather similar in a certain book, and it didn't turn out well, either for you or the lady. For my own part, the less I know of magic, the better. I was made a similar offer a long time ago, and I rejected it. I have no need of such power, and my faith lies with the Lord Jesus Christ.'

'You need time to think,' says King Arthur. 'What's more, you should bear in mind that we are all Christians here. Although I must tell you that there are many good Saracens, Jews and outright pagans, and many very bad Christians. Even if you have not met any of the former, it's certain you have had dealings with some of the latter.'

'Your words smack of heresy,' I say, putting my hands over my ears. A pointless gesture because it does not stop me from hearing him.

'Magic may be used for good as well as evil,' he says 'and it is insulting to suggest otherwise.'

'I suppose you mean well,' I answer, 'but the only magic that would interest me would be a spell that would convey me back to Sir Roger. We can carry on looking for the Grail, but it won't worry me in the least if we don't find it. Indeed, I tend to think it would be better if we didn't. There are too many people who want it for the wrong reasons. Even King Edward might abuse it; there are others that certainly would.'

'The Lady Crystal Plantagenet?' asked Merlin.

'The so-called Lady Crystal; there are others around Edward's court who are just as bad.'

'With proper training, you would have ten times her power. Moreover, the Grail would knock her out completely. You really ought to take it to her; it would work the most wondrous cure.'

I am caught in a trap, it seems to me. Remember, I am not certain I am clear of Crystal's enchantment. What if this Merlin is simply trying to make me do as she wants? I am by no means convinced that he actually exists. He might simply be part of the spell. I need to find a way of putting him to the test.

It is tedious to relate the rest of the negotiations. Essentially they keep offering to teach me sorcery and I keep refusing. King Arthur grows increasingly irritated. That's the trouble with kings, even imaginary and fictional ones. They expect you to fall in with their plans, however ridiculous or inconvenient. They don't like to be told 'no'. At last, they send me back to the Queen. To 'think' as they put it.

Again, it is boring and repetitive to describe the passing days. They are more or less as previously set out apart from variations to the dinner menu.

On the third night I have a vivid dream about a group of mice attempting to pull a knife from a hunk of cheese. At last one succeeds, and is hailed as King of the mice. Then I wake, and by the light of the little oil lamp at my bedside, see that I am being watched by a large black dog, something between a greyhound and a mastiff, or perhaps an alaunt.

'Hello,' I say, stretching out a hand to stroke his head, 'you're a beauty aren't you?'

'Some people seem to think so,' he answers, wagging its long, whippy tail.

'Saints preserve us!' I cry. 'First King Arthur, now a talking dog. I think I'm going out of my head.'

'I am not just a dog,' he says, 'I am a Black Dog. To be specific, the Black Dog of Hergest Court. I'm fairly unique.'

'There are no degrees of uniqueness,' I answer. 'You are either unique or not unique.'

'Oh, very well, I'm very rare. There are many black dogs, but very few Black Dogs. Do I smell beef?'

At the side of the bed, sitting on the dresser, is a night livery, made up of a cup of small ale, some thick pieces of bread and, on this occasion, some finely sliced beef. I take a slice of the beef and offer it, and the Black Dog wolfs it down.

'That's the best beef I've ever tasted!' he said appreciatively. 'Is there, by any chance, some more of it?'

The rest of the beef follows quickly.

'Perhaps I can have just a piece of the bread?' he asks, tilting his head to one side after the way of scrounging hounds. I sigh, and offer the bread, which he wolfs down with every sign of relish.

'That's the best bread I've ever tasted!' he adds. 'Of course, the trouble with being a Black Dog, as opposed to a black dog, is that hardly anyone thinks of feeding me. Indeed, most sons of Adam and daughters of Eve tend to be wary of one. But I have feelings just like any ordinary dog! And I do like to be fed. Of course, being black doesn't help. There seems to be a common prejudice against my colour of fur. Quite irrational, but there you are. And people tend to react badly to my red eyes.'

'But your eyes are not red,' I object. 'They're brown; quite a pleasant light shade of brown in fact, not red at all.'

'Well, that's how you see them. That means that you are only a moderate sort of sinner. If you were a saint, they'd appear blue, and if you were a really wicked person, they'd seem as red as coals. It's surprising just how many truly wicked people there are around.'

'Yes. Lancastrians for the most part; although that crazed creature, Crystal Plantagenet, is no Lancastrian, more in the way of an independent sorceress. It's because of her and her evil spells and enchantments that I'm stuck here wherever *here* is — far from my husband and with no way of getting home.'

'This is King Arthur's court, that's simple enough. It isn't part of the world you understand, but it's real enough. I often visit here when I'm not needed elsewhere. There are pickings to be had, and one meets such interesting people. You ought to ask for an introduction to Sir Gawain. Now *he's* a real sport, and lets me go hunting with him like any commonplace hound. Arthur's not so bad either, once you get to know him. Bit stuck in his ways, a bit holier-than-thou, but, at the end of the day, a decent enough sort of bloke.'

'You have a lot to say for yourself, for a dog.'

'I can just bark if you like. I thought you'd welcome the conversation.'

'What I should really welcome,' I say, 'is a set of directions that will take me out of this madhouse and back to good old Yorkist England in 19th year of Edward IV. Not that I expect you can help with that.'

'Oh,' he says, 'I might. How about giving me a bit more of that bread?'

I watch as he gobbles down what's left of the night livery. 'The trouble is,' I say, 'is that I don't know where I am, or whether any of it is real; including you. You must admit, a talking dog is somewhat improbable. I could be dreaming, or perhaps I've simply lost my mind. If I were to tell King Edward, for example, that I'd had a long conversation with a dog, he'd have me locked away in Bedlam so quickly that my feet wouldn't touch the floor. It's hard to trust when nothing seems real.'

'Well, you'll have to trust someone, won't you, if you want to get out of here? From what I gather you don't trust King Arthur either.'

'Well, no I don't. Because reason tells me that if King Arthur ever existed (which I doubt) he'd be long dead by now. So the gentleman purporting to be King Arthur can't possibly be him, can he? It stands to reason.'

'What if it told you that not everything fits into what you call 'reason'? Look at me, for example. God gave me the job of appearing at Hergest Court whenever a member of the family is due to die. Is that reasonable? Why doesn't God supply a Black Dog to every family? Of course, in point of fact I do a similar job in a few other places, as I'm told to do, but I certainly don't do it for everyone. Reason doesn't come into it. Do you suppose you can contain God, and all his wonders, within the narrow span of your little brain? After all, it's only a bit bigger than mine, and I certainly can't. If I wasn't real, I wouldn't have been able to eat that food, would I?'

'That's all very well,' I say, 'but if this whole place is just a dream, or part of an enchantment, or whatever, the food would naturally *seem* real. It could all be an illusion, everything. So I just don't know what to do.'

'Please trust me,' he says. 'Although I'm a Black Dog, I'm still a dog, and it's against our code to hurt those who feed us.'

'That's all very well, as long as you are a dog, and not a demon.'

His face takes on a hurt expression, insofar as a dog's can. 'I work for God, so I can't be a demon, can I? That *certainly* stands to reason.'

'If you work for God,' I muse, 'you must be some sort of angel.'

'I don't know about that,' he says, 'but if I am, I'm a very junior one. Not even listed in the book. I'm just a Black Dog. Do you want to go now, or later?'

I hesitate for a moment. 'It isn't quite that simple. Before I wake up in the 19th year of King Edward IV, I need my proper clothes and equipment.'

'Try looking in that press over there,' he says.

Hesitantly I drag myself out of the bed and make my way to the press. I grope about in the uncertain light and find that everything is there, including my service poniard, the sharp blade of which catches my right index finger. In my excitement, I forget even to swear. Instead I drag everything out and retire to the garderobe to dress and undertake my ablutions, not forgetting to bandage my finger with a small piece of torn linen. It all takes some time, inevitably, and when I emerge the sun has begun to rise in the east. At least, I presume it's the east. One really cannot be sure of anything in a locus where it is possible to have a rational conversation with a hound.

'About time,' the Black Dog grumbles. 'I was just about to organise a search party. Now, are you quite ready?'

'Yes.'

'Then take hold of my collar, close your eyes, and say a Paternoster.'

His collar is made of thick leather, so wide that my fingers can barely close around it. I close my eyes, begin the prayer, and immediately feel myself lifted from the ground. How I avoid panic, I do not know, but somehow I maintain my grip on the collar, keep my eyes fast shut, and think of England. My ears are filled with a sort of rushing sound, like every storm you have ever heard and every fast running river all combined into one noise.

We touch land with only a slight jolt, and I even manage keep my feet, though only by bending my knees in a sort of clumsy curtsey. I open my eyes, and there we are, at the fringes of a wood. The Black Dog inclines his head. 'The year is 19th, Edward IV,' he says, 'and you are safe landed in the Marches of Wales.' He leads me a few more paces away from the trees. Some way off, set on a ridge of land, is a sizeable house, built largely from timber and daub, extending from a core of old stone.

'That is Hergest Court,' he says. 'All you have to do is walk to it, and the people there will take care of you. I doubt it's more than a mile.'

'Are you not coming with me?'

'Alas, no; no one in the family is booked to die at the moment, but if I make an appearance it might throw them into unnecessary panic. Best if I stay out of sight.'

'When will I see you again?' I ask.

'Oh, quite soon,' he says. 'Please keep some food about you, just in case.'

I stroke his head and rub his ears, just as if he is one of my own. Then I begin the long, solitary walk to the house.

*

On The Road

I never reached the house. Instead, I woke and found myself back in the swaying litter, somewhere on the road north. I asked Juliana where we were, but she hadn't a clue. The creature had no concept of direction or place; we could have been entering Plymouth or Berwick for all she knew.

I was as weak as a kitten starved of milk, and could barely raise a hand. Yet my mind was beginning to work again.

'What was the last town we passed through?' I asked her. 'Surely you must know *that*?'

She pressed a flask of some vile-tasting liquid to my lips. Horse piss, or at least something equally horrid.

'You must rest, my lady. Don't try to talk. Sleep if you can.'

'I've slept enough. And I've had enough evil dreams; I don't want more. The last town?'

'Doncaster, my lady.'

Doncaster. Some way to go yet, and those damned, stupid re-enactors in the way. I swore that if they delayed us I would find means to have the whole crew of them hanged from the trees.

Despite my resolution, I drifted off again. This time, by the grace of God, there were no dreams or visions, or whatever you call the experiences I have described. Just a peaceful dark, where I knew nothing.

There were days of this. Much of the time I was asleep; even when awake I could barely move, was not sure what to do with myself.

Roger was never far away; he was very worried about me. Still fearful I might die. He looked into the litter every few hours — possibly more frequently, I was not always awake. At night, when we were halted, I was aware of him next to me in bed, sometimes caressing my back, sometimes reaching for my hand. I could only grunt. Only rarely did we exchange real words.

At last, on one of his visits to the litter, he said: 'We are but an hour from Middleham.'

'Thank God,' I said. 'I feared I might never see it again.'

'Alianore, you have never even *liked* Middleham.'

I did not answer. I lacked the spirit. What he said was true, but it was also irrelevant. I *needed* Middleham. I needed Richard and Anne. If you had asked me to explain why this was, I should have failed.

'Is there a fog?' I asked, looking beyond him.

'Mist,' he said. 'Thick mist. Nothing we cannot manage. We are on the road.'

'The mists of Middleham,' I said, and fell asleep again.

*

Middleham Again

My next memory is having broth spooned into my mouth by no less a person than the Duchess of Gloucester. (There's an experience not everyone can claim.) Anne's kind, gentle face reminded me of a statue of the Blessed Virgin. Or Queen Guinevere. Now, there's blasphemy for you. That or something like. I was so relaxed, so assured of my safety, that nothing mattered. Nothing could touch me now I was at Middleham. It was, in my mind, a sort of sanctuary.

My children and my dogs clustered around me, all glad to see me, as I could see from their broad smiles and wagging tails. (The children had smiles, the dogs had tails, just to make that clear.) All too soon though Authority — I am not sure in what shape — shooed them out of the room on the grounds that I needed to rest. It was true — I did.

That bed, so soft, so comfortable, so warm, so spacious, was a foretaste of heaven. I slept peacefully. If I dreamed at all, it was of being up on the moors with Richard and Anne and our hawks, or of being pleasantly occupied with Sir Roger. So I woke with a smile on my face, and somewhat stronger.

It took some time before I was back on my feet, fully dressed and ready for duty. A fortnight, no less. As luck would have it, there was little on the intelligence desk that required attention. My excellent clerk, Norbert, had handled everything appropriately in my absence. (Well, I had trained him, and he was sharp enough to cut a quill.)

'I think we had better speak to Richard,' Roger said. 'I haven't told him the half of it, but I think he has the right to know about his sister.'

'Hmm,' I said. 'You do know that once we tell him he can't be untold? It could get horribly complicated. It touches on family honour and all sort of dangerous aspects, and the presentation doesn't bear thinking about. Imagine if the Crowland Chronicle got hold of this! They'll twist into such a shape none of us will recognise the tale. Then there's the French. They'll love it! A wonderful piece of tattle to demonstrate how wicked and foolish the English are. The other thing is — I don't like the cut of Ursula's jib. Not even slightly.'

'She seemed a delightful, innocent girl to me.'

I sighed. 'Roger, she was *playing* you. She's about as genuine as a five-penny groat. Crystal Plantagenet my bum! What if she has a dark side? She sent shudders up my spine, that one.'

'I still think Richard must be told.'

I sighed. 'Very well. But in that case he gets the full show of betting; we tell him *everything*.'

*

We did so, although we chose our time carefully, waiting for a time when we could be alone with Richard and Anne; or at least, as alone as is practicable. Both of them had attendants with them, but they were all trusted and discreet people who would not reveal everything to the whole castle and town. Lady Warwick, fortunately, had gone to bed at an early hour.

There was a lot to tell, of course, and how much of it they believed I cannot say. Some of it, like Roger's exorcism, I had difficulty in believing myself and I had been there in the chapel to see it. They kept looking at one another, and I began to wonder what they were thinking.

When I came to the part about Ursula, Richard could no longer restrain his disbelief. It had to be nonsense, he said. This creature, whoever she was, must be an imposter. It was the only possible explanation.

'Lady Warwick knows the truth,' I said. 'So does my lady the King's Mother. I can only suggest you ask them both. If they both deny it, then perhaps the young woman — this Crystal Plantagenet as she calls herself — is indeed an imposter. But that would beg a question. From whence does the money come to support her? And another — what is the purpose of the imposture? "Crystal" makes no demands. Indeed, she went out of her way to ask to be left in peace. I must admit, though, I took a dislike to her. I'd prefer her not to be related to us.'

'I thought she was charming,' Roger objected. 'And I have to say, Dickon, she looks *remarkably* like you. For a woman that is. There's a definite family resemblance. That's the least that can be said. I only wish you could see her for yourself.'

'So do I,' said Richard, 'and perhaps I shall. If she is a counterfeit, I shall see through her easily enough. The issue that arises is that this can scarcely be kept from the King; God be loved, I doubt he will rejoice to have such news. But how can I keep it from him? He has the right to know.'

'It may be wise,' I suggested, 'to establish the truth beyond doubt. If this is just some — false mummery, a deceit — it would become a trivial matter, below his Grace's attention. Something to be dealt with by the local justices perhaps. Such a case might be better suppressed. If it is so.'

'That is good counsel,' Richard said decisively.

'One thing is sure,' I went on, 'the matter of the Grail is over.'

'It is? It seems to me you have barely started. What will you say to the King?'

'I will say I have risked my life in the past, and would do again for a good cause. But not my soul or my sanity. Those are too precious. There are evil forces out there, working against us. Look at Roger, filled with a parliament of demons. Look at me, seeing one vision after another. Me! Is there a person in England *less* likely to see visions? I've always laughed at such trash. I'm convinced that my visions are the work of the Devil, and Bishop Russell was inclined to agree. Wrangling with demons and devils is well beyond my pay grade. I'm not qualified and *I will not do it*! If the King wants to put me in the Tower, so be it. I'd sooner be in the Tower than in the pit of Hell, or in Bedlam.'

I don't blame you,' said Anne. 'I've never seen you in such a state as when you came home. You were babbling in your sleep about Black Knights and Black Dogs and I know not what.'

'I feel safe here,' I said, 'though I can't explain why. I shall be very wary of leaving until I am quite sure the evil can't make another attempt to destroy me. I suppose if we move to Barnard Castle, or Sheriff Hutton, or somewhere like that, it should be all right. But I'm not sure I'll dare to leave this household ever again.'

Richard rose to his feet, took my hand, his face full of concern. 'Alianore, you are quite safe here. To be sure, I shall have extra Masses said, and the whole place censed with holy water. Yet I have to say, this must have shaken you badly. You don't sound like yourself at all. Are you sure you're fit to work?'

'If "work" means run the intelligence desk and wait on Anne, then of course I'm sure. Missions outside —' (I gave an involuntary shudder.) 'That I'm much less certain about. I think not. Not for a long time, at any rate.'

'And Roger? Have your demons quite fled?'

My husband sat up rigidly. 'I am your man, and will do as you command. I ask for no special consideration. Come to that, if the King wishes me to continue to seek the Grail, I shall. I'm not afraid.'

'Roger,' I said, 'you should be! This evil is not something that can be fought with a sword. It needs a saint, just as Bishop Russell told me, and good, dear man though you are, you are no saint.'

Richard looked extremely pensive, as he often did. 'I feel,' he said, 'that we should give the whole matter a serious coat of thinking about. Nothing should be done in haste. Let us all reflect on it for — say, a week.'

'There is also the matter of Uncle Jasper,' Roger pointed out. 'The man may well be stirring trouble as we speak.'

'We have a possible identification, nothing more,' I said. 'We've already warned Hastings of that. I need to update him, and I shall suggest he puts a Welsh specialist on the job. As he should in the first place. I suppose he was trying to get us to cover it to save money.'

*

The Mists of Middleham

The hardest reports to write are those in which you wish to tell your principal nothing, without actually making it obvious. I sent Hastings a heavily edited account of our activities, stressing that Roger and I had both been seriously ill, saying that I still was, and not mentioning our encounter with Ursula. I told him we had gone to Warwick in pursuit of a rumour about the Grail that had turned out to be nonsense. Uncle Jasper might or might not be in the country. It needed someone in Wales who knew the country well. I could not be Roger or me, as we were searching for the Grail in Yorkshire. (It could, I told myself, just as easily exist within the bounds of Middleham Castle as anywhere.) I added that we were both too ill to do the task justice, and suggested the King find someone else. I added there was danger to the soul in the business, and recommended they used a churchman. Preferably someone as close to a saint as could be found. (And good luck with that, I thought!)

Even after several revisions, this report did add up to much; but I couldn't be bothered to make any greater effort. I really did not care if they threw me out of Yorkist Intelligence altogether. I could still wait upon Anne, and live quietly. One day, when I felt able to travel again, I might even be able to return to Horton Beauchamp.

Richard said he would interview Lady Warwick at the first opportunity. However, that opportunity was slow to arise, because when Richard was not occupied with business, Lady Warwick had a way of being absent on some work of her own. The Guild of St. Anne seemed to have more meetings than usual, but quite apart from that she was often out riding across the moors or confined in her room, claiming to be ill or indisposed. Richard was patient and did not press the matter.

When he did manage to raise the subject with her, she admitted it was true.

'No wonder Rous's books cost so much!' he cried.

'Now, now Dickon!' she wagged her finger at him as though he was a little boy. 'Surely you don't begrudge your sister a modest living, do you? She asks for very little, and has no great household. Many a country gentlewoman has more splendid attendance. Besides, I'm sure you don't want to embarrass your lady mother. *Do you?*'

This was case of defending by means of an attack, and it was an effective tactic. Richard seemed completely nonplussed.

'Moreover,' Lady Warwick went on, 'Ursula has great plans to be entirely self-supporting. She and Rous are involved in alchemy, and as I understand it they are very close to success. Once they have quite mastered the art of turning lead into gold, she will not need any further subventions. I have, of course, helped to pay for the equipment and elements required, but it should prove an excellent investment. I expect a return of many thousand percent. Better than shares in a copper mine or a brewery.'

'She practises *alchemy*, my lady?' I could not hold back my surprise.

'As I said. She's a very clever girl.'

'That was not the impression she gave me,' I said to Richard. 'Not the impression at all. It seems there is more to her than appearances show.'

He snorted with amusement. 'People have been practising alchemy for years, but I've never heard of anyone succeeding. I *have* heard of it being used to trick gullible fools out of their money. My lady Mother, you should be wary of letters from 'princes' offering to make you rich. They never do, you know.'

Lady Warwick scowled. 'You'll see,' she said.

One of Our Countesses is Missing

On the morning following this discussion, Lady Warwick rode out of the castle with her woman and a small escort made up of her own servants, for she had several men on her establishment to manage her errands and her horses, as was fitting for so great a lady. Her purpose in leaving was to buy thread from a particular stall in Masham that she had long patronised.

No one thought anything of it. She was not in any sense a prisoner at Middleham, and this was an excursion she made quite regularly, as much for exercise as purchase. Nor was anyone in the least concerned when she did not return for dinner. That was pretty much expected. Her failure to appear for supper was another matter.

'Perhaps,' ventured Anne, 'she has decided to spend the night with the Scropes of Masham; or maybe could not find what she lacked, and so has gone on to Ripon, or even York.'

'In either case,' Richard said, 'she would surely have sent word to us.' (Nine times out of ten, Richard could put his finger on the nub of any question, and this was no exception.)

Anne began to look worried.

Richard decided to send one of his more trusted yeomen to Masham to enquire. The fellow was a giant of a Yorkshireman called Bradley, who rode off at once into the mist that was suddenly descending on the castle. Such weather is unusual in summer, and it made me feel uneasy — mists, I thought to myself, are not always natural. It was tempting to say as much to someone, but I decided not to in case they thought that I was going potty.

It was full dark before the man returned. The Countess was not at Masham. (Lord Scrope had turned out men to look for her.) Nor was she at Jervaulx Abbey — he had checked. Nor had anyone seen her on the road to Ripon. Or anywhere else for this matter.

This was odd, because countesses with their escorts are not that common a sight in the remoter parts of Yorkshire, and although the locals can be taciturn they have eyes in their heads and rarely need to be told what day it is. It was as if Anne's mother had vanished into one of the local cave systems, or into thin air.

'We shall gain nothing by stumbling around in the dark,' Richard said, in his decisive way, 'but as soon as it's light, we shall send out search parties in all directions. I shall myself take the Masham road. Francis shall follow the way to Leyburn, Roger to Coverham. We shall ask every person we meet, visit every likely sheltering-place. If any word is found of her, we shall each of us send it back to Middleham by a sure man.'

'What of me?' asked Anne.

'You stay here, in case your mother returns. She may have need of you. In the interim, you should search her rooms, see if you can find anything to suggest where she might have gone. If word comes to you that she's found, recall the other parties. If word comes from Francis or Roger that they have found signs of her, send someone to me, and I shall decide what is to be done. We shall spend the day in search, go as far as we can. Failing all else, we meet back here for supper.'

I could not find fault with this; it seemed quite sensible. Although, if Lady Warwick had strayed from the road and somehow lost herself, then there was a great deal of ground to cover, and no certainty that any of the search parties would locate her. To search the moors thoroughly would require all the household, and all the men from Middleham town besides. Perhaps even that might not be enough. We might have to turn out the monks of Jervaulx and Coverham, and the men from every hamlet and farmstead for miles around, such was the size of the task.

We slept somewhat uneasily, and then after an early breakfast the three search parties set off, the men looking serious, even grim. Anne and I, meanwhile, retired to Lady Warwick's rooms and began our search. It was indeed a search, for Anne's mother had always been notably untidy; nothing was ever in its place, nor was there a place for anything. We detected she had taken some of her clothes, but even that was hard to determine, given that many more had been left behind. Her store of money was also gone, not so much as a penny left in the coffer she used to store her coin, as had all her jewels, of which she had a fair collection. At last, Anne found a note, hidden under a cushion. It said:

Dear Anne,
I am gone to help restore King Harry to his throne.
Please tell your husband I intend to have my lands back.
You and he may remain at Middleham until further notice.
Your loving mother,
Anne Warwick.

'Oh, Mother!' cried Anne. 'What are you about?'

On the face of it, it made no sense at all. King Harry had been stone dead for eight years at this time. Some people (like Margaret Richmond) reverenced him as a saint and visited his tomb. The Countess herself had told me she had conversed with his ghost in a dream — or a vision, or whatever it was.

This was now a political matter, and downright scary. The Countess, whether she realised it or not, was dabbling in treason. Since Richard and Anne were responsible for her, they were also touched by it. If word reached the King of this, serious questions would be asked. It would be awkward at best.

'You must send to Richard at once,' I said. 'He must be told of this without delay. He is going to have to decide what to do.'

'I don't understand,' Anne howled. 'Has she lost her wits? King Harry is dead!'

'Yes. But what if someone is pretending to be him? It wouldn't be the first time, you know. King Richard II was said to be alive and well in Scotland long after his death. Some people chose to believe it, and acted accordingly. This could be a similar case. Your mother could believe the old King lives. Someone may have told her so. Not necessarily by natural means.'

I had in mind the so-called Guild of St. Anne. If those creatures really were speaking to the dead, perhaps it was not merely to Aunt Joan. Perhaps some of the dead did politics and sought to stir rebellion. Who could say? It occurred to me that I might have been better accepting Lady Warwick's invitation to join.

We sent a messenger off to Richard with a note from Anne sealing within it the original note from the Countess. Then there was nothing to do but wait.

Before Richard returned, we had a message from Roger to the effect that Lady Warwick had been seen on the road to Coverdale. The informant was some random shepherd who had watched her ride by. This news we also sent on to Richard, for it was very pertinent and made it probable that he was wasting his time looking for her in the vicinity of Masham.

In mid-afternoon, Richard rode into the castle, looking grimmer than ever. His first order was to recall the other search parties. His second instruction was for food to be served to all the men who had ridden with him, and for it to be made ready for the return of the others. Then, rather to my surprise, he asked me for a briefing on the latest state of play in Scotland.

'Confused,' I said. 'Albany is making trouble, undoubtedly. On the other hand, his own position is weak, and his King's allies are intriguing against him. I've been feeding him some information — not in my own name, of course. I have used the cover name of a disgruntled Scottish exile here in England. Angus Mac Whine of that Ilk. I've told him is in imminent danger of arrest, and advised him to flee abroad. I have hopes that he will panic and escape to France. If he does, it will make the border safe, because King James has no interest at all in war. Mar is still under house arrest, and there is talk he will soon be thrown into prison.'

'Good,' said Richard, shortly. 'It appears I may have no choice but to leave the rule here to Northumberland for a while. I shall feel the easier in doing that if there is no immediate threat from our friends in Edinburgh. The Countess must be be recovered at all costs, and I can trust no one but myself with the task. The woman is almost certainly out of her wits, but that will be no defence if it becomes generally known that she is trying to restore Henry VI.'

'Just to be clear,' I said, 'it is certain, isn't it, that Henry of Lancaster is dead?'

'Unless he had a hitherto unknown twin brother.' Richard let out a deep sigh. 'I saw his body, Alianore. The King ordered his death, and it was done. Then I was off into Kent, to deal with other rebels. They were uncertain times, as you know, after Tewkesbury.'

'I myself was busy nursing Roger after the wounds he took there. So I'm afraid I rather lost track of events. Well, if Henry VI is definitely dead, either the Countess is deluded or there is an imposter in place. The great question is, who else is involved? If anyone? She may merely have imagined the matter, or someone may be leading her on. There are no papers here to suggest that she has confederates, but that is not to say that there are none. Then there is this matter of the Guild of St. Anne that I broke to you. Necromancers. What if there is treason in their dealings?'

Richard grunted. 'I did not take that seriously. A meeting of silly women, hoping to talk to their grandmothers or their dead husbands. But perhaps I should have done.'

I shrugged. 'There is evil out there. From my own experience, I suspect someone is casting enchantments. For what purpose? Was it to hamper our search for the Grail? Or is there some other motive? And is Lady Warwick at the centre of it, or some other person?'

'Do you have someone in mind?'

'Lady Warwick mentioned that Ursula of York — or Crystal Plantagenet as she calls herself — and that fellow Rous practise alchemy. That makes me suspicious, especially given they are linked to the Countess. What if it is more than alchemy? What if, together, they are the source of the enchantments?'

'It seems a stretch, Alianore.'

'I've no better ideas. What's more, it may be that it's significant Lady Warwick fled as soon as we discovered the links. What if she has gone to Guy's Cliff? Indeed, where else could she go?

'To one of a hundred places.' He sighed. 'You forget, old Warwick had any number of supporters and even more relatives. Any one of whom might conceivably harbour his widow. She might even have gone back to Beaulieu Sanctuary. No one could touch her there. Not even my brother.'

'Well,' I said, 'if you are going in search of her, you will have to start somewhere, and Guy's Cliff is my tip. I suggest you question that fellow Rous at length; you might start by checking his accounts against his invoices for Lady Warwick's books. Just don't disturb the Boggart. It's a very nasty piece of work, even by boggart standards. I suspect it of Lancastrian sympathies. It may even be related to the Beauforts.'

'My search will be methodical,' Richard said. 'Enquiries will be made everywhere, and we shall track her down. Someone like Lady Warwick cannot simply vanish into the mist. She will be noticed.'

'My worry is that we're not dealing simply with normal people. Remember, there are enchantments in play. Something very dark is behind all this.'

'Enchantments?' he laughed. 'This does not sound like you, Alianore.'

'I know. Yet I told you what Roger and I suffered while we were away. I am serious, Cousin Richard. You must take great care. Invoke the saints. Carry a relic or two. Be prepared.'

'I do not fear the Devil,' he said. He meant it, too.

*

One of Our Dukes is Missing.

Richard left next day, taking with him Francis Lovell, Rob Percy, Roger and all of the most trusted men he had at Middleham. They intended to make for Skipton as their first objective and make enquiries there.

For my part, I had to make some sort of report to Hastings, so I wrote to him, making the most of the latest news from our Scottish friends, then going on to add, almost as an afterthought, that Lady Warwick had gone on pilgrimage to St Winifred's Well in Wales, and that Richard, having had no news of her, had gone off to retrieve her, thinking she might be in some danger. That was as good a cover story as I could imagine, given that at this stage I had no intention of mentioning Henry VI, or enchantments, or Ursula.

Another letter, signed by Richard, went off to Northumberland to tell him he was temporarily in charge of the shop. I doubt whether this grieved Henry Percy's heart. However, to my relief, he did not see fit to come to Middleham and sit in Richard's office, but remained in his own country, which was the best place for him.

It was necessary to keep Anne occupied, for she was naturally worried for her mother, and indeed for Richard. There were hawking expeditions on the moors, that included all her ladies; we rode to Masham to visit the Scropes thereof and patronise the market; we even ventured to Richmond, which as always took up almost all of the day by the time we had visited the various shops and stalls and dealt with the local gentry and their pestering.

On a particularly fine day, we made our way to Aysgarth Falls, which is a very beautiful place, for all that it is pretty much in the middle of nowhere. (Unless you count Bolton Castle, which is not *that* far off. We ended up visiting the Scropes (of Bolton) and staying the night, as no one could break into Lady Scrope's conversation long enough to make an excuse to leave. She was, by the way, half-sister to Margaret Richmond, not that that was her fault.)

Anyway, it was at Aysgarth Falls that I found the cup. A small, earthenware drinking vessel that someone had evidently dropped while collecting a drink from the river. It was nothing to look at, but it was a pleasing shape so I thought it might be useful to keep pins in, or serve as a stand for my pens, so I picked it up. Considering where I found it, it was remarkably clean. In fact, I scarcely needed to rinse it. The strange thing is, that no sooner had I tucked it in my saddle bag than the melancholy that had hung on me for weeks — ever since falling ill at Warwick, in truth — completely lifted. I felt myself again. So much so that even Lady Scrope did not seem to be particularly tedious that evening. At the time, I thought nothing of this change.

The days slipped by, and then the weeks. At first, Anne received quite regular letters from Richard, explaining where he was and describing the enquiries he had made, all to no avail. He could no longer find any trace of Lady Warwick.

His last letter was dated from Coventry — after that, there was silence. Or there was silence until one afternoon Francis Lovell rode into the courtyard, accompanied by a decidedly ragged tail of fellows.

Francis did not look well. He rarely did these days.

'Richard is missing,' he told Anne.

'Missing!' she screeched. 'What do you mean – missing?'

Francis sighed. 'We rode into this fog. It covered the road. When we came out of it, Richard was missing.' He glanced at me. 'So was Roger Beauchamp. We looked *everywhere* for them. We all thought they could not be far off, even if they'd strayed from the road. Yet we couldn't find them. Rob Percy and most of our men are still down there, turning over every house in the district. But I thought someone should come back to report; so here I am. I have it in mind to return and carry on the search.'

'This is enchantment,' I said.

'What?' They both stared at me.

'Two grown men do not simply vanish into thin air. Certainly not two as sensible as Richard and Roger. They have been searched for, no doubt thoroughly, and they are not to be found. It can only be that they've been taken against their will. They will be prisoners somewhere. This is what I feared all along.'

'Then what are we to do?' asked Anne.

'We are going to kick arse,' I said. 'I just need to work out how.'

'A relief column?' Francis suggested.

'You could call it that,' I said, 'but we need at least one specialist. I shall go to York to try to recruit him. A few more archers would not go amiss either. All our best fighters are with Richard — *were* with Richard. What we have left here are the halt and the lame and the beardless boys. Apart from Patch the Jester, and I doubt he is much use in a fight. ' I turned to Anne. 'May I offer five pence a day?'

'Whatever it takes,' she said.

'I shall bring them back here, then we follow Richard's route. I've also just thought of someone else who might lend us men, over in Lancashire.'

'There is just one little thing I want to make clear,' Anne said. 'When this column, or whatever you call it, sets out from here — *I am going with it!*'

It was not often that Anne reminded me of her father, but that morning I saw him in her. He was in an angry mood. No prisoners would be taken.

*

The Exorcist

Next morning, Lovell and I rode to York. We set out as soon as it was light, and made our horses work for their oats, as it is a full day's journey.

The Archbishop was not at home. This was no great surprise, given that his Grace was an old and sickly man, who, when he was not at court, was usually ill in bed at Cawood Castle. Fortunately, his suffragan, the Bishop of Dromore, was in the building.

After the usual preliminaries, Francis went straight to business. 'We are in need of an exorcist, my lord,' he said. 'Can you recommend a suitable man?'

'A heavy-duty, fully qualified exorcist,' I added. 'Not some charlatan.'

Of course, the Bishop wanted to know more. Such men always want to know more. So between us, Francis and I told him the whole tale, which took quite a few minutes.

'Hmm,' said the Bishop. 'This is serious. The Duke of Gloucester missing you say.'

'And the Countess of Warwick,' I said.

'Vanished into mist,' Francis added.

'And you're quite sure it's an enchantment?'

'Quite sure.'

'This needs our top man. Father William Senhouse of St. Mary's. A Dominican, you see. Very learned, very skilled. Just the chap you need. I shall give you a letter for him. He must leave all else aside for so important a case.'

Thank you, my lord,' Lovell said. He was almost beaming with gratitude.

'There is one small snag. He is already on a case. Quite a worrying one. He left York three days ago. You will find him at Valle Crucis Abbey.'

'Where on earth is *that*?' I asked. I would have used sharper language, except one must be polite to bishops. I had never heard of such a place.

He nodded solemnly. 'In the northern parts of Wales, not far from Chester. Father Senhouse is so famous that he is summoned to all the most complicated disturbances, anywhere north of Trent and sometimes even as far south as Peterborough. You want the best we have — it is he.'

'Great,' I said. 'As if dealing with enchantments is not bad enough, we have to venture into Wales. The Duchess will not like this.'

The Bishop held up his hands. I noted they were surprisingly leathery for those of a clerk. Perhaps he spent a lot of time digging his garden. 'I'm sorry, my lady, but so it must be,' he said.

*

While we had been engaged with the Bishop of Dromore, our servants had been seeking out lodgings for us, for we could not hope to regain Middleham until the next day. They had secured places for us with Master Snowshill, near the Minster. Not the finest lodgings in York, but good enough for our purpose.

We were on the way there we can upon a familiar figure coming the other way. Much to my surprise, it was Feather Hat himself, the pretended Robin Hood.

'What do you do here, fellow?' I demanded.

He took off his hat and bowed deeply. 'My lady. How agreeable to see you again. My lads and I are in York to have words with the Abbot of St. Mary's about a certain unjust loan. We hope to make him repent and be more generous to a good knight of our acquaintance.'

'Re-enactment, right?'

He looked rather shamefaced. 'Well, it's part of the legend you see.'

'But the good knight does not really exist? Or the unjust loan?'

He looked awkward and shuffled his feet. 'Not really, my lady. We're just having fun.'

I sighed, and indicated my companion. 'This is Lord Lovell. He and I are about to undertake a *real* adventure. One with actual dangers. Now, as it happens, we have vacancies for a limited number of archers. Five pence a day and all the ale you can sup. What do you say to that?'

Robin stared at me in amazement, then turned towards Lovell. 'Is this true, my lord?'

'True as you like, my man,' said Francis. 'What's more, if you are honest fellows, and both serve us well and survive, you may live to be taken on strength by the Duke of Gloucester himself. As good a service as you can find this side of Trent, or indeed on the other. Now, will you come or not? Plenty of others will not sniff at five pence a day.'

'We are your men, my lord.' He bowed again. 'My lady. A real adventure! It's beyond our dreams. And to be paid too!'

'Report to Lord Lovell at the West Door of the Minster, first thing in the morning,' I said. 'I trust you know how to handle your bows?'

'My lady, we are but re-enactors, but the least of us can take out a horse-fly at three hundred yards. We are your men!'

He bowed, and vanished again, I suspect to the nearest alehouse, a mean establishment that men called 'Betty's'.

*

In the night, I had a very particular dream.

I dreamed of Ursula, or Crystal, whatever you choose to call her.

She stood before me, dripping in cloth of gold. There was a coronet on her head, as good as a crown.

'This is how it is, Alianore. I hold your husband hostage, to say nothing of my brother, Gloucester. If you would see them again, fetch me the Grail. You know where to find me.'

Then she was gone.

*

The Road to Valle Crucis

Robin did not fail us. He was there next morning, as arranged, with his entire band, including 'Marian'. They were all, I was glad to see, suitably horsed. (Where they kept those animals in the woods I do not know, but they must have had some arrangement.)

So, we returned to Middleham in more secure numbers than before. Even so, I knew we should only be able to leave a very thin garrison behind, made up of greybeards and young boys, and it was as well that the Scots were relatively quiet. Anne was still determined to journey with us, but she agreed that I should be her only woman so as to keep the company as martial as was possible. Her other ladies would stay behind and entertain the various children, including mine. As would my woman, Juliana.

Next morning we were out of bed early, for there was much to do. Some of my emergency requisites needed topping up, while sundry children and dogs had to be patted and reassured that we would not be long away. We took an early dinner, about eleven o'clock, and we did not linger over it. Anne told the usual queue of petitioners to come back another day. Just after noon we out of the castle and on our way down Coverdale.

The mists were back, and it grew a little hairy over the tops, for that road, if you can call it a road, is as steep and narrow in places as any in Wales. Soon, however, we were descending into Wharfedale. From there it was a simple enough ride to Skipton Castle, where we were to spend the night, the mists rapidly thinning to nothing once we were on this lower ground.

Skipton was another of Richard's holds of course, although (as we had not brought even the normal riding-household with us) it was a little less comfortable than we would normally have found it, with only the caretaking staff in places so that we had to manage as best we could.

We were in truth quite a small company. I had Patch to attend me and a couple of our archers from Horton Beauchamp, chosen for their ability to stay awake on horseback, a skill that was less than universal among our people. There was Anne, of course, with Francis Lovell, with the fellows he had brought back with him and the scrapings of the Middleham people, most of them Yorkshire chaps with little to say but a distinct air of business about them. You would not have wanted an argument in a dark corner with the least of these men. Then we had Robin Hood and his band of re-enactors, an uncertain quantity but good cooks for sure.

Next morning we rode through the market place and along the high road to Colne. By 'high' I mean in this case not that it is a principal route, but that it seeks out high ground along the way. It clear day, with the sun soon warm on our backs, and there were beautiful views from this vantage point, if you enjoy the sight of innumerable acres of moors, rough pasture and dark woodlands, held together by a few scattered homesteads, the best of them scarcely fit for the occupation of pigs, let alone rational creatures.

Anne and I played a game of 'spot the church tower'. Neither of us made much of a score, as the population hereabouts is so sparse that for many of the locals an attendance at Mass is as good as a pilgrimage. This is thin, poor country, where to have half a dozen chickens and a pig practically makes you an esquire.

From Colne we passed along many dark and murky ways, through assorted tiny villages that seemed to have very few visible inhabitants, until we reached the valley of the mighty Irwell, an unfriendly-looking river that fell sharply in places, drove the occasional water wheel and led us, eventually, to within a short distance of Pilkington Hall, our designated stopping place.

I had ridden this way before, on the occasion when Roger and I had successfully retrieved Richard's banner from Wigan Church, and our host, then and now, was Sir Thomas Pilkington, Richard's leading retainer in the North West. We were made very welcome indeed. Sir Thomas seemed no older (although he must have been pushing sixty at the least) still bluff, still loud, still an amusing and generous host.

The Mists of Middleham

He introduced us to the local ale, produced by his brewer, Master Lees. It had the new-fangled hops in it, which would have roused Roger's hackles had he been with us. (Roger is a member of Society for Ale's Defence (SAD) and the Campaign for the Restoration of Ale that is Pure. (CRAP). He abominates the use of hops which he considers a crime against humanity. He would have been shocked to find the practice had spread so far north. At this time it was usually confined to such degenerate areas as Kent, Sussex and London.)

When Sir Thomas heard of our mission he insisted on tagging along, just as I had hoped.

'Have to protect the ladies, don't you know,' he cried, tugging on the ends of his very white whiskers. He was a game old devil, even if he had been born in the time of Harry the Fifth. 'Besides, you'll be riding through Cheshire. Bandit country. Need every blade, what?'

He rode with us in the morning along with his eldest son and two or three stout fellows from his immediate household. The only problem was that this led to an ongoing debate with the Yorkshire lads about the best way of frying fish and how to play stool ball, and similar topics, although it was all kept very friendly.

We passed through Manchester, a very small town with some elements of the cloth trade and the biggest church we had seen since leaving Middleham. Then across the Mersey at a place called Stretford and into Cheshire, where the lanes ran between steep green banks and there were far too many trees for comfort, given the reputation the place has for outlaws and unruly gentlefolk.

Cheshire, like Lancashire, is a palatinate, which may be defined as an area where there is even less law and order than usual, except as the whims and customs of the local gentry may determine. See also the Welsh Marches. However, we were a heavily armed company, and if anyone thought of getting in our way they thought twice and got out of it.

Patch had procured a trumpet, or clarion, or some such brass instrument from somewhere, probably the herald's store at Middleham. When he was not singing the *Nut Brown Maid* he was playing something he called *'Gary Owen'* on this trumpet by way of advertisement. I must admit, it really was quite tuneful, and it helped pass the time. I presume this Gary Owen was some Welsh fellow, back in the day. Perhaps a friend of Llewelyn or Glyndŵr or whoever.

It had words to it too, some of them quite rude. I only remember:

We'll beat the bailiffs out of fun

We'll make the mayor and sheriffs run
We are the boys no man dare dun
If he regards a whole skin.

So we reached Chester, which is what passes for a city in those parts. They say it has as many as five thousand inhabitants. Behind its red stone walls there are several churches, an abbey, two friaries, a nunnery and a castle. We lodged at the mayor's house — or some of us did, the rest being lodged with sundry aldermen, sheriffs and similar riff-raff elements. Anne made it clear that this was an informal visit, and there was no need for processions or illuminated addresses, which relaxed things a little.

There was a minor banquet at the mayor's house, with a good choice of fish and plenty of oysters. Patch did his usual half-hour, and as none of the Chester people had heard the Rivers joke before it went down well, with several people falling off benches and rolling about in the rushes on the floor.

Here we also procured a guide capable of showing us the way to Valle Crucis Abbey, because quite frankly none of us had a clue as to where it was, and once you enter Wales there are no signposts, very few milestones and even the local peasants do not necessarily speak English. (Those that do might well take pleasure in misdirecting you to Fishguard, or Cardiff, or some other place that makes Middleham on a wet Sunday seem like Bruges at carnival time.) There are no maps of course, or at least none worth talking about. You can follow the coast to Conwy, that's simple enough. The interior, though, is another matter. They have mountains and moors that make Yorkshire look like a particularly flat part of Norfolk, and places to shelter from the prevailing weather are few and far between. You do not want to get lost in that kind of country.

Next morning, Anne and I went shopping immediately after breakfast. This involved walking along the Rows which are a sort of raised pavement more than a tall man's height above the actual street, an excellent arrangement that saves your feet from getting covered in mud and horse crap. We took Sir Thomas Pilkington with us by way of escort, more for the form of it than for any real necessity.

Sir Thomas walked in front of us, saying friendly things like: 'Dogs, scum, peasants, make way for the Duchess of Gloucester!' in his quiet, amiable way. We rapidly became the centre of attention. I don't flatter myself that this was solely because of our looks. It was partly down to Sir Thomas's heralding, but perhaps also due to the fact that most people hereabouts looked like a fashion parade from 1390.

Chester is a place that attracts tourists. Half of Wales goes there when they want to purchase something more sophisticated than homespun or laverbread. Ireland is only just across the sea so Irish visitors are also common. As for the English, they come from as far away as Northwich just to soak in the cosmopolitan atmosphere.

Our purpose was to buy a personal weapon for Anne. She had only her eating knife about her, and I felt that a suitable poniard would be a good investment. It was true that she would probably not need it, as she had me acting as both lady-in-waiting and close personal protection officer, and was travelling with a group of chaps who would have scared the crap out of an oversized troop of mercenary *landsknechts;* but you can never be too careful in a place like Wales where even the squirrels carry axes and daggers.

The poniard was not hard to come by in a place like Chester and was quickly secured. Then, of course, we became distracted among the stalls. The town has a surprisingly good quality of mercer, and there were veils, girdles, garters and gloves that even Elizabeth Woodville would have thought good enough for second-best. Before we knew it, Lovell was chasing after us, asking if we knew what time it was. You would have thought that the mayor or someone would have been able to provide him with such basic information, but apparently not.

Anyway, after a somewhat hurried dinner, we set off, passing over the Dee by the stone bridge provided just outside the city. There were a few houses on the far side and then we were in open country. The land looked like rough pasture, although at first there were plenty of woods. Occasionally we passed through a little settlement, but the further west we went, the rougher the pasture, the thinner the woods and the smaller the settlements. Eventually we saw a sign before us that said: *'Croeso y Cymru'*. Underneath some helpful soul had scrawled the translation: 'Bugger off Saxon Pigs.'

Almost from this point the road narrowed to the extent that we had to ride in pairs, and sometimes in single file, and before long I realised that we were climbing steadily, and that there were huge mountains ahead of us, as far as the eye could see. The day being so clear you could see the tops of most of them, which made them all the more impressive.

Dwellings were now a rarity. You might see, at most, two or three clustered together, and then there would be a long gap to the next little grouping. We were growing thirsty, and eventually we found that one of these places sold what they called ale, and had enough in stock for all of us. Our guide assured it was the best option this side of our destination. We paused and had a cup. It was sour, thin stuff, but better than nothing. It was a hot day and there was little shade. Around us was moorland, with a few stunted trees and a scattering of stunted sheep. Nothing much else at all, unless you counted sundry birds, including buzzards that circled high above us, and the gorse that flowered brightly.

The climb continued for what seemed like many miles, but at last we reached the summit and began to descend. The road (if you could call it that, sheep track might be more the word) turned back on itself almost in the shape of a horseshoe, and gradually our surroundings became greener, more wooded. At last we saw the abbey before us and to our left, set in a steep-side valley, a surprisingly large establishment to be located in such a wilderness. A Cistercian house, of course. In such a remote place, it had to be. Our guide spread his hands and grinned amiably — his task was over.

We rode up to the gatehouse, where a monk held up his hand to halt us.

'I'm sorry,' he said, 'but no women are allowed beyond this point.'

'This is not a woman,' I said, gesturing towards Anne. 'This is the Duchess of Gloucester, the King's sister-in-law, and I am her attendant. Now, either get out of our way, or fetch your abbot. Be swift about it too, as the Duchess does not stand about waiting on menials.'

'Away fellow!' roared Sir Thomas, spurring his horse forward. 'Do not dare to question your betters.'

The monk fled, and we rode on into the precincts. It was, considering its remote location, a very fine building indeed and much larger than I had expected. We were not kept waiting long.

A monk led us inside. We were asked to leave our weapons in the cloakroom, and they made quite a pile. I must confess, I did not offer up my secret poniard. In those days I felt quite naked without it, and no woman wants to feel naked in a monastery, Cistercian or otherwise.

The Abbot was Welsh, as you might reasonably have anticipated in such a place. (You wouldn't have expected him to be from Milan, that's for sure.) His name was Dafydd ap Something-I-couldn't-pronounce-if-I-tried, and he was a tall, vigorous fellow in middle-age, who looked as if he could have been a blacksmith or a stockman if he hadn't chosen to go into religion. He was polite enough, and expressed himself honoured to meet the Duchess of Gloucester, although very surprised. Were we not somewhat off our usual path? He would be very glad to show us the best way to Shrewsbury, even to send a monk with us as guide, but first we must accept the hospitality of the house. If we wished to rest, that could be arranged. If we preferred to offer prayers of gratitude for their our arrival, he would show us the best chapel in the place. Food and drink would, of course, be available for all, and right promptly if required.

He had barely finished with these courtesies when a black-robed figure appeared in the doorway. It was not hard to guess that this was the exorcist, Father William Senhouse. Who else would be so clad among the white habits of the Cistercians? He was a bull-necked fellow of middle years who looked like he could demolish a stone wall with his head and shoulders.

'My prayers have been answered at last!' he cried, with the enthusiasm of a man proclaiming a new king. 'The Grail is here! It has returned!'

*

Valle Crucis

We gathered in the Chapter House for what I can only describe as a conference. There was, after all, a great deal to be explained on both sides.

Abbot Dafydd had gathered three or four of his monks by this time to act as his supporters. Father Senhouse sat next to him. There were still seats for most of us, though a few of the lesser men were left standing by the door, Patch among them, bright in his motley in an array that mostly comprised stern-looking warriors. Given that I was in attendance on Anne, I got one of the best seats of all, right next to her. There was a strange atmosphere for this meeting — an intense silence that at first no one seemed anxious to break.

At last the Abbot spoke up, his lilting voice a little firmer now he had had time to think.

'We have long had in our possession a relic that some call the Grail. It is a perilous thing, not to be touched by profane hands, and of such power that no wise man would wish to possess it. It has many powers, many properties. We do not boast of it, or encourage pilgrims to visit it. On the contrary, we prefer to keep it secluded from the world, for it might easily be abused by the wicked.

'One of its properties is that it has the power to — I scarce know how to explain it — to simply vanish. This it has done many times, but usually only for a few days. A week at most. Lately, however, something has changed. It left us at Christmas and did not return. Our prayers were not answered. At length, I concluded that the Devil was at work, or one of his agents. Therefore I sent for Father Senhouse, whose fame is well known to we churchman. He was our last hope.'

The exorcist bowed his head.

'I prayed for its return. Conducted several ceremonies that need not be described. I found myself fighting great evil. What I can only describe as the forces of black sorcery. Still my prayers continued, and now, by the Grace of God, and by the intercession of his Most Blessed Mother, the Grail has returned. You have brought it, Duchess, knowingly or not. You, or one of your company. I can feel its presence.'

Francis Lovell laughed out loud. 'Are you out of your wits, man? We have come from Yorkshire, not Camelot. Do we look as if we have the Grail about us? Do you suppose we would not have noticed if we had?'

'I believe,' said Abbot Dafydd, 'that it may be a convenient time to show you the replica.'

The Mists of Middleham

With a nod, he despatched one of his monks, who returned in a few minutes with a modest, earthenware cup, such as you might buy at any market. A cup which was remarkably similar to the one I had found at Aysgarth Falls.

'Is that it?' Francis hooted. 'You cannot be serious, man.'

'Our Lord lived in poverty, among the poor,' Abbot Dafydd said. 'Did you imagine that His drinking cup would be such as King Edward has at his hand? A thing of gold or silver, laden with rich jewels? No, my lord. Think on it.'

There was an intense silence that seemed endless.

'I believe I have it in my saddle bag,' I said.

I was at once the cynosure for all eyes, which is not pleasant.

'I will fetch it,' I added.

'I will come with you,' said Father Senhouse. 'Such a relic should properly be handled only by a priest. Even then with the greatest reverence. In your saddle bag, forsooth! How did you come by it, woman?'

'How did I come by it my Lady Beauchamp, I think you mean,' I said acidly.

'I will come with you too,' said Robin. 'I trust no priest but good Friar Tuck. (And even he, only so far.)'

So the three of us made our way to the stables, where I soon found my saddle hanging on a peg. However, the officious priest would not allow me to retrieve the cup but insisted that he alone should do the delving.

He grunted as he discovered various items that did not answer to his purpose; but then his hands grasped the prize and drew it out into the light with a cry of triumph.

'Here is it is!' he cried. 'Just as I knew it would be.'

'Why,' said Robin, 'how can you be sure, priest? I vow that such a paltry thing could be found at any market, even in such a place as Edwinstowe — which is a very poor market indeed. Scarce worth visiting. A man would think himself robbed if he had to pay a halfpenny for such a cup. I have thrown better into a ditch before this time.'

'You lack faith,' said Father Senhouse, shaking his head. 'I wonder at it. Can you not feel its power?'

Robin and I looked at each other in bewilderment. We could not.

*

Father Senhouse carried the Grail — as I suppose I must call it — back to the Chapter House, bearing it with as much care and reverence as if it were a Monstrance. Robin and I formed a modest procession behind him, and watched as he placed it most carefully on a shelf near the abbot's seat. He stood back and bowed his head. I settled back in my place and then something very remarkable happened.

I cannot speak for others, but it seemed to me almost as if there was a glow that formed behind the Grail, feeble at first, like a candle, but growing, ever growing, until it was like a small sun, impossible to look upon. I closed my eyes — I had no choice — slid off my chair, and fell to my knees.

When I dared to open my eyes again, I found that everyone else was kneeling too. The light had faded, almost to nothing, and the Grail was just the unimpressive little bowl we had first seen.

Everyone looked completely awestruck, and you must remember that most of our company were hard men, accustomed to arms, ready to fight and kill whatever stood in their way, not at all the sort to be easily intimidated. Some were offering up prayers. Others were simply staring, unable to believe what their eyes had seen, shaking their heads and checking the reactions of the company. A few were literally prostrated.

A good relic should stir a degree of awe, perhaps even religious fervour. This went well beyond anything that any of us had experienced. It was as if we had been given a glance of heaven itself, of something so wonderful, so powerful, that our poor wits could not deal with it. The abbot was right, I knew. This thing was far too much above us to be used as a weapon in our petty disputes, or even to strengthen the King in his dealings with foreign powers. We were not fit to look at it, let alone make it a tool for our sinful purposes.

'Father Abbot,' said Lovell at last, breaking the profound silence, 'I rejoice that this relic has been restored to you, but you must know it was not our purpose in coming here.'

'Not your conscious purpose,' interjected Father Senhouse, 'but clearly the work of God.'

'Perhaps. But there are two complications. One is that King Edward himself sent Lady Beauchamp and her husband a commission to recover this Grail and bring it to him. That commission still stands, and has the force of law.'

'Not the law of God,' said the exorcist, 'only that of the civil power, which is inferior.'

'Sir, good luck to you if you would speak so to King Edward!' Lovell shook his head. 'Having seen what I have seen, I swear to you that I would be more than happy to leave the relic safely in my lord abbot's custody. It's a fearful thing and belongs not in secular hands. However, The King's writ binds us. This we must consider at further length.'

'A legend attaches to the Grail,' the abbot said. 'It will put a curse on he that misuses it, and on all his kindred and friends. Finally, after such misuse, it will return here once again, but not in our lifetimes. It will hide itself until the proper time comes for it to be revealed. I beg you, therefore, to let this matter lie.'

'I would not handle it for a pot of gold,' said Sir Thomas explosively. 'Nor would any sane layman after what we have seen. It is not for profane hands to touch.'

'Let me speak of our true purpose in coming here,' Lovell went on. 'We came here, Father Senhouse, to consult with you, on the recommendation of the noble and reverend Bishop of Dromore. We have urgent need of your services. Thus stands the case: The Duke of Gloucester, the Countess of Warwick and Sir Roger Beauchamp have vanished into thin air. We believe they are being held captive under an enchantment.'

'Indeed?' said the exorcist. 'And what evidence have you to suggest such a phenomenon?'

'Let us discuss that over supper,' suggested Abbot Dafydd. He was rubbing his belly and I suspect he had hunger pangs.

After that, and a few more speeches, the meeting broke up, and we retired to supper, which for those of highest rank was at the good abbot's table. A very splendid table it was too considering that we were surprise guests and that Anne was probably the first duchess to be entertained at that place in a century or more.

Lovell, Anne and I between us explained what had happened, and Father Senhouse asked many questions, all pertinent I must say. From time to time he nodded his head, or grunted, and at length said he would pray on the matter, long into the night, and consider what was to be done.

Although they had some very decent wine to offer, the main drink was mead, which came in quart pots and had most of us legless before the first course was done. If there had been tension at first in our dealings with the abbot that was now all forgotten, and Patch was soon giving his usual performance, including the Rivers joke which the abbot and his people had not heard before. At the time it was all very funny, and I laughed until my sides ached, but you had to be there, and three quarters cut to appreciate it.

*

Anne and I were not allowed to sleep within the monastery. Whether we were regarded as a threat to the chastity of the monks, or they to ours, I am not sure.

Anyway, we were conducted to what was called a 'guest-house' in the outermost ward. I suspect it was a converted piggery, or something of that sort. The threat we posed was thereby neutralised.

Within it was what might politely be described as a dormitory. It was low-roofed and oppressive, lit only by a single oil lamp of singular feebleness. There were three reasonably large beds, supplied with hard straw mattresses, a scatter of pillows and a few blankets. There were very few other amenities, certainly nothing so degenerate as a glass in which one might inspect one's face.

Anne and I had each, in our time, known worse, but even so this lodging was little short of an insult. Even as I was, my brain half befuddled by the monks' wretched mead, I was outraged.

It took me a fair few minutes to realise that we were not alone. There was an old woman, sitting on a stool in the darkest corner. At first I took her for a servitor, albeit an extremely inattentive and mannerless one. Then I realised there was something familiar about her. The mead had dulled my wits, or I should have known her at once. It was Tegolin.

'Welcome to Valle Crucis, my ladies,' she said in her very Welsh voice. 'I have to say, Alianore, it has taken you long enough.'

Anne stared at me. 'You know this woman?'

I nodded. 'This is the Lady Tegolin, your Grace. I think I may have mentioned her. At one time, long ago, she was a sort of governess to me. Or a tutor, anyway. I was only very young, of course.'

Tegolin climbed stiffly to her feet and made Anne a curtsey of sorts — the sort that one queen might give another, out of politeness.

'You deceive the Duchess, Alianore,' she said. 'I am more than that, madam. I am what some call a wise-woman, and a seer. Were I anything less, I would not have made the long journey from my home to this place to meet you, would not even have known that you were coming. Nor, at my age, do I make such a journey lightly, or for the pleasure of setting eyes on great ones. I am here because you must be *advised* — warned. It is my duty, no less.'

Anne sat on one of the beds, the one she had selected for herself. She gave me a look as if to say: 'Is this creature for real?' It was an awkward moment. I thought I remembered Tegolin reasonably well, but the years had flown by and I had not seen her (except in dreams) for a good twenty years. She was, in truth, as much a stranger to me as to Anne, and I had no idea — no idea at all — what she was going to say. It could well be embarrassing. Still, there was nothing I could do.

'These monks,' Tegolin said, 'will never part with the real Grail. It's far too precious. They'll fob you off with a substitute, and, believe it or not, they'll be doing you a favour. They keep their replicas close to the true relic, close enough to absorb some of the power. It will fade completely after a month or so, be no more potent than your own wine cup. The good news is it will not destroy you, as the real one quite possibly would. Even the duplicate will be quite perilous for a time. Be wary of it. Look at it, by all means. Touch it if you must. Nothing more. Above all, do not be tempted to work spells.'

'*Spells?*' Anne repeated in her very best Duchess voice, which was surprisingly scary. 'Do I look like someone who works spells, woman? I am the Duchess of Gloucester, no witch or necromancer.'

'I know,' said Tegolin with a nod of her head. She was quite unmoved. 'However, my lady your mother is another case. I grant you she is only an amateur, no further on than the basic certificate. Unfortunately, that makes the matter more dangerous. Especially as she is involved with another, one who has reasonably advanced skills.' She sniffed. 'Still an amateur, but a gifted one. Working together, they can do some quite impressive work. The Grail in their hands, coupled with their ignorance, would be exceedingly dangerous. Even the substitute could cause very serious disruption. Very serious. You do not want to know.'

'My mother is missing,' Anne said. 'We have no idea where she might be.'

Tegolin chuckled. 'That at least I can answer. She is at Guy's Cliff, near Warwick, with her fellow who calls herself Crystal Plantagenet.'

'As I suspected all along!' I cried.

'They have spent the last few weeks working on a drawing spell to bring Alianore and the Grail to them. I have done my best to block it, but it really isn't that simple. I'm growing old, and they are sapping my power. At one time I could have clapped a stopper on the whole business, but now I need assistance. In plain terms, I need you both.'

*

That night the Black Dog returned to me.

'Is there any food?' he asked.

There was a poor excuse for a night livery, made up of oysters and coarse bread. I fed it to him, piece by piece, and he wolfed it all down.

'Those are the best oysters I've ever tasted. And the best bread. Is there nothing more?'

I held out my empty hands.

'Miserable fellows, these monks,' he said. 'You'd have thought they could run to a piece of cheese at the least.'

'I'm very sorry about the inadequate catering arrangements,' I said. 'What do you do here?'

'I'm here to help. You're a very difficult person to help, Alianore. You actively *resist* it. I've been trying to help you. King Arthur and Queen Guinevere have been trying to help you. Merlin too. Then the Grail was actually presented to you, at Aysgarth Falls, and — nothing! Have you any idea how that came about? Let's put it this way — the very top, top management were involved. The Grail doesn't just move for anyone. It really doesn't. We're all a bit disappointed, to speak the truth. You seem short on sensitivity, not to say faith. You're so darned — prosaic. That's the word. Prosaic.'

'I can't help it,' I said, 'I've always been that way.'

'You don't listen enough. Try less talking and more listening.'

'Now you're beginning to sound like my mother.'

'Perhaps Lady Audley was right. Consider that. Now, do you trust me?'

I hesitated only fractionally. 'Yes.'

'Then take hold of my collar. You're going for a ride.'

'Where to?'

'The same place as last time, but this time we're going into the house. You'll see why when we get there.'

'Let me get dressed,' I said. 'I'm not wandering about Wales in my shift.'

'Hurry up, then,' he urged.

'Now you sound like Sir Roger.'

Still, I wasted no time. Then, when I was more or less ready, I grasped his collar and closed my eyes.

*

We landed on soft, lush, summer grass. Time had obviously shifted, as it was full light. From the position of the sun I saw it was morning. A river was flowing to our right, loud in its gurgling.

'Don't worry,' said the Black Dog. 'We are out of real time. No one will notice your absence at the abbey; you should be back before they wake.'

'It's very confusing,' I said.

'Come on.'

We walked by the river for a while, the Black Dog padding at my side. However, after a little way, we turned away from the water and climbed a slope as the ground took us to the house. In places the grass was so high that this walking was hard going but, I consoled myself, the house was not far off. Suddenly a thought struck me.

'Did you not say you didn't want to be seen?' I asked.

'That was then. In the circumstances, I don't care if we scare the crap out of them.'

'I see.'

As I drew closer to the house; some of the local rustics left off their work to lean on their tools and stare. I couldn't really blame them. After all, it's not every day that such people see a strange gentlewoman crossing their fields on foot and alone but for her dog. One of them removed his hat and addressed me in Welsh. I smiled back in a vague attempt at politeness.

It was then that they noticed the Black Dog. His impact on them was astonishing. They dropped their tools and ran off in all directions, as if the Devil was on their heels.

The Black Dog laughed. Well, not exactly. This particular dog could talk, but to expect him to laugh as well was a bit much. He made a strange sound that I presume was a dog's equivalent of laughter.

At the gate of the house I was met by an upper servant of some kind, an elderly fellow who wore a smart livery and a grey beard. He inclined his head at me in a questioning manner and waited for me to speak. Then he too saw the Black Dog, cried out in horror, and ran off into the house as fast as a greyhound in pursuit of a hare, bawling his alarm.

'Do you think by any chance my eyes appear red?' the Black Dog asked.

I looked at him. 'No, they're still brown.'

'They are for you,' he said.

Inside was a fine hall, surprisingly large for such a place. A gentleman — so I took him to be from his clothes — came running down the stairs from the floor above. He was a dark-visaged fellow of middle years, quite well made. He had a drawn sword in his hand.

'Who are you?' he demanded. 'A fiend from Hell?'

'Dame Beauchamp, in King Edward's service,' I said, making him a curtsey. 'This is my associate, the Black Dog. Prepare to die.'

Why I said those few last words, I am not sure. However, his face turned white, the sword dropped from his hand, and he too ran off.

'This is fun,' I said. 'Now all we have to do is find Uncle Jasper and my work is complete.'

'Uncle Jasper is not here,' said my companion. 'But try upstairs. Chamber on the left.'

I pulled out my poniard. This did not feel safe. I began to climb the stairs, the Black Dog not only keeping pace but bounding ahead, in the manner of dogs. On the top landing he put his nose against the first door to the left. Then he barked. That was a surprise. But then again, he *was* a dog.

Within was a single, very large bed. On it were Richard and Roger, both fast asleep. Yet it was no ordinary sleep. I prodded them, one after the other. At first, neither stirred. Then Roger opened his eyes.

'*Alianore?*' he asked. Then went straight back to sleep.

'The enchantment is powerful,' said the Black Dog.

'Can we take them with us?' I asked.

'No, Alianore. If you're dreaming, and put a piece of gingerbread in your pocket, is it still there when you wake?'

'Of course not. Are you saying this is just a dream.'

'It is and it isn't. It's hard to explain, but if you think of it as a dream, that's easiest.'

'Then what are we to do?'

'What you are to do is to return to the waking world; then return here with the Grail. Bring friends. These people are the Vaughans of Hergest. You are in the Marches. Everyone here is a dangerous bastard. The Grail will break the enchantment.'

*

I woke in my bed, astonished. It was past dawn. Anne was already awake and in the process of dressing. Tegolin was fully clothed and was performing one of my tasks, helping Anne.

'Slept well?' asked Anne.

'Not exactly.'

'I had this strange dream. There was a big, black dog standing next to your bed. The odd thing was, it had the most beautiful blue eyes you've ever seen.'

I was silenced for a moment as I took in what she had said. Had she dreamed it, or had she seen the Black Dog visiting me? Or had it *all* been a dream?

'I think they are at Hergest Court,' I said.

Tegolin laughed. 'Have you only just worked that out?' she asked.

*

'The Vaughans of Hergest,' Tegolin said, 'are a ruthless family. Yorkists, of course. Old Sir Thomas — Black Thomas as he was known, and rightly — fought for Edward at Edgcote, and was captured. Earl Warwick had him beheaded, and it is said that a black dog — his dog — came for his head and carried it home. Certain it is he was buried at Kington, but his spirit is restless. Many tales are told of it, and the local *gwerin* fear him dead even more than he did in life.

'As for his wife, Elen ferch Dafydd ap Cadwgan — she is known, for she still lives — as Elen Gethin. Elen the Terrible in the Saxon tongue. When she was younger, she dressed as a man; took a bow to an archery contest, and there shot dead her own cousin. He had, of course, killed her brother, but it was certainly not very ladylike. So she gained her name — Terrible. It fits her well.'

'She sounds like my kind of woman,' I said, 'but in any event, if these people are Yorkists they are sound enough. Not politically unreliable. At least I am not likely to walk in and find Uncle Jasper there. But why would they have Richard and Roger as prisoners? That makes no sense.'

Tegolin grunted. 'In fairness, I'm not certain they are prisoners. More like guests. I doubt very much they know who it is they entertain. That is what I have seen. But I cannot be sure.'

'Well,' I said, ' if *you* can't be sure, what hope is there for the rest of us? I am going in there mob-handed, not taking any chances. Sir Thomas's son — I suppose it is he?'

Tegolin nodded. 'Watkin Vaughan. I know nothing against him. He's a great patron of bards, a good Welshman.'

'This Watkin — what a strange name! — may have been turned. Perhaps Uncle Jasper is there, after all. He may even be behind this talk of restoring Harry VI, mad though that is. When did madness stop these people? King Edward is both heir-male and heir-general of Edward III. You would have thought that settled the matter. But no, Lady Richmond still has hopes for her son, Henry Tydder, who has about as much claim to the throne as I have. None. We can take no chances.'

Anne stood, and asked whether she was fit to be seen. She was. Tegolin had performed a surprisingly good service as tire-woman.

'I am not clear as to how we know Richard — and Roger — are at this Hergest place, wherever it is. If I am not clear, how do we explain it to the others?'

'Information received,' I said. 'We simply say we've had a report, and the details are on a need-to-know basis, and they don't need to know. Anne, you are going to have to pull rank if necessary. I know it's not your way, but the plain truth is you are Number One around here, and by a long, long way. We need to square Lovell, I suppose, but the rest will have to do as they're told. That includes the clerics.'

'Let us say a prayer together,' said Tegolin, holding out her hands. 'Form a circle, my sisters. We must summon our strength.'

We did as she said, and on her instruction closed her eyes. The prayer she then recited was in Welsh, so I can't claim I understood it. But then again, I don't understand much Latin either. I doubt whether Father Senhouse, or the Church in general, would have entirely approved, but I cannot say, or indeed think, that there was anything heretical in it. All I know that I could feel the power surging through me. It was quite astonishing. I felt like two Alianores.

We opened our eyes, and blinked at one another.

'Don't worry,' said Anne. 'From now on, I am in charge. We are going to get Richard back, and *nothing* is going to stand in our way.'

*

We went to our breakfast in the abbot's lodging.

'Francis,' Anne said to Lovell, 'we have received information as to Richard's whereabouts. This lady,' she gestured towards Tegolin, 'tells me that Richard and Roger at are a place known as Hergest Court, lying under enchantment. We are going there, in full force, and we are taking the Grail and that priest with us. This is not up for debate. I am authorising all necessary force. The paperwork can be sorted out when Richard and Roger are restored to us,'

'My lady — are you sure?'

'Quite sure. I hope the abbot will not make difficulties, but if he does, we are taking the Grail anyway. And the exorcist, even if he has to be tied to his horse. I trust that will not be necessary.'

Francis nodded. 'I shall warn Sir Thomas, and Robin, have our men prepared.'

'We negotiate first. But I am not staying here all day, or even all morning. There is not a moment to be lost.'

We proceeded to the abbot's table, and there, as we sat to our breakfast, Anne presented him, and Father Senhouse, with the full show of betting. Warwick himself could not have been firmer.

'Father Abbot,' she said, 'if the decision were mine alone, this precious relic would be left with you; for I understand its power and the dangers arising from it. Yet my lord husband lies bound by enchantment, and for the good of the entire realm he must be released from it.

'Therefore I intend to take the Grail, and Father Senhouse with us. With your consent and blessing I hope, but without it if necessary. The priest shall have custody of the Grail. As far as possible, none other shall touch it. It may be that we are forced to obey the King's mandate and take it to him — we are all his servants and bound by loyalty. If that comes to pass, I shall urge the King to return it here, where it belongs, and not seek any other advantage but the privilege of having once set eyes on it. For that is more than any of us is worthy to do. I shall do more than urge — I shall beg.'

Abbot Dafydd turned several shades paler than his habit, and that, of course, was white. Then he began to bluster. He came out with a long list of denials, excuses and prevarications, some of them in Welsh. To be fair, Welsh is a beautiful, lyrical language. I could listen to it all day. However, none of us understood a word.

'Nice abbey you have here, Father,' I said quietly. 'It'd be a shame if anything happened to it.'

'Sir, be reasonable,' said Francis Lovell in his gracious, diplomatic voice. ' We do not ask lightly. We have a missing duke, countess and knight, and believe the Grail will help us find them. You can be sure of an eventual reward for your cooperation.'

The abbot chewed this over for a few minutes. Then he spoke.

'My lady Duchess, I thank you for your goodness,' he said. 'Your mission shall have my blessing and my prayers. This whole House will pray for you — and the return of the Grail.'

*

The Battle of Near Presteigne

We rode south, all of us, including Tegolin and Father Senhouse. He kept muttering something about 'impiety' but was partially consoled by his possession of the Grail, which he carried in a lined box, kindly provided by the monks.

It was only when we were crossing the long, stone bridge at Llangollen, where the road is carried over the troubled waters and cascades of the Dee, (Afon Dyfrdwy as the Welsh call it) that a thought struck me.

'How do we know it's the Grail, and not a replica?' I asked.

'We don't,' said Tegolin. 'I told you about the monks and their tricks, and we may well have a replica. All I know is that I worked a swap in the chapel before we left. So there's a fifty/fifty chance that we do have the real Grail, not the false one that the monks were trying to fob off on us.'

'You *touched* it?'

'Yes, and so did you, when you picked it up at Aysgarth Falls. Did it do you any harm? I think not! You should not fall into superstition, Alianore. What is a priest, but a man? What is a man but the other half of the human race, created from dirt? What is any man or woman, but a sinner? The Grail will only harm the wicked. It should be treated with reverence, but when all is said and done, it's no more sacred than that tree.'

She pointed to an oak that stood on the far bank, its roots undermined by the flow of the river.

'Christ did not touch that tree,' I said.

'No, but God created it. And Owain sheltered under it.'

'Owain?'

'Owain Glyndŵr. Or Owen Glendower as you English insist on calling him in your ignorance. This is his country.'

'Is it?'

'He knew Valle Crucis better than you know Middleham. And his house at Glyndyfrdwy is but a few miles away to the west. Or it was, before you English burned it down in Bolingbroke's time.'

'Well – Bolingbroke!' I said. 'What do you expect? A murdering usurper, like all the Lancasters. And now you have King Edward, a descendant of Llywelyn ap Iorwerth. You Welsh should be made up. Instead, half of you are rooting for that wretched Tydder fellow, who is half English and a quarter French. Not much more Welsh than I am myself.'

'You were not born in Pembroke. Nor are there prophecies about you.'

'No, I was born at Heighley Castle in Staffordshire, which is a very tolerable place to be born. As for prophecies, they are twelve a penny. People on remember the ones that come true and forget the nine hundred and ninety-nine that don't. And there are prophecies about me, Tegolin. I distinctly remember you saying that I could be Queen.'

'And so you could have been, if you had not rejected the path. You had your chance and turned it down. Now you wait on the woman who took your place.'

'Anne? Do you say Anne shall be Queen?'

She nodded. 'It is written.'

'Good God,' I said, 'that mead must be strong stuff!'

*

We rode to Shrewsbury, and then through the Marches by way of the Hereford road. It is fine country, and we were sufficiently numerous and well-armed not to be accosted by the local brigands, although occasionally bands of ugly-looking fellows emerged from the trees or appeared on the skyline, obviously scrutinising us and asking themselves whether we were worth it. The answer appeared to be 'no'.

'These are lawless lands,' Lovell said conversationally. 'I should not care to travel this way alone, or even with my squire. Fortunately, they seem inclined to leave us alone.'

'It isn't just the local ruffians who trouble me,' I said, 'it's the question of what enchantments or demons stand in our way. For I shall be very surprised if there are none. It is well that we have Father Senhouse and the Grail. To say nothing of Tegolin. Believe me when I say she is a serious wise-woman. One way or another we should be able to deal with anything, but we should still be cautious. Anything could happen, and it could happen fast.'

I had barely finished speaking when a mist descended, like a curtain before us. In truth it was not so much a mist as dense fog. You could not see ten yards.

'This is no ordinary mist!' cried Father Senhouse. 'Smell it! This is the work of the Devil!'

It was true that the fog had an odour about it. Like a privy neglected by the gong-farmers for about twenty years.

'It certainly stinks like the Devil's arse,' cried Robin.

'It does indeed,' said the priest. 'It is evil and unnatural. I must pray at length. All of you, down! Get on your knees.'

The Mists of Middleham

'Wait!' said Tegolin. 'Let us try to use the power of the Grail. Let an arrow touch the holy relic, then shoot that arrow into the fog. If this is an enchantment, that will surely defeat it.'

Robin was already off his horse. Now, hurriedly but expertly, he strung his bow. Took an arrow from the quiver at his waist. 'Armour piercing,' he said, referring to the head. 'Will that serve?'

Tegolin nodded, and we all looked towards the priest. For a moment he hesitated, but then gave a gesture of consent, dismounted, and drew the Grail from its hiding place.

Robin took off his hat, and knelt. Then, cautiously, reverently, he advanced the point of the arrow into the cup, until it made contact. There was a very faint glow, a hum, almost too quiet to hear, that seemed to indicate approval.

He withdrew the arrow, fitted it to his bow, and drew to the ear. Then he loosed.

From out of the fog came a loud cry: 'Ouch!'

The fog was already thinning; almost before we knew what was happening, it was gone.

'A miracle!' cried Father Senhouse. It was hard to argue with him. If it wasn't, then I have never seen one. The vile stench had gone.

We all knelt upon the turf, and thanked God and his saints. It was only right.

Then we heard the voice, very loud. 'What the flipping heck do you think you are doing? I am sore wounded! What fool shoots an arrow into fog?'

(This is an edited version of what he said. He was actually a good deal ruder, but I am conscious that children, priests and servants may one day read this account.)

We saw, now that the fog was gone, some rustic fellow in russets, a shepherd or some such. Robin's arrow had pinned him to a beech tree.

'You goddamned knaves!' he cried. 'For the love of God, help me!'

Sir Thomas climbed onto his horse and advanced, for the fellow was a good hundred and fifty yards away, and no gentleman cares to walk so far.

'No need for language, fellow,' he told the man. 'Keep a civil tongue in your head. You're in the presence of the Duchess of Gloucester.'

'I don't care if it's the Queen, and the Pope and the Scottish Ambassador. Get this arrow out of me. I'm in agony and I can't move.'

181

We made our way forward to inspect him, gathering beneath his tree, which was only a step or two from the highway. It was Tegolin who took practical action, cutting away at his clothing with her small eating knife until she had uncovered the injury.

'Only a flesh wound, you big baby!' she cried. 'You need not tell me you're English, not Welsh. Now, stand still and stop whining. We shall have this sorted in no time. Alianore, go to my saddle bag and take out the green bottle and one of my pieces of linen. You're lucky, fellow. It could be a broad head arrow, stuck inside you, and then you'd have something to complain about. It's a bodkin, and it's gone straight through your shoulder. Someone lend me a half-decent blade, and I'll cut the arrow in no time. Then we can withdraw it, no trouble at all.'

Robin produced a large hunting-knife, and Tegolin inserted it into the gap between the fellow and the tree and sawed away. The knife was uncommonly sharp, and in seconds the fellow was free of the tree and able to stagger forward. Tegolin cut away more of his clothing. Then she took the linen, poured whatever was in the bottle onto it, and gently washed the wound, front and back.

'Now,' she said, 'I need a strong man — no, two strong men — to take hold of this fellow and keep him still. The arrow must be removed, there will be a lot of blood, and he is probably going to cry and struggle like the baby he is. Alianore, more linen. Much more. This will need dressing.'

Lovell and Robin took hold of the man, securing him almost as if he was a prisoner being taken before the Bench. Then Tegolin took and grip on the shaft of the arrow and pulled. Carefully, but not timidly. The wounded man howled, but in no time at all the arrow was pulled and the blood flowed. She took the linen from me, and applied more and more of the green bottle liquid, but still the blood kept emerging, back and front.

'Father,' she said, as if inspired, 'pray pour some water into the Grail, then bless it, and soak the wound. That will be a sure way of keeping this from turning septic.'

The priest did not hesitate. He took water from his own leather drinking flask and used it to fill the Grail. Then he said some words of prayer in Latin, made the sign of the cross, and advanced. As if taking part in a rite, he slowly, carefully tilted the Grail until the liquid poured out, all over the man's shoulder.

What happened next astonished us all, even Tegolin. The blood was washed away, of course. That was expected. However, not only did it cease to flow, but the wounds closed up, back and front. There was no sign of it, not even the smallest scar. It was as if the arrow had never pierced the fellow. Tegolin stood there, staring, the redundant linen in her hands, her bottle dropped in the grass.

'Another miracle!' cried Father Senhouse. 'A further miracle of God and the Grail! Let us pray!'

Those still on horseback dismounted, and we all fell to our knees, forming a semi-circle around the tree and the healed man. We prayed in earnest then, for perhaps a quarter of an hour, our priest plumped up like a pigeon, so pleased was he to see the power of the Grail demonstrated. No one could claim this was a trick, or that our eyes had deceived us. It was real.

The wounded man was still shaking his head with disbelief when we rose.

'Am I out of my wits?' he asked. 'I was just walking to Shrewsbury, in search of work, and all this happens. That arrow felt real. You folk look real. But am I dreaming?'

'It is very real, my son,' said Father Senhouse, 'and you have just been blessed by a miracle of God. You say you seek work?'

The fellow nodded. 'Yes, sir. I've been turned off. I thought I might find a new master in Shrewsbury.'

'Are you a local man?'

'From Bishop's Castle, sir.'

Father Senhouse looked about him. 'We have need of a guide do we not? Does any man here feel sure of the road? I think not. We are all foreigners in this land. Perhaps this man is another gift of God.'

'Do you know the way to Kington, my man?' asked Lovell. 'To Hergest Court?'

The fellow nodded. 'To Kington, well enough. I can show the way, sir, and willingly if I am paid.'

'Threepence a day, with food and drink. What say you to that?'

'I say I will do it, sir, and willingly. But I want a penny extra danger money within five miles of Hergest Court. They say Black Thomas and his dog walk the lanes. Evil spirits.'

Father Senhouse came as close to a laugh as a man of his stamp can. 'You need fear no evil, my son. I am the premier exorcist of the Archdiocese of York, and have about me the most powerful relic in Christendom, the virtue of which you have witnessed with your own eyes. The Devil himself is no threat to you in such company, let alone some paltry evil spirit from the marches of Wales.' He spat expressively. 'The evil spirit will run like a hare when we appear over the brow of the hill.'

'Then I am your man,' said the fellow. 'I'm Adam Carlisle of Bishop's Castle, a labourer by trade. Though I can do anything asked. I carry that quarterstaff,' he pointed to a stout weapon, lying unnoticed in the grass, 'and fear no mortal man. For I am the champion wrestler for twenty miles around, and now my wound is healed — praise God and His saints — I'm ready for anything.'

'A stout fellow,' said Robin approvingly, 'and such as would be welcome to my outlaw band. When all this is over, Adam, you may come with me to Sherwood, or Barnsdale, or both.'

'Outlaw?' cried Adam. 'I thought someone said something about the Duchess of Gloucester.'

'So they did,' said Lovell, gesturing towards Anne 'and there stands her Grace.'

Adam took off his bonnet, and bowed in her direction. 'Forgive me, my lady,' he said. 'My wits are all muddled.'

'It's all too complex to explain here out on the road,' said Lovell. 'Later perhaps. In an alehouse. For now, we must make progress.' He looked around. 'Now, how shall this fellow travel? He must share a horse. Who is best placed to take a double burden, given that he is no featherweight?'

After some debate, it was decided he must share with Marian, for she was by far the lightest of the company. (She was dressed in a man's clothes, and had passed for a youth back at Valle Crucis.) I sensed this did not altogether please Robin. He warned Adam to be careful where he put his hands, or he might find himself with another arrow, but this time better placed.

*

Adam soon led us off the main highway and down various byways, some so narrow that a horse could barely pass. He assured us that this was a short-cut, saving many miles, and perhaps it was. He knew the country, and we did not, so who could say? We had no map and only a vague idea of where we were.

We came at last to the place of his birth — as he claimed — the settlement of Bishop's Castle, a vile little town set on a hill, a place that made Middleham look like Paris by comparison. There was indeed a castle, as you might have expected from the name, but it was a tumbledown assembly of stones inhabited by pigs and stray sheep. (This was very much sheep country.)

So we lodged in a glorified alehouse called *The Three Tuns*, which turned out to be owned by Adam's uncle, one Master Roberts. (People the world over always give trade to their relatives if they can. It is a mark of common humanity.) There was no wine to be had, so we had to be content with what Roberts called his XXX ale. It was tolerable, and so was the mutton stew he served up, as long as you had a taste for mutton and cabbage. The locals, at least half of them Welsh, droned on with comparisons of their black-faced sheep, while Lovell, increasingly drunk, tried to explain to Adam who we were and what we were all about. By the end of the evening I had almost forgotten that myself.

It was all very cramped, and I had to sleep in what was more or less a cupboard, with Anne, Tegolin and Marian. It was as well that we were all relatively cleanly, or at least that none of us stank, or it would have been insufferable; worse than a ship's cabin at sea. I was not sorry when dawn came, for the mattress was stuffed with straw and fleas.

The things I do for the House of York! I thought, as I combed out my hair in the very limited space available.

'This day should take us to Kington,' Adam informed the company, 'riding as we are and making good speed. I believe we shall be there well before nightfall, as long as we do not sit an hour on each alehouse bench. Dinner at Knighton, I think. I know a right good place. Another uncle has it.'

Surprise me! I thought. Still, we rode on through good, wooded country, with many climbs and as many descents. We hardly saw a soul, for people are not thick on the ground in that part of the world. Here and there was an assart with a cottage in it and a couple of rooting pigs with half a dozen hens. Some had a man or a woman working the land, who paused to stare at us and watched us pass. The villages were few and far between and very small.

At Knighton, we ate well in the hall of what called itself an inn in those parts. (I was reminded of a byre, it both looked and smelt like one. Then we rode on again, climbing out of the valley in which that town (or village) sits, and through dense woods.

'I like not this country,' said Francis Lovell. 'It's perfect for an ambush. We should send out scouts, to right and left, but they need to be on foot, and good woodsmen. A horse would never pass through such thickets are these.'

'A job for my men and me,' said Robin, for he was in earshot. 'We fear no forest. We shall guard the flanks, if you, my lord, will keep the pace of the main party slow, for we shall make no great speed.'

'It would be well,' said Sir Thomas Pilkington. 'God curse me if I do not have a pricking at the back of my neck, such as I've not had since I ran into a pack of Stanley's rogues near Tyldesley church. Lovell, I suggest me and mine to the front, with that guide fellow, who should have some idea where we are, and Lady Beauchamp's archers. Women in the middle, with the priest and Patch. You and the Middleham fellows protecting the rear. Swords out. Axes too. I shall show my banner to the rascals and see them run!'

(There was, I must point out, no enemy in sight, but Sir Thomas was mad keen.)

Robin divided his men into three groups. One section, led by Marian, was to lead the spare horses, and these fellows rode just ahead of Anne and me. The other two carefully strung their bows, and took an arrow or two into their hands, ready for action. Then Robin led one party off on our right flank, while his lieutenant, calling himself Little John, took the other half to the left.

They vanished into the trees. Quite literally after a few moments, because their green clothing merged in very well.

We waited. Lovell took up his position at the head of the rearguard, while Sir Thomas led us, as he had proposed.

'Forward, banner!' he cried, when he judged the time was right. Off we went, as slowly as the horses could be persuaded to walk, like a mounted funeral procession.

At first, nothing happened. I was just beginning to think all was well when a protesting flock of birds flew up from the trees to our right, and almost at once arrows began to fly.

'Down!' Sir Thomas ordered, and we all of us scrambled down from our horses, and took what cover we could. I persuaded Anne into a convenient dry ditch, and found the priest and Patch were already taking refuge in it.

'Archers,' cried Sir Thomas. 'Advance through the trees. Be careful only to shoot at clear targets – Robin and his men are on our flank. Rest of you, on me; advance!'

Within seconds they had vanished into the wood, pursuing the enemy, ducking from tree to tree in fine skirmishing mode. Meanwhile, Lovell came up with some of his men to protect Anne (and me) with the others held back in reserve. As I studied our fellows I noticed, perhaps for the first time, just how young they were. They clutched an assortment of weapons, from swords to bills. Only one or two had a bow.

There was a lot of shouting from the wood in front of us, where I presumed Robin and Sir Thomas were fighting, and, I hoped, not against one another. All was silent behind us, until with a sudden roar, a whole host of spearmen came running through the trees. The enemy was on both sides!

I drew my poniard, not that a poniard is much use against a spear, but it gave a feeling of security. Lovell and the Middleham youths leaped the ditch and began to deal with the newcomers, and some of our reserve, unbidden, came running to join the party. So did Marian's horse-holders. They were all game enough.

For a few minutes it all looked very hairy indeed. Those spearmen, everyone looking like a giant, were a darn sight closer than I liked, yelling their incomprehensible slogans. Father Senhouse was praying, very loudly, as if he thought they were demons.

'Patch,' I cried, 'sound the recall. We need everyone *here*, now!'

Fortunately, he had his clarion, and he blew it. Whether the notes produced signified 'recall', 'advance' or 'come to the kitchen door' I cannot say. Nor can I boast that it made any difference. All was utter confusion.

Then one of the enemy spearman dropped, just feet from me, an arrow in his back. A black arrow as it happens, not that it matters. I was puzzled for an instant, before I recall the second group of Robin's men. They were obviously on their way to help, and taking our opponents in the flank.

The chaos continued. It still looked very uncertain, but then, ever so slowly, our spear-wielding friends began to give ground. Our Middleham lads had put up a stiff fight, and the growing number of arrows from side or even rear was enough of an addition to make the spearmen wary. Then Sir Thomas and his party came back from their excursion, roaring defiance as they approached us, and suddenly our enemies all seemed to remember they had bread in the oven at home. They withdrew in disorder, pursued by the most enthusiastic of our warriors, Sir Thomas charging through the trees as though he were eighteen, drunk, and trying to impress a girl.

Meanwhile, we mustered our forces. There were a few minor wounds, but nothing Tegolin, Father Senhouse and the Grail could not sort out between them. The enemy left two or three dead on the ground, all from arrows shot by Little John's party, and I've no doubt many more had wounds to lick. A discussion between Robin and Lovell rapidly came to the conclusion that the attack from our right had been a mere distraction, made by perhaps three or four archers. The main force had been the spearmen, and they might well have triumphed had it not been for our flank guard.

Sir Thomas returned, prodding a prisoner along with the tip of his sword, and singing:

> 'We had joy, we had fun,
> 'We had Welshmen on the run,
> 'But we soon felt really sick,
> 'As they ran away too quick.'

(It was something like that anyway.)

'A prisoner for questioning,' he announced, reverting to normal speech.

'String him up by the thumbs from that tree!' I ordered.

This was done in haste. Robin's men in particular seemed anxious to oblige.

'Now, fellow,' said Sir Thomas, 'whose men are you? Who is your lord?'

The man swore at him in Welsh, provoking a hiss from Tegolin, the only one who understood a word.

'Does he only speak Welsh?' I asked. 'It's possible. I suppose one way to find out would be to start carving a few important bits off him with my poniard.'

The look in the man's eyes suggested he understood.

'I am saying nothing!' he said.

'Oh yes, you are,' I told him. 'Because we will start by lighting a fire under your feet. That will just be the first course unless you talk.'

'Archers,' ordered Sir Thomas, 'establish a perimeter. I want no surprises if this dog's little friends find the balls to return. Not that I think it likely, but better safe than sorry.'

Robin and the other archers did as they were told, forming a defensive circle around us. Anne was standing by, examining her hands.

'Are you all right, my lady Duchess?' I asked.

'Yes. Just stung by pismires, or nettles, or whatever was in that ditch.'

'See what you have done!' I shouted, turning back to the prisoner. 'How dare you assault the Duchess of Gloucester! Or me, come to that. You had better start talking, and swiftly.'

Sir Thomas punched him in the belly, hard. 'Speak!'

'We only wanted the horses. We didn't know who you were,' said the fellow, as if that excused him.

'*You only wanted the horses?* Scum! Filth! Why not work, and earn the price of a horse? Now, whose men are you?'

'No man's men, as such. We live under the protection of Sir Robert Whitney of Whitney.'

'Who the devil is he?'

'He used to be my brother-in-law,' I said. 'One of them, that is.'

A cold finger ran down my spine.

'Every great man around here has thieves under his protection,' the prisoner explained. 'It's the way of the March. He looks after us, we look after him. But we don't wear a livery or sign indentures. It's what you might call — *unofficial*.'

'And why would you want horses?' I asked.

He grinned at me, ape-like. 'Profit, of course. What else? Jasper has needs.'

'Jasper?' I repeated.

'Jasper Tudor. He forges a dragon to dismay you Saxons.'

It was then that Sir Thomas struck. He drew back his sword, pierced the fellow just below the ribs, drove the blade into his heart. The outlaw slumped in his bonds.

'I had more questions to ask!' I protested.

'By what right did you slay this man?' Anne demanded.

Sir Thomas bowed his head towards her. 'By the power invested in me by this sword, I judged him guilty, madam.' He saluted her with the sword, then used the long grass to wipe the blood from it. 'We are in the Marches. There is no law as you understand it. If by some remote chance he had been brought before a jury, they would have all sworn he was at Pontypridd on this day, and set him free. My way is a more effective justice.'

'You might at least have given me time to confess him, rogue though he was,' Father Senhouse said sententiously.

Sir Thomas snorted. 'Do you usually confess rats, Father? He belongs with the Devil who has him.'

'You may just have started a blood feud,' Tegolin said.

'Don't give a damn, woman! Let them come. Would you allow filth like this to shoot arrows at the Duchess? I'll be hanged before I tolerate it.'

'Richard would not like this,' Anne said.

He shook his head. 'Madam, what do you imagine Duke Richard does when we go against our Scottish friends? Does he holds seminars with them to discuss the Battle of Halidon Hill? No, he does what he has to do to keep you safe at home. That is why you *can* be safe at home.'

He turned to Adam. 'You, fellow. Guide. Well done for leading us into an ambush. Now, what is the name of this place?'

Adam, who had been fighting boldly alongside the Middleham division, doing some execution with his quarterstaff, looked hurt. 'I know not, sir. We're in the middle of nowhere. Near Presteigne.'

'Then,' said Sir Thomas, 'this field shall be known henceforth as the Battle of Near Presteigne.'

*

At Presteigne we paused for refreshment, for the men had all been involved in serious exercise and had a raging thirst.

I drew Francis Lovell aside, telling him that I had need of a word.

'Francis,' I said, 'I have been thinking. What if this all hangs together? The missing countess; Richard and Roger being enchanted, the Grail, everything.'

'Go on.'

'Lady Warwick runs off to restore Henry VI, which is impossible. She's either been tricked, or is deluded, it matters not which. When people get stupid ideas in their head, it's very hard to persuade them to see sense, no matter how obvious the truth. It's highly likely that she's at Guy's Cliff with Ursula of York, or Crystal Plantagenet as she calls herself. A woman deeply alienated from her family.

'Then there is this of Robert Whitney. He was married to my sister, Constance, and he was at Mortimer's Cross, but what his politics are now, God knows. We are a divided family. Besides, in this part of the world a man may go to bed Lancaster and wake up York, or vice-versa. It's a strange chance that outlaws under his protection should attack us.'

'How would they know who we were, or even that we were coming?'

'Pitchers have ears, as they say. I doubt you can take a company of our size through country like this without the chief men becoming aware of it. The other thing is, after Constance died he married again. A Vaughan of Hergest Court. I remember we had a wedding invitation. We didn't go. We sent them a chafing-dish or something. Not that it matters. The point is, the two families have that link. If they are both against us, we have to assume they could array a force at least equal to what we have.'

'I see,' he said, and looked serious.

'Where are your other men? The ones Richard took with him? Not least my man, Guy?'

'I left them at Coventry,' he said. 'As far as I know, they're still looking for Richard.'

'Looking for Richard. That sounds like a story. Never mind, we need them. I know, we'll send Patch to fetch them. He's useless in a fight, but as a minstrel he can pass anywhere. No one ever stop minstrels, they're like heralds.'

Francis frowned, no doubt consulting the map in his head. 'It will take days,' he said. 'It must be eighty miles if it's an inch. Then it will take at least a day to recall such a scattered company, for they'll be spread out over every town and village for miles. I don't see how they could join us in much less than six days at best.'

'At least we should know that a relief column is on its way. On top of that, Patch can carry a letter to the Sheriff of Herefordshire. I can put a Yorkist Intelligence seal on it; that and yours next to it should resolve any doubts. Tell him to pipe all hands aboard Hergest Court. That should not take more than two or three days at most. Again, a relieving force, just in case.'

'Hmm,' said Francis.

'You know that fellow mentioned Uncle Jasper? Well, if he's around it makes matters even more dangerous. We could be facing a major Welsh rebellion. I wish Sir Thomas had not been so impetuous. I had plenty more questions to ask, and that makes me wonder about him too.'

'About Sir Thomas?' he asked, sounding incredulous.

'As an intelligence officer I must consider every possibility, however remote.'

'My God, Alianore, you might as well suspect me! Pilkington is the most loyal of the loyal.'

'Perhaps. But you must assert yourself and take command even so. You are a peer, and outrank everyone here apart from Anne.'

'I'm no great warrior – Thomas is.'

'Nevertheless, you must pull rank. You see, it occurs to me we could be walking into a trap, and if we are, the Grail will fall into the hands of the enemy, which would be a disaster. What if Jasper and Ursula are working together to that end?'

'Ursula is the King's sister!'

'Yes, but as I said, alienated from her family and, I suspect, very ambitious. She could not claim the throne in her own right. But what if she married Henry Tydder? That would unite York and Lancaster, and two weak claims might just add up to one strong one. What if they had the Grail too? Who knows what support they might achieve! All the old Lancastrians for sure, but perhaps some of ours too. You know how unreliable some people are. Thomas Stanley, for example. I'd not trust him a yard. Not with that wife of his, Tydder's mother.'

Francis shook his head. 'I think you're getting into the realms of fantasy, Alianore.'

'Perhaps, but nothing else fits so neatly with what we know to be true. As for our immediate course of action, I think subtlety might be in order. We could try to storm the place, but if this is a hostage situation, that could be perilous. For all we know, the place could be stuffed with men-at-arms.'

'Then what do you propose?' he asked.

*

Hergest Court.

We walked, Father Senhouse and I, along the narrow road that climbs slowly from Kington up to Hergest Court. Our companions were lodged in Kington. It was late afternoon and the priest was already complaining.

'I really do not see why we could not have kept our horses,' he grumbled, not for the first time.

'Because, Father, we are supposed to be a distressed gentlewoman and her accompanying priest. No threat to anyone. The more pathetic we look, the better. Remember, we were parted from our companions in a sudden mist, and got lost. We are desperately seeking shelter. Once inside, we look for Duke Richard and my husband. We use the Grail to break any enchantment, if they are under one. Either way, we release them. With two knights, the Grail, and the finest exorcist in the country, I shall fear nothing. Lovell comes to our relief at dawn, with everything he can throw at the place. By that time, with any luck, we shall be barricaded in a defensible room and able to defy the garrison. Any questions?'

'I should like to know why you think they are under an enchantment.'

'Because of information received. Please understand, I cannot reveal all the secrets of Yorkist Intelligence. It's forbidden. Think on this though. Men like my husband and Richard of Gloucester are not easily imprisoned. They are fighters. To the death if necessary. They must be under some form of restraint.'

At the gate I was met by the same upper servant I had seen in my dream (or vision, or whatever it was) in the company of the Black Dog.

'My name is Lady Beauchamp,' I said, 'and this is the Reverend Father Senhouse, of St Mary's York. Please be good enough to take us to your master at once.'

He surveyed me us some interest, and for a moment I wondered if he understood English. In the Marches, and certainly in Wales itself, there are many who do not. However, he bowed. 'You would seem to be in some distress, madam,' he observed. 'Do you wish to lean on my arm? There are quite a number of steps, you see.'

I told him that was quite unnecessary, and allowed him to guide us inside. The house smelt of newly-strewn herbs and fresh paint and was not nearly as dark as I had expected, the shutters being open and strong sunlight illuminating the rooms. There were indeed a number of steps, and my legs were surprisingly weary by the time I had climbed the last of them. The fellow showed me to a seat, and went off to fetch his employer. The good news what the place did not seem to be swarming with armed ruffians.

A few minutes went by before the master of the house appeared.

'I am Watkin Vaughan, lady, how may I serve you?' he asked.

It was the fellow I had seen, when I had visited with the Black Dog in my dream. (Or whatever it was.) His voice was strong and decidedly Welsh.

I was just about to open my mouth when Father Senhouse answered for me. I must admit, he did it very well, without a stumble, remembering our cover story beautifully.

Vaughan called out a series of rapid orders, mostly in Welsh, and before I knew what was happening someone fetched a blanket to me and handed another to the priest. Another fellow arrived with cups of wine, and a third appeared from the kitchens – as I suppose – with bread, cheese and slices of meat. Elizabeth Vaughan, the lady of the house supervised all, and then fussed over us as though we were two lost babes. This was hospitality, by any standards. Rather to my surprise they did not ask any of the awkward questions that I had anticipated, but gave us time to recover.

Only over supper did they begin to make a few gentle probes. We explored our ancestry, a common topic of conversation among the Welsh, and it turned out we were quite closely related. His uncle had married my sister, Margaret. (The younger Margaret that is, by this time Lady Powys by her second marriage and by no means to be confused with my half-sister, also Margaret.) This seemed to please them both. Being part of the family, no matter how tangentially, is no small thing in Wales.

'It is strange,' said Watkin, 'but you are not the only wanderers to have found refuge here. We have two men under our roof, gentleman by their clothing, who arrived one evening, quite out of their wits. We have them upstairs, for we can barely persuade them to open their eyes. They sleep like men drugged. Though I know not the drug that could make a man sleep for weeks on end, barely stirring.'

Father Senhouse gave me a significant glance. 'I have seen such cases in my — er, pastoral work. If you will allow me to see them, I shall pray over them. It is my experience that such cases often arise from spiritual issues. I do not want to prejudge, of course.'

'It so happens that my husband is missing,' I said, 'with his — his friend. We have been searching the Marches for them. If you will permit...'

'Certainly, certainly,' said Watkin. 'It would be a relief to us both if they were known, and returned to their kin. Would it not, *cariad*?'

'In faith, it would,' agreed his wife, nodding vigorously, ' and if the good father can help them with his prayers so much the better.'

We left the table, all of us, and followed Watkin up those same stairs I had climbed with the Black Dog. I knew before he touched the handle that he would show us into the first room on the left. There they lay on the bed, Richard and Roger, just as I had dreamed.

'There is evil here,' said Father Senhouse. 'I smell it. Not, you understand, with the nose of my body, but with my spiritual nose. Fortunately, I have a flask of holy water about my person, and a very powerful relic. We shall not be overcome. Let us pray.'

So we knelt, and the good father led us in prayer for what seemed half an hour. Then he brought out his holy water, poured some into the Grail, and used it to make the sign of the cross on Richard's forehead.

He began to stir at once, and the priest moved to the other side of the bed and repeated the process with Roger. By this time, Richard was already sitting up, blinking like an owl.

'Where am I?' he asked. Then he set eyes on me. 'Alianore?'

Roger was awake too. 'Alianore? I thought I saw you in a dream. Is this a dream too?'

I hurried to his side, and squeezed his wrist. 'No dream. You are both back. Thanks to the Reverend Father Senhouse and the Grail.'

'Gratitude belongs to God alone,' the priest said, though he looked rather pleased with himself.

'No one has told me where I am yet,' Richard said, swinging his legs off the bed. He sounded quite testy, but I suppose so great a lord did not to be found in such disarray, dressed only in his shirt and in mixed company at that.

'Master Vaughan, Mistress Vaughan; this is his Grace, the Duke of Gloucester,' I said, making the introductions like a chamberlain. 'Your Grace, I have the honour to present Watkin Vaughan, Esquire, and his lady, of Hergest Court in the Welsh Marches. Whose unknowing guests you and Roger have been for some weeks as you lay under enchantment.'

'Enchantment? So that was what it was! I had an idea I had had too much ale and cheese. Such dreams! God be loved, did you say you have the Grail?'

'Here it is,' said Father Senhouse, and Richard fell to his knees and venerated it. Roger was not so far behind, and in no time we were all back on our knees, praising God for the destruction of the enchantment.

At last, Father Senhouse broke into our prayers. 'The forces of darkness are very strong, and I feel them closing. Mistress Vaughan, be good enough to bring salt and water, so that I may consecrate a much greater volume of holy water than I have left. I intend to asperse the entire house. Darkness is falling fast, and I fear we may soon be under spiritual attack. The Grail will surely protect us, but nothing should be left to chance.'

Elizabeth Vaughan hurried off, and I followed her, for it seemed to me that Richard and Roger would wish to dress, and probably use the privy, so they were best left with the other men for a time. We descended to the kitchen, and in no time at all the servants there produced the necessary items. The priest had followed us down the stairs, and met us as we returned to the hall. He nodded approvingly, and began by blessing the salt. Then he blessed the water, and added a surprisingly small pinch of salt, before saying even more prayers. All in Latin, of course, and no doubt efficacious, though I barely understood a word.

He pointed at one of the Vaughan's servants. 'Boy, you shall follow me with the holy water. There is not a minute to be lost. We must asperse every door, every window, every drain and shaft, every chimney, and every room, forgetting nothing. Let us begin.'

From some discreet crevice of his habit he produced an aspergillum, and off they went about their lengthy task. I was a little surprised he did not use the Grail as his source of water, but I suppose he did not want the boy to touch it. He left it in its box on the high table.

I could not help but look at it, though I decided it might be better not to touch, just in case. It was, on the face of it, the very same cup I had brought from Aysgarth Falls. Yet at the same time it was identical to the replica the monks of Valle Crucis had produced. Absolutely identical. Was it in fact the true relic, or the replica? Yes, I had seen its power, but Tegolin had explained that. Even the replica might have power for a limited time, just from being kept in close proximity to the true Grail.

I remembered what Bishop Russell had said, all those weeks ago. The true Grail might be exceedingly dangerous in the wrong hands, and the 'wrong hands' included some of the people at court. Perhaps it would be better for everyone if this really was a replica, and the true Grail back at Valle Crucis, where the good monks would merely venerate it, not exploit it. I said a quiet prayer that this should be so.

Richard and Roger came downstairs, now fully dressed of course, very hungry. The Vaughans were swift to arrange for food and drink, and we enjoyed what amounted to a rere-supper, although in my case, as I was already quite full, it was chiefly a matter of taking wine, enjoying the occasional taste of some delicacy or other, and squeezing up to Roger, given that I was very pleased to have him back.

'Now, Richard is himself again,' the Duke said, when he had consumed a very large bowl of mutton broth, 'and I should be very pleased if someone would explain what in the name of God has happened, how I came to be here, and what is to be done next.'

So, I tried to explain, with very occasional interjections for Father Senhouse when he considered I was not giving the Grail, God and the Church in general sufficient praise. The one point I could not explain was how Richard and Roger had been brought to this place. The mundane answer was that they had probably been brought by cart, and dumped. The other possibility — less likely, but not unimaginable — was that the enchantment had transported them, that they had literally flown through the air.

Richard laughed at the idea, but to my surprise Father Senhouse said it was entirely possible. This was clearly an act of sorcery, and witches were known to fly, with the benefit of powers given by Satan. It was therefore not beyond the bounds of possibility that they could make others fly.

'But why *here*?' Richard persisted.

'You were not brought *here*, my lord,' Watkin Vaughan pointed out. 'You were found, wandering and lost, and brought here by my servants for shelter. Perhaps it was not intended you should have so good an end. There are many lawless men in these parts who might well have made an end of you. Or you might have died from exposure, out in the woods.'

'There is also reason to believe Uncle Jasper is working in these parts,' I said. 'The intent may have been to deliver you into his hands. To be killed, or deployed as a hostage.'

'In which case,' Father Senhouse said, 'we must presume that your Grace was delivered by the power of God, and guided to the shelter of these good people. It may even have suited your adversary that you should stay here, lost to the world, at least for a time. Now that you have been released from the enchantment, it may be the sorcerer by attempt further mischief. Either by sorcery — against which I have already made strong provision — or by the hand of man. It is possible we shall face attack.'

'Francis Lovell will be here at dawn,' I said, 'with the Duchess and a force of men. They are lodged in Kington.'

'*Anne*?' Richard cried. 'Anne is here?'

'She insisted. What's more, we have sent for reinforcements. I expect the Sheriff of Herefordshire to be here in a day or two. More of your men from Middleham in about a week — they have been searching for your Grace in the district around Coventry. Taken together, we should soon have a significant force.'

'A week is a long time,' Richard said. 'Still, it's far from hopeless. Much depends on what support Jasper Tydder has raised, if any. If the worst comes to the worst, this a defensible house. How far off is this Kington?'

'Less than two miles,' said Watkin Vaughan.

'So near? Then let us bring them up at once, while the light lasts! Concentrate what forces we have. I shall write a note for Lovell. You have someone to carry it, Vaughan?'

'I will send one of my boys,' said Watkin.

'Excellent!'

Richard was given an ink, quill and paper, and rapidly scribbled a note.

Francis,
All is well; bring all your forces to Hergest Court on receipt of this.

Richard Gloucestre.

He sealed it with his signet ring and the boy was sent running.

'As Roger and I have had enough sleep to last for months, we shall keep watch through the hours of darkness, 'Richard said. 'Vaughan, if you could spare us a man or two, I think that will suffice to give alarm.'

'I will watch with you,' Watkin volunteered.

'As will I,' said a voice. It was a very tall, elderly woman who spoke, clad all in black. She was in the business of descending the stairs; not the ones leading to the room where Richard and Roger had been lodged, but a quite separate stair at the far end of the hall. I assumed at once that this was the fabled Elen Gethin. She was certainly no youngster, but her steps were confident and there was no hint of a stoop. What was unusual about her was that she was carrying a bow — a war-bow at that, of fit size for any warrior.

'Mother!' said Watkin, rising to his feet. Richard and Roger imitated his courtesy.

'I was listening at the squint,' she said, her voice loud and confident. 'I see that our guests are well again, for which I am grateful to God. But did I hear correctly? Is one of these gentlemen the Duke of Gloucester?'

'It is I, madam,' said Richard, advancing and bowing politely over her extended hand. She made him a deep curtsey in response.

'My lord, this house is honoured,' she said. 'You will find us loyal here.'

'I did not doubt it, madam.'

She was pleased by that. She allowed herself to be conducted to the table, to have wine and food set before her. There was certainly nothing wrong with her appetite. The bow she set down, but kept close at hand.

'Not all hereabouts are so honest,' she said, her eyes fixed on Richard as if fascinated by him. 'Some still yearn for old Harry the Sixth, or sympathise with the exile in Brittany. That fellow, Henry Tydder. There is word that his uncle, that *murderer*, is in the land again, seeking to stir trouble. Then there are those who do but seek profit for themselves. *Their loyalty is to their purse.* Do you understand me?'

'Quite, madam.'

'If there is any threat to this house, or the guests within it, you may rely on me. I may be old, but I am still as good an archer as any in fifty miles around. So I will stand watch with you, and think it an honour.'

'The honour will be mine, madam,' Richard said.

*

Francis Lovell led the troops in just as darkness closed on us. There were many introductions to be made, but Richard and Anne had eyes only for one another. Wine and mead were distributed to all, and billeting arrangements put in hand, Lady Elen and Elizabeth Vaughan bustling about, giving their orders. Some could be accommodated in the hall, on pallets, others in the stables or in storerooms. Those of us highest in rank were given proper guest rooms.

The night seemed endless. The bed felt damp, or at least musty, and it was surprisingly cold for the time of year. There seemed to be a whole household of owls hooting at each other in the woods and once, just once, I heard a dog howl in the distance. Then the storm broke — and what a storm it was! Thunder, lightning, torrential rain, everything that could make a noise. I perhaps managed three hours sleep, and during that time I had more weird dreams than you could shake a stick at, not one of them comforting or reassuring. What I wanted was Sir Roger. At the barest minimum he would have kept me warm and comforted, and that was exactly what I needed. Of course, he was not there, but on active patrol with Richard, in case the enemy made a sneak attack.

Lying awake in the darkness, I considered my life. I had once been the youngest in a large family, alternately ignored and ordered about. Then I had found myself in a nunnery, until they decided I was not an asset to the abbey. Next my time in Warwick's household, where I had met Roger and performed my first duties for Yorkist Intelligence. Then, as a result of rejecting a most unsuitable marriage I had found myself involved in a very dangerous mission, which I might well not have survived but for Guy Archer and Roger. Then, eventually (to cut a long story short) I had married Roger and found a degree of contentment, serving in the Gloucester household and performing my intelligence duties. Roger had been a key part of all the good times. How I had missed him!

Morning came, and there was no sign of any enemy.

'It may be,' Richard said over breakfast, 'that all this talk of Jasper Tydder is just that — talk. That any turbulence in this area is nothing more than the customary disorder found in the Marches.'

'That Uncle Jasper is in the country seems probable,' I said. 'My sighting of him is confirmed by local rumour. That's a remarkable coincidence at the least. The question is — what is he about? The last time he came to town he started a full-scale rebellion; but that was when King Harry and his son were still alive. One possibility must be that's he's here on private business. He has — or had — a mistress and children in Wales. The suggestion is he's in this area. Perhaps he is, but unless we hear of armed revolt — something more than the usual sheep-stealing and so on — where do we even start?'

Unexpectedly, Elen Gethin spoke up. 'You might try talking my son-in-law, Robert Whitney. He has some very strange friends.'

'Yes,' said Lovell, 'we met some on our way here.'

'Do we know of this Whitney?' Richard asked.

'He was with us at Mortimer's Cross,' Roger said.

'He was also married to one of my sisters,' I said.

'And now to my daughter,' Lady Vaughan added. 'We are close kin, my lady, one way or another. The fellow is a malcontent and protects rogues.'

'So does everyone, Mother, in all fairness,' Watkin said. 'You must not give my lord of Gloucester the impression we claim to be saints. This is lawless country, your Grace, where a man must look to his own, since there is no one to protect him. I'm not sure my brother Whitney is any worse than anyone else.'

'Perhaps a reconnaissance would be in order,' I suggested. 'Roger and I could pay a visit, with a few to attend us.'

'No,' said Richard, firmly. 'We keep our forces concentrated in hostile country. There are not enough of us to divide into smaller groups. We advance together. All of us.'

So, that was that.

*

Whitney-on-Wye

Elen Gethin offered to show us the way — though she assured us that it was but a matter of an hour's ride. Before we set off, however, she demonstrated her prowess with the bow, splitting a willow wand at two hundred paces.

'My lady,' cried Robin, 'if ever you lack for a home, you may join my band.'

Elen smiled at him. 'Thank you, sir, whoever you are. But I've a good home of my own at Nash when I'm not with my son, and have no interest in becoming a professional musician at my age.'

So, we set off, Elen bringing a couple of stout Welsh archers with her to add to our strength.

The local countryside is very fair and thickly wooded, but somewhat short in the way of proper roads. It was, for much of the way, a matter of following the horse in front along a narrow path. There was little sign of population but for the occasional stray sheep or wandering cow.

The manor house at Whitney-on-Wye was, as you might have guessed, set close to the River Wye. It lay behind a circuit of tall walls, and a broad moat, and although not quite a castle, was certainly designed for defence, with one stout stone tower soaring above the lesser buildings. We had reached clear land, away from the trees, and gathered around Richard, who sat on the horse he had borrowed from Watkin Vaughan, and studied the place at leisure.

'It seems peaceful enough,' he said.

We advanced with some caution, though, and I was sent back to ride with Anne, some way behind the front rank. No arrows flew at us, and although the drawbridge was raised, once Dame Elen had shouted to the gateman that she was with us, and that here were the Duke and Duchess of Gloucester, it was quickly lowered to admit us. I noticed that once we were all inside the walls it was just as swiftly raised behind us. Was this a trap? You may think I was on edge — perhaps I was, but I had a prickling along my spine. (It may just have come from sleeping on a damp mattress.)

I had met Robert Whitney before, but it had been many years earlier, when I had been but the least significant of Lord Audley's numerous children, and, to be honest, I could not recall the occasion. It might be he had brought my sister, Constance, home to visit her family. No matter. He was considerably older, greyer and fatter than I remembered him. He talked a lot though, which was in line with my memories. The trouble with relatives is that you cannot choose them, and they are often garrulous and embarrassing, or just plain stupid. Robert Whitney, of course, was all three of these things, and he seemed anxious to demonstrate it.

'My lord of Gloucester! My lady! This is a scarcely believable honour!' he cried. 'What brings you to these remote parts? I'm astonished! Amazed! How we shall feed you all, I do not know. We shall though. Our wine is poor stuff, unfit for you to drink. Do you prefer ale? Mead? We have some of that. Quite good cider too. Will you be pleased to stay the night?'

So on and so forth, without leaving space for answers.

Given the crowd of us that had arrived, the large number of children in the house (some my own nephews and nieces be it remembered) and with servants rushing to-and-fro with jugs of ale and the like, it took time for everyone to settle down. There were not enough chairs, by the half. Most of us had to make do with a bench, or squat down on the rushes, while Robert talked on and on. Even his unfortunate wife, Elen's daughter, could scarcely get a word in edgeways. She stood by, occasionally bidding some servant to fill that cup or fetch such-and-such a plate, and bustled from hall to kitchen and back, making sure all was in order.

Richard, of course, had the best chair by the fire. He looked quite at home, even in that small, remote hall, far from the splendour of Middleham, and his very presence drew all eyes even though, by his standards and those of the court, he was barely dressed.

'We are here for a purpose, Sir Robert,' he said at last, when the babble had died down. 'Of late, there have been several strange occurrences which appear to be diabolically inspired. Acts of witchcraft worked against our very person. It can scarcely be doubted that these are linked to more practical matters — such as the reports we have received that Jasper Tydder, calling himself Earl of Pembroke, is at large in this area and working mischief. Now, I must ask you, have you information regarding this rebel? If so, it is your duty to reveal it, and to assist us to apprehend the traitor.'

'I have heard such tales,' Robert Whitney admitted, 'but beyond that I know nothing.'

'Even though Lord Lovell here, and those with him, were lately viciously attacked by a force of evil-doers claiming to be under your protection?'

'Rogues claim many things, your Grace. I protect no thieves. I am a loyal subject. I fought for King Edward at Mortimer's Cross.'

'That at least is to your credit. I still intend to have your house searched, for rebels, thieves, treacherous correspondence and stores of weaponry.'

'Has your Grace warrant for that?' Whitney sounded both appalled and uncomfortable.

Richard snorted. 'I am Lord High Constable of England and a member of the Council of the Prince of Wales. That's warrant enough, I think.'

'The warrant of the sword besides,' growled Sir Thomas Pilkington. I had almost forgotten him, but he was standing by the screens, hand on sword hilt and ready for action. 'Shall we make a start, your Grace?'

We divided into parties for the purpose. I took Robin and one of his followers, a fellow called 'Will Scarlet' — presumably because, unlike his fellows, he affected a red hood — to inspect Whitney's study, where we had a good hope of finding some interesting papers. Both the men were literate, of course. Indeed, Scarlet was something of a scholar. From what I could gather he'd been thrown out of Cambridge University for scandalous conduct. (Perhaps he had never been blind drunk for three days or had failed to make a woman pregnant — I can't think of anything else that would have been scandalous enough for the masters of that place to notice.)

In truth, we were disappointed. The papers we found on and around his very untidy desk were household accounts, rentals and the like. There was, admittedly, a promising pile of scribblings in Welsh. We had to call Tegolin in to translate, but she assured us that they were all poems about love, and ancient legends and so on, nothing of any interest at all.

'What's in there?' asked Scarlet. He pointed at a small door in the corner, barely tall enough for a child to enter. A cupboard of sorts, as I supposed, albeit one built into the fabric, not a piece of furniture.

Robin lifted the latch, and I advanced into what was a dark and gloomy hole. There was a flight of stone steps, descending into further dark.

'Lights,' I said, drawing out my poniard.

Scarlet found a tinderbox, and between them the two men fussed around until they produced enough spark to light the small lantern that stood on the desk. There was a candle, in a holder, and they lit that too and passed it to Tegolin. Then we began to advance down the stairs, Robin first.

At the foot of the stairs was a man, sitting on a stool in the far corner, trying to make himself invisible. I recognised him at once as the man I had seen at Chertsey.

'You are Uncle Jasper, and I claim my five thousand marks,' I said.

'I am Edmund ab Owain!' he protested.

'Robin,' I said to my companion, 'regard this fellow as a bishop, or archbishop.'

'Ah, "These bishops and these archbishops, Ye shall them beat and bind,"' Robin recited.

He and Scarlet set to work at once. The beating was thorough enough; then, from I know not where, they produced cords, and in no time Jasper was trussed like a fowl before cooking.

'Are you sure this is your man?' Tegolin asked. 'The light is poor, and he looks unfamiliar to me.'

'He is certainly the man I saw at Chertsey. Why, have you ever set eyes on Jasper?

'Several times,' she said. She addressed some words to the man in Welsh.

'I am Edmund ab Owain!' he repeated.

'He is Edmund ab Owain,' Tegolin repeated, after the fashion of a parrot.

'Then why does he hide in cellars?' I asked. 'Very suspicious behaviour for an innocent man I should think, even in Wales.'

'It is a penance!' the fellow protested.

'A likely tale,' I said. 'Tell it to the judge. Or in this case, to the Lord High Constable.'

Robin and Scarlet half-carried, half walked him to the hall, where Richard still sat in his chair by the fireplace.

'Uncle Jasper, your Grace,' I said, by way of introduction. 'We found him curled up in a cellar, hoping we would go away.'

Robert Whitney was also on his feet, his face redder than a particularly red beetroot that had been painted red. 'How dare you insult me! How dare you insult my guest! This gentleman is Edmund ab Owain, a good friend of mine.'

'Yes, of course he is,' I nodded, walking towards them. 'That's why he was at Chertsey, visiting old Harry of Lancaster's tomb, and that's why Margaret, Lady Richmond, was at such pains to protect him. Because he was just an innocent Welsh gentleman on his way to Oswestry Market. You must think I came down in the last shower. He answers the description of Jasper Tydder, he's the right age and build, and *he is Jasper Tydder*.'

'I am Edmund ab Owain!' the man protested. 'It is no crime to visit Chertsey Abbey.'

Richard spoke for the first time. 'Is there anyone here who knows Jasper Tydder, calling himself Earl of Pembroke? If so, come forward.'

'I was at the siege of Bamburgh,' said Roger. 'I saw the man Jasper there. As your Grace knows, that was seventeen years ago. This fellow has the look of him, but if you put me to my oath, I could not swear to it.'

'I have seen Jasper many times,' said Tegolin, 'most recently, in the flesh, when he raided Wales ten years ago. This is not the man. For one thing, he's not quite tall enough. For another, Jasper is a warrior. He would not hide in a cellar.'

Richard gave her a thin smile. 'Madam, my brother King Edward and I are warriors, I dare swear, but we ran away to Flanders when the odds were against us. A wise warrior knows when to retreat as well as when to fight.'

It was then that Dame Elen walked into the hall. (I believe she had been searching the outbuildings, but it may equally have been that she had been comforting her young grandchildren.)

'That is Jasper Tydder,' she cried, pointing a bony finger. 'The murdering bastard who killed my right-near kinsman, Sir Roger Vaughan of Tretower, at Chepstow in 1471, in the aftermath of Tewkesbury.'

'A brother-in-law of mine,' I pointed out.

'Indeed, my cousin,' she cried. 'We demand his death! Take his head off, my lord, before you have your dinner.'

'How can you convict on such evidence?' asked Robert Whitney. 'Two of us say this is not Jasper. One (an old woman!) says it is. This knight,' he pointed at Roger, 'says he cannot be certain. No magistrate would condemn a poacher of conies on such a basis.'

'What have you to say for yourself, prisoner?' Richard demanded. 'Are your Tydder, or not?'

'At least get the pronunciation right. It is *Tudur* not Tydder.'

'It sounds identical to me,'

'Well it isn't.'

'Some say "Tudor",' suggested Sir Thomas.

'They are wrong. It is *Tudur*. Although actually, it isn't. Not under the Welsh patronymic system. My father was Owain, and his father was Maredudd, and *his* father was Tudur. So how anyone can call me Tydder, Tudor or Tudur is beyond me.'

'I'm none the wiser,' said Richard. 'Who are you claiming to be now?'

'I'm not claiming to be anyone. I am Jasper ab Owain.'

'Uncle Jasper!' I cried.

He glared at me. 'No uncle of yours, whoever you are.'

Elen marched up and spat in his face. 'Murderer! Your Grace, you have an admission from his own mouth. He must die!'

Richard sighed. 'I am satisfied,' he said, speaking to our prisoner, 'that you are the attainted traitor Jasper Tydder, here in Wales to foment rebellion against King Edward. Therefore it is my duty, as lord High Constable of England, to sentence you to death, by beheading. Sentence to be carried out as soon as we can find a suitable axe and a half-competent executioner. (I will not have you butchered.) May God have mercy upon your soul!'

'Amen!' cried most of us.

'Burn in hell!' said Elen Gethin.

'Hang the bastard,' suggested Thomas Pilkington. 'We're not short of rope, and there are plenty of trees.'

Richard frowned. 'No. He is a nobleman, and entitled to a nobleman's privileges. My sentence is given, and shall not be varied. The king's pardon alone being except, and that will not come.'

'This is a poor sort of trial,' objected Robert Whitney.

'I suggest you read up on the powers of the High Constable,' Richard said coldly. 'There are excellent books on the subject. Notably by one Carson. I should hold my tongue if I were you, lest the next business turns to an enquiry into your harbouring of this notorious traitor.'

It was then that some fellow came running into the hall. 'To arms! To arms!' he cried. 'We are under attack!'

*

The Mists of Middleham

It was astonishing to see how quickly Richard sprang into action. His first order was to Sir Thomas, telling him to take a dozen men to the gate to ensure it was secured and the drawbridge in our control. Then he ordered Robin to take Jasper back to where he found him, and lock the door on him, posting a guard to be on the safe side.

Next he spoke to Robert Whitney.

'Whitney,' he said, 'you have your chance to prove yourself. If you are for Tydder, say so, and we shall lock you up with him. If you are with us, you will share the hazards of battle. But be warned. If you play false, there will be no trial for you. You'll be cut down where you stand. Decide swiftly.'

'I am your man,' said Whitney, which was very sensible in the circumstances.

'Then show us your armoury. Roger Beauchamp and I have not a piece between us, and Lovell is not much better provided. We must contrive what we can.'

'The rest of you men — to the walls! Make every arrow count. Anne; ladies — prepare a dressing station. Father Senhouse — to the chapel with you, and the relic with you. Pray for us.'

Elen Gethin raised her eyebrows. She had already strung her bow. 'I am for the wall-walk,' she said. 'I know not who comes against us, but if I am to die, I swear there will be ten of the bastards dead at my feet.'

Off she stalked, waiting for no leave, and I believe she took up station on the highest tower and did as she had promised.

You would have laughed if you had seen the four knights when they returned from the armoury. They looked like an old illustration of Simon de Montfort, with scarcely a piece of plate between them. Lovell, who had brought some of his own kit, was best provided, but he had shared out some of his best defensive protection so that they each had something. Still, they all had a hauberk at the least, though with enough rust on them to fill a bucket. Lovell had a good sword, the others had a war-hammer apiece. It was better than fighting naked.

'To the walls!' cried Richard 'Amaze the welkin with your broken staves!'

Off they rushed, roaring with delight, like boys running to a picnic.

'What's a "welkin"?' Anne asked, when they were gone.

'The heavens, I believe,' I said.

'Then why not say "heavens"? And what staves?'

'I think he was talking figuratively. He means they're going to bash, bash, bash the enemy until they break their weapons.'

'But then they'll be defenceless. With broken weapons.'

'It doesn't do to be too literal, Anne. Believe me. That's what I've been all my life. Is your poniard to hand? Lady Whitney, we need to cut up sheets for bandages.'

'Not the best ones!'

'No, the spares will do. If clean. Better get some water on the boil too.

'Why, is someone having a baby?'

'To clean the men's wounds. This could get very messy. There's a lot of noise out there.'

Indeed there was; albeit a lot of it was mere roaring and abuse. You'll recall we had a moat around us, and the drawbridge was raised and under our control. In the circumstances, all the enemy could do was to shoot arrows; there was no immediate route for them to come to close combat. To do that, they would need to cross the moat and climb the walls. Not impossible, of course, but not to be achieved in five minutes, or even half an hour.

The wounded men began to make their appearance, fortunately only in ones and twos. All were arrow wounds, some nasty due to use of broad heads, which had to be dug out. Tegolin took the lead, for she had more skill in surgery and nursing than the rest of us put together. The men were thirsty, and I saw to it there were all provided with ale. Then a thought struck me.

'I need water-carriers,' I said.

I adjourned to the kitchen, where one or two serving women and a couple of boys too young for fighting were huddled. I had them fill buckets and fetch cups, and with them I ventured outside, with the idea of providing refreshments.

The courtyard was an interesting place. Arrows, mostly spent, were falling around us, and although they were few they made life uncomfortable. Many of our horses were out there, and they were stirring and whinnying, for horses are not stupid and know when there is danger. One took an arrow in its rear quarters and began to kick and plunge, which did not make matters any better.

It was hard work taking the water around the defenders, and involved much crouching and climbing tight stone stairs, with the occasional arrow flying about one's ears to make life interesting. Still we worked along the defenders, most of whom were busy returning shots, and I believe they were grateful for our efforts.

Eventually, I reached Roger.

'Alianore! What are you doing here?' he demanded.

'Water-carrier,' I said shortly. 'Also I want to know what is going on.'

'It's dangerous! Get back in the house.'

'Men can't fight without water.'

'Oh yes we can! How do you think we managed at Towton?'

We were behind a merlon, so relatively safe.

'At least tell me what is going on.'

'There are *thousands* out there. God knows where they have come from.'

'I've heard these Welsh lordships can produce large numbers of fighting men, even if little else.'

'True. Anyway, they are drawing our arrows. We only have a limited number. When we run low, they will find a way to wade the moat, or bridge it, and assault the walls. There are not enough of us to hold them when that happens. We are in the county town of Shitshire.'

'I see,' I said. 'Then we had better string up Uncle Jasper while we can.'

Roger grunted. 'If they want him, we may have to trade him. It might be the only answer.'

'I think we can assume they do want him. Either that, or Robert Whitney has a pretty serious quarrel with the neighbours.'

'Get back inside!' he ordered.

I set off to do as he said. As I did, the first arrow with burning tow attached to it came over the walls. It hit the thatch of the stables and, fortunately, went out at once. If too many of those hit home we shall have fiery steeds! I thought.

I ran back into the house, though not in a straight line just in case I was somehow observed by the enemy. One never knows. Inside I shouted for more water. Fire was a danger now, even if thirst was not.

By the time the water had been poured into sufficient buckets, and a suitable team assembled (including even Anne) the thatch on the stable roof was already alight. I had the boys hurl the water onto it, for boys are good at such work, but I feared it would soon be out of control.

'We must release the horses,' I said to Anne. 'The whole place could burn.'

We hurried inside the building, with Lady Whitney, opening doors and untying horses with a will. These were our best animals, together with those belonging to Robert Whitney, and the poor creatures could smell smoke and were already beginning to panic. Our task was probably more dangerous than I appreciated at the time, but we escaped with barely a kick. Most of the horses simply made their way out into the courtyard, only the odd awkward one needing to be blindfolded and led.

By this time we were choking ourselves, and glad to be back in the open air. The courtyard was chaotic with horses rushing about, trying to find safety, others struggling against their reins where they had been tied, and arrows still finding their way over the walls and landing on random targets.

The boys had done a good piece of work with the buckets, and were already rushing away to fetch fresh supplies. The roof smoked, but the fire had not really caught hold as I had feared. No doubt the previous night's storm had done a great deal to damp things down.

I ventured back into the stable, more out of curiosity than anything. It occurred to me that there were saddles and other useful items inside that would be worth securing. However, my eyes were drawn to something that stood at the far end, covered by a large piece of coarse canvas. Wheels stood out beneath it. A cart for sure! I thought. We can use that to rescue whatever needs rescuing. So I covered my face — there was still smoke inside the building — hurried over and drew the canvas aside.

It was not a cart. It was a gonne!

Old enough, I suspected, to have been used in the first siege of Harlech, seventy years earlier, and not very large, but still a gonne. Not a siege-piece as such, more portable than that, suitable for the field.

'Everyone get in here!' I shouted.

It took some shifting, that gonne. Even on wheels they are damned heavy things, and this one's axles had seized up, no doubt because it had not been moved for ten years or more. Choking, coughing, all of us lending a hand, we somehow budged it. Turned it towards the exit. Pushed it along at an average speed of about half a mile an hour, out into the courtyard.

By this time we were all choking again, and panting. Shifting gonnes is damned hard work, especially when it is not your usual business. For one thing, it breaks your fingernails, that I can tell you.

As you know, I always used to carry a small horn of powder with me on my missions, in case I had to blow a lock or create a diversion. However, it was nowhere near enough to fire this thing. Nowhere near. We needed more. Where might it be?

I divided our little party into three groups. One, led by Lady Whitney, to continue to damp down the stable roof. (It was pretty much under control, but you cannot be too careful). Another, led by Anne, to collect every small stone and piece of metal they could find. I wanted at least a bucket full. The last group was my own, and very small. I just took the youngest kitchen-boy to help, and asked him to show me the armoury.

That room was a scene of chaos, as you might guess. Richard and the others had stripped it of almost everything useful, and what remained was lots of broken weapons, a few pieces of rusty mail bought second-hand from Richard the Lionheart, and the odd chest of arrows. There was, however, one small cask that looked promising. I broached it with a rusty old dagger and there within was the gold I sought, so to speak. Powder. Old, no doubt, but undoubtedly powder, and nice and dry to boot.

It was, believe it or not, light enough and small enough for me to carry. Of course, I was fit in those days, not as I am now. I told the boy to drag the chest of arrows out too for good measure. Our men on the walls might well be glad of them.

We arrived back in the courtyard just in time. Robin had used all his arrows, and was wandering around looking for spent ones to replace them, as were several of his men. The chest of fresh arrows was better than a Twelfth Night gift to them. I had never seen men grin so wide, not even Roger when I woke him up while naked and carrying a quart of old ale one Christmas Day.

I asked Robin himself to stay with us, on the grounds that we had need of his strength. With his aid we shifted the gonne again, until its barrel pointed into the tunnel of the gatehouse. Then I used a jug to pour in what I guessed to be a suitable amount of powder. I do stress, *guessed*. I had not be trained in this. We rammed it home with a small cushion and the handle of a spear; not the ideal tools, but the best we could contrive. Then we filled the barrel with all the stones, nails and broken pieces of iron we had been able to find. A good bucketful. Rammed it all home with another small cushion, until it was stuffed solid.

I returned to the armoury, found a piece of slow-match, lit it from a lantern, and made my way back to the gonne.

This all took a good time, and we were not a moment too soon. The defence was failing, our arrows were now in very short supply, and, as I gathered from reports, the enemy were filling the moat with brushwood and other solid matter and starting to cross. Soon there would be hand-to-hand fighting along the battlements and then their numbers would tell.

Elen Gethin came down from her high tower. She had expended all her arrows, and I suspect she had not wasted more than a couple. Her eyes were fierce, and she had a wicked dagger in her hand, thin and sharp, designed to pass through the gaps in armour.

'Whatever happens,' she said, 'Jasper Tydder shall not live. I will see to it myself.'

She meant it, too.

Just then, the drawbridge came crashing down. To this day I do not know whether it was the result of men scaling the walls and breaking its mechanism, or whether we we betrayed by traitors within. My money is on the latter. Soon the gates were bulging as men pressed against them, some hacking away with axes. It did not look good. I stood by with my slow-match.

'Madam,' said Robin. 'Let me fire the piece, lest the barrel bursts.'

I hesitated, then handed over the slow-match. He was right, there was a good chance it would burst and if it did he was only a peasant, more easily spared than someone of noble birth. Besides, it was a man's job.

'Stand clear,' Robin ordered. So we fell back. Indeed, I ushered Anne and Lady Whitney back into the house, reminding them there were still wounded to be attended, and that Tegolin was more or less alone. For my part, I was curious. I stood on the threshold, watching.

The gate gave way with a splintering crash, and there was a roar as the enemy burst through. There was a frightful crowd of them, and they all looked jolly cross. Our men, led by Richard, began to hurry down from the walls to meet them.

'Stand clear!' Robin repeated. Then he touched the burning slow-match to the hole in the barrel. For a second, there was nothing. Then – BOOM!

He was enveloped in smoke, but emerged from it unscathed. The barrel had not burst. Several of the intruders had though. As the clouds of smoke drifted away, they became visible, some clearly dead, many lying on the ground, bloody, groaning and missing important parts of their bodies. Into this shambles our men charged, Richard to the fore with Sir Roger and Sir Thomas guarding his flanks.

'A York! A York!' was the cry.

It was still a desperate fight. Robin snatched up his bow, shot off the last of his arrows above the heads of the defenders, then drew his sword and plunged into the melee.

Inside, I found that Father Senhouse had left the chapel, and was working miracles with the Grail. Our wounded scarcely had to be touched with the water poured from it before they became as fit as fleas, their wounds healed. All that was necessary for Tegolin to do was to cut out arrowheads and withdraw the shaft. The Grail did the rest, and most of these fellows were so game that they immediately rushed outside to rejoin the fun.

It was then that I heard the distant sound of a clarion, sounding an extremely urgent note. I knew what that note meant. Charge!

I ventured outside again. Our men were fighting boldly, but were they gaining ground? Even as I watched, I saw that they were, and that the enemy was falling back at an increasing rate. This made no great sense, as we were sorely outnumbered. Unless —

That clarion sounded again, and very much nearer. It had to be a relieving force.

It was only then that I remembered the letters Francis Lovell and I had sent from Presteigne, carried by Patch. It was too soon for our Middleham men. It had, therefore, to be the Sheriff of Herefordshire, whom we had ordered to Hergest Court. Obviously, he had followed us on. The sensible man!

*

The Sheriff turned out to be Sir Richard Delabere, and by a remarkable coincidence he was yet another of my brothers-in-law, being married to my sister, Anne. (That is my full sister, Anne; not my half-sister Anne, who is another person altogether, married to Sir Thomas Dutton and widowed at Blore Heath. Yes, it is confusing, but don't blame me. I didn't name my siblings.)

Most of the enemy got clean away, vanishing into the forests as though they were but smoke. A fair few were dead, and those that were captured were made to throw down their weapons and banners in the courtyard of Robert Whitney's house, making a lovely pile. Then they were stripped of everything of value, including their boots, and sent bootless home. Richard said there was no one important enough to hang, so he let them off with a caution.

The wounded, of both sides, were taken into the hall and treated with water from the Grail. All emerged healthy, even those who had seemed half-dead, although those with pieces missing had to manage without. At least their stumps were sound. Considering the ferocity of the fight, the numbers involved, and the firing of the gonne, the butcher's bill was surprisingly light. Three killed on our side and about fifty on theirs. Barely enough to fill a decent pit. Even the wounds to the horses were nothing that Tegolin and the Grail could not put to rights.

We feasted late into the night, even though not all the tidying had been completed. We were, of course, a very numerous company indeed, with the fellows the Sheriff had brought with him, and it seemed to me that Robert Whitney and his wife would have very little left in their stores by the time we were gone. Still, if was perhaps fitting they should feel come consequences. Richard had effectively pardoned Whitney, but it seemed to me the fellow was at the least guilty of misprision of treason. So he got off lightly.

It may be that everyone drank a little too much, and that we all slept a little too long; however, it was understandable. Everyone, without exception, had had a hard day. If Delabere and his men had not arrived at the right moment it might have been worse. We might all have been dead; or most of us at the least. Some indulgence was inevitable in the circumstances. We did not merely celebrate our victory. We celebrated the fact that we were still alive.

It was only when someone realised that Jasper had not had his breakfast — or his supper either, for he had been completely forgotten in all the excitement — that we discovered he was gone. I was not altogether surprised to find that Tegolin was gone too.

What was more shocking was that Father Senhouse's box had gone with them — they had taken the Grail! Or so it seemed.

The priest produced it from some crevice in his habit, and grinned. 'They have taken the replica,' he said. 'The real Grail has lain under my pillow each night, and last night was no exception.'

He held it up so all could see, and there was a great deal of cheering.

For my part, I was uncertain. I remembered what Tegolin said about swapping the Grail over with the replica back at Valle Crucis. How could one be sure? The Grail and its replica were twins.

There were two possibilities:

1. We had the Grail and they had the replica.
2. They had the Grail and we had the replica.

I decided that I would keep this thought to myself for the time being.

'Now,' said Richard, 'all that remains is to proceed to Guy's Cliff and deal with the other horn of this conspiracy; I suspect Jasper is half way to Brittany by now. In any event, I have no intention of chasing him all over the Brecon Beacons. His rebellion is smashed. Besides, I long to meet this imposter claiming to be my sister. Let us hope that Lady Warwick is with her, in good health, and capable of being returned to her right mind.'

*

Guy's Cliffe.

On our way from Whitney to Warwick we met the remainder of our friends from Middleham. They included, to my particular satisfaction, Rob Percy, Guy Archer and Patch the Jester. Patch had done an excellent job of collecting everyone together and marching them in the right general direction, and although they were too late for the battle at Whitney, they were a most welcome reinforcement. (Sir Richard Delabere and his men, being but shire levies, had quite naturally gone home, their service complete.)

It took us five days to accomplish the march, which was fair going considering that one of those day was a Sunday, spent at Worcester, resting and worshipping. Father Senhouse insisted that we all make offerings to Our Lady of Worcester in thanksgiving for our recent delivery from our enemies, and we naturally complied. Richard, of course, was a very pious man, and Robin had a particular devotion to Our Lady, which surprised me, but which he said was included in all the best legends of his hero.

We arrived in Warwick late on the afternoon of the Tuesday, and put up at the castle, which was more than big enough to lodge us all in comfort. A select group of us gathered in what had once been old Warwick's solar — a large and impressive room, unsurprisingly, with a good view down to the river — to plan our strategy. Not that there was much to plan, in truth, but Richard liked to hang up a map and gesture towards it with a stick on such occasions, and to make the whole operation a lot more complicated than it needed to be.

I could have summarised it in a sentence. Rock up at the front door in serious numbers and kick the crap out of anyone who offers resistance. Indeed I doubted there *would* be resistance. There was Rous, who was about as dangerous as a day-old kitten. There was Ursula and her woman. Then there was the Boggart, who would only come out to play if anyone was stupid enough to knock on its door. *That* was about the only issue worth stressing and repeating. All in all, it was about as scary as taking over the pie shop in Middleham. Or so I thought.

That night I had another dream. A long and complex dream of which I only remembered the half when I eventually woke. It featured Robin Hood, King Arthur and the Black Dog, with the so-called Crystal Plantagenet in the leading role. I smashed her repeatedly in the face with a quarterstaff, which was deeply satisfying, but she just popped up again, smiling and sneering. So you see she was annoying even in dreams, which I always think is a bad sign. Also featured was the Holy Grail, but in the dream it was a shining object, made of gold, held by King Arthur, or Richard of Gloucester, or perhaps both. They seemed to me to be all but identical twins, which was very strange. I was not at all sure whether I could tell them apart.

Anyway, although the dream left me with a headache, I went down to breakfast in a reasonably contented mood. There was small ale, and bread, and oysters, and it was well enough. There was, however, very little talk.

We rode in cavalcade to Guy's Cliffe, but just as we drew near Richard's horse came to an abrupt halt and would not take a step further. Lovell advanced, meaning to persuade the animal, but exactly the same thing happened to him. None of the horses would pass that point. Moreover, when we dismounted to investigate, we soon found that none of us could proceed either. It was like walking into an invisible wall. Literally, a wall. If you banged your head against it, it hurt as if you had butted a castle.

'This is enchantment indeed,' cried Father Senhouse, who had advanced very boldly on foot and hurt his head and his dignity alike. 'I have never seen the like, but it must be evil, and powerful evil at that. We shall pray.'

So we knelt, and Father Senhouse led us through a long litany. Then he produced holy water and his aspergillum, and let loose. There was a hissing, and a certain amount of steam, but the wall remained as solid as before.

'Try the Grail,' said Richard, who growing impatient. As a soldier I imagine he saw the Grail as a sort of heavy artillery.

The exorcist drew it out. Then he said a long, Latin prayer, held the Grail before him, and advanced.

It so happened that I was right behind him. There was a strange sound, like the howling of demons, and the wall, or whatever it was, became visible. It was green. Bright green. In that sea of green was an aperture, not very large, and Father Senhouse advanced through it, with me at his heels. Yet we were no sooner through than the aperture closed behind us. In other words, we were through the wall — which promptly became invisible again — but no one else was able to follow. Instead, we were trapped inside.

'What devilry is this?' he asked.

I was just about to suggest that we retreat — for if the Grail could get us in, it could surely get us out — when the mist descended. A vile, stinking mist, or rather a fog. You could not see your hand in front of your face, and for once I am not exaggerating. All I could see was something rather like a candle flame, save that it was green. I felt compelled to advance towards it, and as I did so the mist began to thin, though it was still difficult to work out where we were. The priest was with me, the Grail still clutched in his hands, and as we walked forward I made out what could only be one of the buildings of Guy's Cliffe. It was in fact the tower, and we were soon standing in front of the door leading into it. I turned the handle, and inside everything was entirely normal. There was no sign of mist at all.

Inside that entrance hall, Father Senhouse and I had a serious discussion. Should we try to win back, or should be climb the stairs and try to take of the evil at it source? For I had no doubt the source lay above our heads, in the shape of Crystal Plantagenet, and the exorcist was in full agreement that evil was there, whether it was she or another.

'I am going to say prayers of protection,' he said, 'but be in no doubt, my Lady Beauchamp, that we are in the presence of extreme evil, and that there is greater danger here than ever there was at Whitney-on-Wye. That was mere physical danger. This is spiritual danger, such as I have never experienced in my career. This is no mere casting out of devils, such as those mischievous sprites that throw milk pails about, or tweak the noses of children, or prevent butter churning. This is degrees above all that. I think it may be wise for you to stay down here, while I tackle it. It's my job, after all.'

'It's a threat to the security of the kingdom, which makes it my job too. Don't worry, Father. I'll let you take the lead. For one thing, you have the Grail. For another, you have the training. But I will back you up. There may be demons up there, but there are also people. Two women at least, perhaps three. I can take them on while you do the serious stuff.'

I drew out my poniard. I was ready to kill anyone who stood in our way, even Lady Warwick if necessary. That was how desperate we were. I wished we had Roger with us, or Guy Archer at the least. Still, we must make do. It was my fault for following the priest. Why had I? All I can say is that I felt *impelled*. I should really have let Richard and Anne walk ahead of me, and Francis Lovell too. Well, this was my punishment for discourtesy.

Father Senhouse prayed for a long time, while I sought to follow him, or at least make the proper responses. Yet I was on edge and could not concentrate. The truth was we were going into action.

*

Carefully, and as quietly as possible, we climbed those stairs.

'Father,' I whispered, 'when you reach the top, whatever you do, do not knock upon the right hand door. There's a boggart in that room, and it's really scary. It chased Roger and me right out of the tower.'

'A *boggart*?' he repeated. 'What is the diocesan exorcist thinking about? A boggart is nothing! A sub-deacon should be able to deal with one of those. Two Hail Marys and a sprinkle of holy water should do the trick. Boggart indeed! Not even up there with poltergeists, and poltergeists are child's play. Why, when I was training, we used to let first years tackle boggarts just for practice. It makes me wonder if it's someone's pet. Did you say there's a priest here?'

'More than one I believe, though I've only met the one called Rous.'

'John Rous?'

'You've heard of him?'

'He was up at Oxford before my time, but his reputation lived on. A strange man, a very strange man. Priested of course, but more interested in alchemy and antiquarianism than theology. A notable liar too, apt to flatter his betters, and at this time still on our list of suspicious persons.'

'Suspicious persons?

'Those with opinions that might be heresy, or worse.'

'There are worse things even than *heresy*?'

'It's one thing for educated men to question details of dogma in debate. Another to worship the Devil.'

'What?'

'It all fits. He could well be the one working this evil; these enchantments. I confess I am always suspicious of those who meddle with alchemy. By its very nature, it leads men to seek out forbidden knowledge, and even to have dealings with demons.'

'But he seemed harmless. A fool.'

'So such people often do, my daughter. But when a priest keeps a boggart as a pet, you must admit it does seem a tad suspicious.'

'Then this place could be a nest of sorcery and witchcraft. With this Crystal Plantagenet.'

'Again, the pattern fits precisely. Women are frequently weak souls, easily led and predisposed to sin. We may have what you might call a gang. Rous at the head, with female acolytes. Very dangerous indeed! I thank God we have the Grail. Better in this kind of warfare than a hundred bombards.'

It was then that we heard the tread of feet coming up the stairs. We were trapped between whoever it was and the chamber above, where Crystal (or Ursula) lurked.

'Rous!' I hissed. 'Let me go down and take him out.'

'He's a priest!' he objected. 'You cannot kill him. At least not until he's been degraded and handed over to the secular arm.'

'Father,' I said, 'with all due respect to your cloth, we are in a desperate hole. It's the pair of us, against whatever we are dealing with, and I don't like the odds. The last thing I want is someone cutting off our retreat. I need to deal with him. He's an old fellow, and shouldn't take much sorting.'

He sighed. 'Very well. But try not to kill him. It'll make a lot of paperwork if you do.'

So, poniard in hand, I made my way down again, keeping as quiet as possible. I had the advantage of being above our opponent and I also wanted the advantage of surprise, if I could retain it.

As it proved, it was not Rous. It was Guy Archer!

'Guy!' I cried. 'Is the wall down? Is everyone here?'

He shook his head. 'I had a scout around. The wall, or whatever it is, has a gap at the back. I found it and came in search of you.'

It seemed harsh to say that he should have gone back and brought the entire team. Instead I welcomed him, grateful for what was a superb reinforcement. This man could deal with the likes of Rous with one hand tied behind his back. Even the Boggart might not fancy its chances.

When we reported the circumstances to Father Senhouse, who was still crouching where I had left him, he seemed gratified.

'This can only mean the enchantment is weakening. It may well be attributed to the presence of the Grail, which is surely fighting against it. It may be that the entire 'wall' will quickly collapse now. The Devil can fight God, can put up a mighty struggle; but ultimately, goodness and light must triumph over evil. By God's grace.'

'Indeed,' I said.

He frowned. 'All the ills of the world are caused by sin. Free will allows choice, and many of us make unfortunate choices. The difficulty, you see, is that evil often presents itself in pleasing forms. If it was always as unpleasant as a boggart, for example, it would soon be recognised as such, and defeated. The truly dangerous evil is that which presents itself as goodness.'

'Father,' I said, 'these thoughts are interesting, but this is not the time or place for a sermon. What is the plan?'

'I intend to hold the Grail before me, and let them do their worst. Its power will destroy them. It's only a question of how.'

'Then Guy and I will cover your flanks. I'm not sure we'll be much use against an enchantment, but at least we can serve as a distraction.'

Guy drew out his sword. 'Which side?' he asked.

'You take the right,' I said.

We crept up the remaining stairs to the top landing.

'Not the right-hand door!' I hissed. Although the warning notice was still in place, I thought a reminder was not wasted.

'I shall deal with that later,' said Father Senhouse. 'Pooh, a mere boggart! The priests here at Guy's Cliff must be a singularly useless bunch, or deeply corrupt, or they'd have dealt with it themselves. Senior exorcists have more important things to do than pop boggarts.'

It was I who advanced to the door and turned its handle. Father Senhouse followed, brandishing the Grail, with Guy to his right with his naked sword. We took a last look at one another, then, having exchanged nods, I kicked the door open.

Inside was Crystal, as she called herself, sitting in the best chair, dressed as I had seen her in my dream, in cloth-of-gold, with a towering headdress. Lady Warwick sat next to her, on her right hand, engaged in reading some book. The serving-woman bustled about in the background, tidying the room as I supposed.

'Ah, Alianore!' said Crystal. 'You have brought the Grail, just as we wished. You are a good girl!'

Father Senhouse spoke in a most stentorian voice. 'The Grail is here,' he said, flourishing it. 'It will put a swift end to you, foul sorceress! Do you imagine that my nose cannot smell out the evil of this place?'

'Oh, that's the drains, you silly man,' Crystal replied. 'I've have told Master Rous to fetch the builders to it, but he is a forgetful fellow.'

'We've no intention of giving you the Grail,' I said. 'Far from it. Moreover, you should be grateful for that; it would certainly destroy you.'

'I don't think so,' she said. 'Take it from that foolish priest now, and fetch it to me.'

'No chance!' I said.

She stretched out a hand, just as she had in my dream, or vision or whatever it was. And, just as in that dream, it felt as if I had been kicked by a horse. I sat down heavily, gripping at my belly.

Lady Warwick dropped her book, stood, and hurried over to me. 'There was no need for that!' she cried. 'Alianore, dear, are you all right?'

Guy was already on the move, the point of his sword aimed at Crystal's chest. He would have killed her, I have no doubt, but her hand shot out again, and he flew through the air backwards, dropping his sword and falling to the ground as if dead.

'Anyone else want some of it?' Crystal asked.

'Screw you, bitch!' I cried, which cost me another flick of the hand, another kick of a horse, this time in the ribs. I felt as if I was going to vomit, but I knew that there more of this power she used, the less she would have to spare.

'You, priest. Bring it here!' she ordered Father Senhouse.

He was praying, some litany in Latin. The Grail was beginning to glow. What was more, it was beginning to buzz, like a whole nest of outraged wasps. To be honest, at that point I was a darned sight more scared of it than I was of Crystal.

'Bring it!' she said, but this time not in her own voice, or in her affected girlie drawl. No, this was an extraordinarily deep voice. The voice of a demon, and a male demon at that.

'Oh, I shall bring it, Belial,' Father Senhouse answered, breaking off his prayers. 'I shall bring it. And with it, I shall destroy your servant utterly, and send you to the deepest pit of hell where you belong. I do not fear you, you pathetic little demon. Nor twenty like you. I am armoured against you, and I serve the Lord.'

He stepped forward, almost eagerly. I swear he had the courage of twenty lions clad in proof. He held the Grail before him, as if presenting a gift. By this time, it was not only glowing brightly, it was buzzing like thirty million angry bees in a particularly bad mood.

That fool Crystal did what I would not have done if you had offered me a Patent creating me Duchess of Norfolk in my own right and ten thousand pounds a year to go with it. She reached out, and touched it.

There was a blinding flash of light, so intense that a thousand wax candles all burning at once would have seemed like a single dying rush light by comparison. Then there was such a scream as I have never heard before or since, and then — blackness. My last conscious thought was that I was dead.

*

'I still do not understand the half of it,' said Richard. He was sitting in the best chair in Warwick's solar, his eyes flicking from Father Senhouse to me and back again as if he expected us to provide him with a detailed explanation.

I'm afraid I was not in any great condition to make speeches. I had come around after an hour or so, but I felt as if I had been kicked by every horse in Middleham stables and I was also exceedingly tired. As for thoughts, those I had were not coherent.

'A clear case of demonic possession,' said Father Senhouse. He was on his feet, which was more than I was, and seemed quite himself. 'However, I do not pretend to understand everything that has happened. It may simply be a case of "they used dark forces".'

'By which, I suppose, you mean that there may have been men, or women, seeking to control these demons for their own purposes? Whether political or otherwise.'

'It may be. Your Grace, this is a complex matter. I should like to examine all the evidence at length; and spend many hours in prayer. Even then, I should be reluctant to come to any certain conclusion. The demonic possession has been dealt with satisfactorily, if I say so myself. As for the Boggart, I shall return to Guy's Cliff first thing in the morning and put that to bed. A simple task.'

'Bring in the man Rous,' Richard ordered.

Master Rous was 'escorted' into the room by Guy Archer and Robin Hood. They both had a grip on him, but it was really quite unnecessary. I doubt he could have fought off a child of ten.

'Now, Rous,' Richard said, 'what are we to do with you? I have little doubt that you are responsible for bringing demons into play, for reasons I can only guess at. What have you to say for yourself?'

'I am an alchemist, my lord. I seek to create gold for the profit of the kingdom, and my investors, such as Lady Warwick. If, by mischance, some incantation or prayer of mine has attracted a demon, or demons, I can only plead inadvertence. It was not by my intent.'

'Fortunately for you, you are outside my jurisdiction. It may be that you will have to answer to the Church court, but that is a matter for the Bishop of Worcester. I dare say you will get off much more lightly than you deserve. Now, tell me of this woman you have been protecting. The sorceress. Do you still dare to swear she is my sister?'

'She is indeed your sister.' It was not Rous who answered, but Lady Warwick, who had just walked into the room. She looked frail, in a way she had not before. 'I myself guided her from your mother's womb. It was my hobby in those days — midwife to the higher nobility. I never charged of course. That would have been demeaning. But I was rather good at it. Your mother had fears for Ursula that in retrospect seem quite absurd, but we are all wise in hindsight. She repented of them soon after, but by that time it was too late. You have no idea of the fears that can trouble women at such times. I believe the Duchess was, for a short time, a little crazed.'

'And no doubt you can explain how my sister became a sorceress, and involved herself with demons?'

Lady Warwick sighed. 'She always was a highly intelligent child. She became Master Rous's assistant in his search for gold, and no doubt that was the start of it. Master Rous has certain books in his collection.'

'Forbidden books?' asked Father Senhouse.

'That you would have to judge for yourself, Father. I know not.'

'Rous?'

'I have — er — a large collection of books, as is necessary for the study of alchemy.'

'Forbidden books?'

'Perhaps one or two.'

'So Rous,' Richard said grimly, 'it may be said you corrupted your pupil. An innocent girl who was effectively your ward. Your case looks very black indeed. The Bishop of Worcester will be told of all this.'

'It was not by my intent, my lord.'

'Then by your negligence!' Richard roared. 'Be grateful you are a priest. If you were not, I would have you summarily executed. What am I to tell the King?'

'As little as possible,' Anne said gently. 'I really do not think it would help anyone to make too much of a noise about this matter. Even the trial of Master Rous, even in a Church court, could become very embarrassing for the family. Not least for your lady mother. I really think the whole business should be — well, for want of a better word, hushed up.'

'Including a full-scale battle at Whitney-on-Wye?'

She shrugged. 'Richard, it was in the Marches. Disorder there is pretty much an everyday event. No one will notice unless you choose to make a song and dance about it. If you do, you'll have to explain how Jasper Tydder escaped. That will not look good. If the question arises, we just say he was a nameless rogue. There was, after all, some doubt as to his identity.'

'So, you suggest this fellow,' he gestured at Rous, 'goes scot-free?'

'No, I suggest that all future books for my mother are charged at seventy-five percent discount.'

'I like that!' Richard cried. 'Did you hear Rous? From this day forward, all books you produce for the Countess of Warwick will be invoiced at seventy-five percent discount. Remember, I have your previous accounts, and I will check that your future prices are as I require. Is that understood?'

'Yes, my lord Duke.'

'What's more, any comments included about me had better be positive. You need to know that I understand Latin perfectly, so don't imagine you can evade that requirement by switching away from English. I shall know. If you give me the slightest cause, I will drop on you like a ton of millstone grit. Be under no illusions on that score.'

'Yes, your Grace.'

'You will also remember that the Bishop of Worcester can be asked to open a case against you if you default.'

'Yes, your Grace.'

Richard turned to Lady Warwick. 'How is my sister, madam?'

'Recovering. She has had a terrible shock. She has asked for a priest. I believe she is entirely penitent.'

'So she should be! As should you, madam. I trust there will be no more dealings in necromancy?'

'There will not,' she answered, hanging her head.

'No more talk of King Harry?'

'No. He is dead, may God assoil him! Crystal — I mean Ursula — told me that he lived, but of course, she lied. Or at least, the demon did. She was possessed, Dickon. I believe it wrong to blame her.'

'She meddled with demons, which is a grave sin. Is it not, Father?'

'Very grave,' said Father Senhouse, spreading his hands. 'However, with due penance and sincere repentance, she may be absolved. We must consider she is young, foolish, badly guided and, of course, a mere woman, of no particular education. All of which mitigates the sin, as long as she now rejects the Devil and all his works, and lives the life of a Christian woman henceforward, without any relapse into wickedness.'

'You are generous, Father.'

'We cannot burn everyone who is a fool. Repentant sinners must and shall be forgiven. If it were otherwise, what hope would there be for any of us?'

'The question remains — what is to be done with her?'

'A nunnery, perhaps? Where better for a repentant sinner?'

'I suggest you return her to her mother,' Anne said. 'The Duchess is the only other member of the family who knows the full truth. Let her decide what is to be done. As she more or less lives like a nun, she would be a good a holy exemplar for Ursula. Time will heal all wounds.'

'I cannot argue with that proposal,' said Father Senhouse. 'The Duchess of York is as pious a woman as can be found in all the land. It is fitting she should have charge of her daughter, and ensure her proper reform. Nothing better could be contrived.'

'So be it!' said Richard.

*

Reunion

Some of the men, led by Lovell and Rob Percy, were sent back to Middleham. Richard realised how thinly the place was garrisoned, and it made him uneasy. It was unlikely that there would be problems with the Scots, but you can never be sure, and the responsibility was on his shoulders.

After another week at Warwick, the rest of us set off for Berkhampstead, where the Duchess of York was living. An old carriage was produced from somewhere — I suspect it was one that Lady Warwick had owned when she was in her pomp — and Anne, her mother and Ursula rode in that. For part of the way, so did I, because I was still recovering from that extraordinary day at Guy's Cliffe and too much time on horseback was uncomfortable and made me weary.

Ursula — she had completely dropped the ridiculous name 'Crystal' — was very quiet indeed, very penitent, to the point that it seemed that every time she spoke it was to apologise. She was also modestly dressed, and might easily have been taken for Anne's waiting gentlewoman. Each time we stopped she sought out the nearest church and fell on her knees in prayer. Father Senhouse, of course, had given her some pretty serious penances, but this was a voluntary extra.

At last we came to Berkhampstead Castle, where at that time the Duchess Cecily was living in some splendour. She was a formidable lady, who somehow gave the impression she was six foot tall, when she was actually about six inches short of that. She was entirely clad in black, but it was the kind of black cloth that would bankrupt most courtiers if they bought three ells of it.

I was rather pleased that it was Richard, not me, who had to explain everything to her. My part was simply to stand in the background, playing my part as Anne's waiting-woman, and that was an easy role, indeed a non-speaking part.

Richard did not tell the full tale, of course. There was elements that he found it convenient to omit, especially those relating to Lady Warwick, Henry VI and necromancy. That Lady Warwick was grateful for this I did not doubt. She stood next to her daughter, and therefore quite close to me, but looked shamefaced, her lips entirely sealed.

The Mists of Middleham

When the moment came to present Ursula, I believe I saw tears spring in the Duchess's eyes. She rose from her seat, more easily than I had expected, stepped forward, and hugged her daughter in her arms. They then made a long series of peculiar sounds, that added up to a sort of conversation, made up of apologies and endearments.

'This child is innocent of any wrong,' the Duchess declared. 'The fault was entirely mine — my folly. My folly for which I ask God to pardon me. I should never have allowed pride to stand between us. I see now that I rejected my own flesh and blood through mere embarrassment; through a lack of faith in my lord husband and those around us, who might have asked awkward questions. Yet equally, they might not. Ursula, my child, I can only beg your forgiveness. I will try to make amends, if I can.'

'Mother,' said Ursula, very quietly. 'All I ask is to be with you, and to serve God. I was a lost lamb, but now I am home, and shall never stray again.'

So it was agreed. Ursula would live quietly with her mother, effectively as one of her waiting-gentlewomen. No one else would ever know. Well, the King must be told. It could not be a complete secret.

'I will handle that,' the Duchess said firmly. 'Ursula will remain under my protection. No one will ever force her to anything against her will. Not even her brother.'

'And now the Grail,' she went on. 'May I be privileged to see it?'

Father Senhouse still had it in his charge. With something of the air of a conjuror undertaking a trick, he suddenly held it before him, even though his hands had been empty a moment before.

'Is that it?' cried the Duchess. She looked terribly disappointed. She had obviously been expecting a more elaborate version, made of gold, with at least a selection of large jewels.

'It is, madam,' said Father Senhouse sonorously. (He had one of those typical priest voices that can fill a room without being raised very much. It must be something they are taught.) 'Moreover, all of us have witnessed its power. It is quite beyond description, and yet so dangerous in its potential that I believe it would be better returned to Valle Crucis. It can save, and heal; equally, if abused, it could destroy. It is not to be profaned.'

We had all fallen on our knees, save for Father Senhouse because, believe it or not, the thing had begun to glow. It was not at its full force, of course. The light was not blinding. It was more gentle, reassuring. Nor did it make that awful buzzing sound. If it is not irreverent to describe it so, it was in a good mood.

'May I touch it?' asked the Duchess.

'With reverence, madam, certainly.'

She leaned forward and kissed it. 'I thank God I have lived to see it,' she said. Her voice had lost its confident, assured note. She sounded like a child.

'We are all blessed by its presence,' said Father Senhouse. 'I pray we may remain so.'

*

The Ending

Richard and Anne decided they did not want to go to court. For one thing, Richard was still uneasy about matters at home, with the North left these many weeks in the hands of Henry Percy. For another, he was not sure it was wise for Lady Warwick to appear before his brother, just in case any awkward questions were asked. Apart from that, Anne in particular was never happy at Edward's court. Her aversion to Woodvilles exceeded even her husband's.

Sir Thomas Pilkington also wanted to go home, and Robin Hood and his fellows had decided to take employment with Richard, as had Adam, our Shropshire guide. So the company that was left to go south was quite select. It amounted to Roger, Father Senhouse and me, with our attendants, such as were left to us, headed by Guy Archer, who was none the worse from his experience at Ursula's hands.

A few days later, there we were at last, back at Edward's court, Holy Grail in the bag and – to be honest – rather pleased with ourselves. We had sent word ahead to Hastings, and half expected to be greeted with some grand ceremonial, because there is little point in having something like the Grail unless you make a fuss about it. However, as so often with Cousin Edward, matters did not follow expectation.

We were, in fact, received almost in private, which in all truth may be conceived a greater honour, because it involved us being admitted to the King's innermost sanctum, his bedchamber, a place which few honest women ever saw, and indeed very few honest men, save princes and the knights and gentlemen of his chamber.

Edward was seated on his great chair, with Elizabeth next to him, resting her slender form on a folding stool. Apart from Hastings, who conducted us into the Presence, we were quite alone. The King and Queen actually rose as we entered, and walked towards us, their eyes fixed on the box Roger was carrying. They reminded me of young children about to receive an expensive present, unable to stand still, almost dancing on their toes with delight.

Duchess Cecily had provided a fine enamelled box for the Grail which Father Senhouse carried with him. The reaction when the box was opened was rather restrained. Indeed, their faces fell. Like the Duchess, they had no doubt expected more in the way of jewels.

'This — is it?' Edward asked uncertainly.

'Yes, your Grace,' Roger answered, 'at least it is according to the Abbot of Valle Crucis. It has already worked several miracles — not least, it has freed Alianore and me from the demons and enchantments that beset us from the moment we began this quest. We are both back to what I can only describe as 'normal'. That may not sound much to you, but to us it is everything. However, it so powerful a relic it is dangerous. In the letter the Duke of Gloucester has sent you, he recommends it is restored to Valle Crucis. I would concur, and I suggest that at the very least your Grace takes counsel from his spiritual advisers.'

'It is a most awesome relic, in every sense of the word.' Father Senhouse added. 'It must be treated with the utmost reverence, or I cannot answer for the consequences. I too strongly recommend that it be returned to obscurity at Valle Crucis, where it belongs and where it is safe.'

'Hmm,' said Edward.

'May I touch it?' asked Elizabeth.

'With reverence, madam. With the greatest reverence. I should advise some hours of prayer in preparation.' Father Senhouse was obviously on his guard. I may be wrong, but I have the feeling he sensed something. The atmosphere was not at all what it had been at Berkhampstead. I could feel it myself, so I'm sure a trained man like Senhouse could.

Hesitantly, she stretched out a finger, and touched the rim of the Grail. There was, or so I thought, a slight hum, just for a moment, and then silence. It did not glow. It looked like the most commonplace of earthenware vessels. She withdrew her hand, an awed expression on her face.

'Edward,' she said, ever so gently, 'may I take this precious relic to my rooms? I wish to kneel in vigil before it all night long, to offer thanksgiving for the blessing bestowed upon us.'

The King beamed at her. 'Of course, my dear; it was by your advice that the quest was begun. Now it is ours forever, and we are safe from all our enemies.'

He then began to thank us. I don't recall the whole speech, but it was a long one, and very grateful. We were to have all our expenses, every penny, and a thousand marks on top, by way of a bonus. Roger was to be given a peerage, and to be elected to the Garter at the next vacancy. Father Senhouse was to have a bishopric, as soon as there was a vacancy. In fact, it was pretty much a case of 'ask and you shall have'.

There was also going to be a great ceremony and a feast as soon as Hastings could make the arrangements; processions, *Te Deums*, jousting, the full catalogue, with Sir Roger and me at the centre of it all. I don't think I said very much, either because I was in a humble mood, or because it all sounded too good to be true. And, as matters turned out, so it was.

*

Very early next morning I was roused from my sleep by a loud banging on our door. Roger went to investigate and found some fellow with a summons from the Queen. I was to attend her instantly.

This, of course, was easier said than done. For one thing I had to wash and dress, and do so in something near darkness, with only Roger to aid me. He was far too clumsy to serve as a waiting-gentlewoman. Moreover, he had been drinking wine in the King's Chamber until very late, or very early, depending on how you view the hours of darkness, and was only half awake.

The Queen's messenger was one of her gentlemen – probably some minor Woodville cousin – hastily dressed and notably unshaven. He grunted something that might have been apology, and with a bow and a gesture hastened me down the stairs. We passed through any number of adjoining chambers, past various snoring personages, for at this unearthly hour not even the most junior of servants or the keenest of priests was stirring. Still partly in my dreams, I lacked the concentration even to wonder what was going on.

Elizabeth's features were ghostly at the best of times, but now she was the shade of best flour. She was wearing nothing but a shift and her chamber-robe, and was stalking around her bedchamber in bare feet. Her women – or some of them – were huddled together in corners, staring at one another in silent horror, scarcely daring to look at their mistress, let alone talk to her. This, I thought, looks like trouble.

She registered my presence, and threw a look at me that would have soured milk.

'*Where is it?*' she demanded. The words came out as a sort of scream.

'Your Grace?' I didn't have the least clue what she was shouting about.

'The Grail! You have taken it! It was there, there in my oratory.' She pointed, arm outstretched, in the appropriate direction. The Grail was certainly not there. There were two burning candles, a rather beautiful gilt crucifix, and the finest triptych you could wish to see. There was even the Duchess's enamelled box, lying open on its side. But certainly no Grail, or anything like it.

I admit to biting my lip. 'Madam,' I said, with all the patience I could muster, 'had I wished to keep the Grail for myself, I could simply have taken it to Horton Beauchamp, and sworn that our mission had failed. Why should I be so superfluous as to crawl into your rooms – with all the risk of detection – and steal it from you? I do not have it, and if you doubt me, you may search where you will.'

There was ice inside me, for I knew at once what had happened. Elizabeth had been an even greater fool than I had previously imagined, and she had not only lost the Grail in consequence, but brought down a curse upon us all, just as the Abbot of Valle Crucis had warned. 'Upon themselves and their family' he had said, and I took that not to mean just the Woodvilles, but the York family as well. It was a disaster, one I had not foreseen, and one that I could now do nothing about.

I think there must have been something in my expression that convinced her of my honesty, for she sat down heavily on her bed, and began to weep. This went on for some time—as well it might in the circumstances.

'What am I to tell the King?' she got out at last.

'That the Grail has been stolen – what else?' I shrugged. 'I dare say he will order a search, and a right thorough one, but I fear it will be to no avail. Not if God himself has removed it.'

'God?' she repeated, her mouth open.

'It would be a bold thief who would enter your Grace's most private apartments, and lay profane hands on so holy a relic. Sir Roger and I have had it in our care these several weeks, and have scarcely dared to look on it. I think Robin Hood himself would be wary of such a deed. All we may safely do is pray it is not lost.'

*

Need I say that although King Edward did indeed order a most thorough search, and raised the hue and cry on every road for a score of miles around, the Grail was never seen again? Though I am quite sure where it is, and there I hope it will stay there, safe forever; for we are not worthy to have it.

The offers of promotion and reward vanished with the Grail; indeed it took fully four years, and a great deal of badgering, to recover all our expenses, and the last of the payments was authorised by King Richard III. As for the curse, well it is certain that bad days were to come for both Woodville and York, but I'm not sure that all can be explained simply by Elizabeth's evident abuse of the relic. It would be harsh to blame *everything* on her. At least some of the disaster was brought about by Margaret Beaufort, Lady Richmond and the wretched Stanleys, and no one will ever persuade me that *they* acted as the agents of Heaven.

*

Roger and I rode back to Middleham, with a very solemn Father Senhouse travelling with us as far as York. The man had little to say, but what he did say was very bitter, on the subject of sinful and foolish women. One night, lodged at Grantham, we did sit and try to make sense of it all, but for all our debate we could not get near the bottom of the central mystery, or who was responsible. My one consolation was the thought that we had had, however briefly, possession of the true Grail, and that the one Jasper and Tegolin had taken was but a worthless fake. It might be sitting on a shelf in Brittany by now, but it would have lost any temporary power it had possessed.

At Middleham, everything there was more or less normal again. There were no more mysterious mists. No more startling visions of the future. Even Lady Warwick was herself again. She had given up the Guild of St. Anne and no longer talked of Henry VI and the good old days. Instead her talk was of preserves and of tinctures of herbs, which was boring but a good deal less politically sensitive.

She and Anne did have one new project. They were delighted with the plan of the book about King Arthur that the knight Malory had left behind him, and decided that they would write it for him, with lots of tales of chivalry and sorcery. I believe it took them fully five years to complete, and then they had that Caxton fellow print it in London. Of course, they could not admit to being the authors. That would have been quite scandalous for ladies of their rank. Instead they used 'Sir Thomas Malory' as a cover, a sort of pen-name. After all, it had originally been his idea, and I dare say it pleased his widow.

As I mentioned previously, Robin Hood and his friends, most of whom had survived, and our guide, Adam, were all taken on strength and given places in Richard's household as yeomen and such. (Marian became one of Anne's chamberers.) They dropped their silly pseudonyms of course, and took on sensible Yorkshire names like Seb Duggleby and Arthur Wilberfoss.

*

Occasionally, I still had dreams of future events I could not explain. The curse of the Grail troubled me, no matter how much a fought to put it from my mind.

I knew that our only hope lay with Richard; but I also knew that his glory would be brief, that the forces of evil ranged against him were too strong. But then, I knew something more. That he would be remembered long after all the rest of us were but forgotten dust. That he and Arthur were essentially the same Being. The Hope and Shield of England, who would come again to free the people from oppression. The Once and Future King.

(There was but one difference. Richard was a real person. I know, because I was there.)

THE END

O God, the Lord of mercies, grant to the soul of your servant, RICHARD, the anniversary of whose burial day we remember, a place of refreshment, the happiness of peace and the glory of your light. Through our Lord Jesus Christ your Son, who lives and reigns with you and the Holy Spirit, one God, For all the age of ages. Amen.'

'Deus indulgentiarum Domine, da animæ famuli tui RICARDI, cujus anniversarium depositionis diem commemoramus, refrigerii sedem, quietis beatitudinem, et luminis claritatem. Per Dominum nostrum Jesum Christum Filium tuum, qui tecum vivit et regnat in unitate Spirius Sancti Deus per omnia saecula saeculorum. Amen.'

Printed in Poland
by Amazon Fulfillment
Poland Sp. z o.o., Wrocław
05 August 2023

250a02a5-3758-4bd0-8c10-2f925644f916R01